THE NEIGHBORHOOD VAMPIRE

THE NEIGHBORHOOD SERIES
BOOK TWO

CHRISTOPHER M. MASON

Published by Candlestick Publishing, LLC.

Author's Website: https://www.christophermmason.com

First Edition

First Printing 2024

Library of Congress Control Number: 2023924393

ISBN 979-8-9874276-5-1 (Hardback)
ISBN 979-8-9874276-3-7 (Paperback)
ISBN 979-8-9874276-4-4 (eBook)

Cover Design by Fay Lane (http://www.faylane.com)
Edited by Nichole Heydenburg of Poisoned Ink Press
Animated Cover Design by Morgan Wright (@byMorganWright)
Character Art by Nicole Deal (@nicoledealart)

For Chloi.

The inspiration behind Max and for those long nights I kept you up.

A SONATA TOLD IN FIVE PARTS

THE INTRODUCTION

QUEEN'S PAWN OPENING

"Well, Mr. White. What can I do for you?" Oliver Raskin asked as he sat down on his office chair. The vinyl cushion was cracked and worn, exposing the foam padding below. The seat exhaled a small puff of air as it bore his full weight.

"Mr. Raskin—" Mr. White began.

"Please, call me Oliver," he interrupted.

"Oliver, I represent Red Heart Distribution," Mr. White continued. "I'm here to discuss the matter of The Neighborhood Witch." He withdrew a business card from a pocket inside the jacket of his pinstriped, three-piece navy-blue suit, and passed it across the desk.

Oliver examined the card, flipping it over a few times. The white card was sparsely populated except for his full name—Jack White—the name of the distributor, and a phone number. In the middle, the logo was prominent—a red heart emerging from a crimson rose with a serpentine stem.

He placed the card on his desk amongst the other various scattered papers and notebooks. Oliver Raskin was not very organized, yet knew exactly where everything was located to the detriment of his wife, Carol. He leaned back into his chair, placing his hands on its chrome plated arms, and scrutinized the man in his office.

Jack White sat upright, not slouching forward or backward. He adjusted his red bow tie, which provided a splash of vibrant color against his perfectly white shirt. Then he readjusted his jacket, so it lay perfectly against his lanky frame, brushing it a few times before placing his hands in his lap.

Oliver scrunched his lips and shifted them to the side, giving a distrusting smirk before saying, "It's my understating The Neighborhood Witch already has a distributor."

"Precisely." Mr. White retrieved a black briefcase resting against the side of his chair. He flipped it open and withdrew a document, presenting it to Oliver. "If you notice, under the terms of our contract in the highlighted areas, it specifically states any and all beer, liquor, and wine purchases must be conducted through one of these five distributors, including Red Heart Distribution."

He slipped his hand into his briefcase to produce another document and handed it to Oliver. Mr. White continued, "Likewise, the specialty deal you received for Red-Hearted Queen clearly states the bottles must be prominently displayed on your shelves and should be the central focus of your wine section. By selling The Neighborhood Witch and giving it such a prominent placement, you are in breach of your contract."

Oliver examined the contract, reading through the lines, trying to understand as much of the legal jargon as he could. A normally talkative Oliver Raskin was rendered silent. An uncomfortable silence filled the room, and it aggravated Oliver. He shifted in his chair, leaning closer to the desk as he continued his reading.

"This brings me no pleasure in delivering the news, as you have been one of our best and loyal customers. We're giving you a chance to remedy the situation if you remove all bottles of The Neighborhood Witch and restore Red-Hearted Queen to its rightful placement," Mr. White added.

Oliver glared at him, sizing him up. Oliver loved a good negotiation and never missed the opportunity to test his skills. He tossed the contracts onto the desk. "And what if I refuse?"

"Then we will have no choice but to take action. As per the terms of the agreement, we will be forced to recall all products, not just those from Red Heart Distribution. We hold considerable sway with our partner distributors as well. You won't be compensated for your losses. Any and all future purchases will be invalid. You'll be hard pressed to sign distribution agreements with any other distributor operating in this state."

Oliver narrowed his eyes, staring proverbial daggers at Mr. White. His heart raced. The normally jovial grocer was now fuming internally. He never lost a business dispute. "Are you threatening us?"

Mr. White closed the briefcase. He glared at Oliver, furling his eyebrows. "I can assure you this isn't a threat."

"Then I refuse," Oliver said in a raised voice. "You can't come into my store and tell me what to do."

"According to the terms of our contract, I can. I'll return in a week. If the situation has not been remedied, then I'll have no other recourse than to pull all inventory from your shelves," Mr. White said as he adjusted his red bowtie. He stood, picking up the briefcase. "The last time I checked, people aren't coming to your store for the cold cuts."

Oliver leapt to his feet and slammed his fists onto the desk. It took every bit of self-restraint to stop himself from punching Mr. White in the face. "Get the fuck out of my store," he yelled. His heart thumped against his chest.

Mr. White nodded and went to the office door. "I wouldn't be late remedying the situation," he said as he pulled on the doorknob. "You'll be hearing from me in one week." He checked his watch and exited.

Oliver let out a drawn-out sigh and plopped back down onto his chair. He propped his elbows on the desk and covered his mouth with his hands. "What am I going to tell them?" Oliver said in a hushed tone. "I can't. Not yet."

"I'm telling you that tree is a fairy tree," Alice said.

"You're telling me that . . . that tree back there is a fairy tree?" Hugo asked. "Wait. Wait. You're telling me fairies are real?"

"Absolutely," Alice responded. "Hold up. You never questioned witchcraft being real, but you're drawing the line at fairies? You have much to learn about the world, Hugo Dodds."

Alice Primrose stood in the dirt walking path of Wildgrove Park with her hands on her hips, head tilted, and a sly smile. The tail of her black, modern Victorian tailcoat swayed in the crisp October breeze. Her curved, black brimmed hat was pulled back, so her emerald green eyes could lock onto Hugo Dodds' icy blues.

Hugo smiled back with a mischievous grin. The ever-impatient golden retriever, Max, pulled and tugged at the leash. She begged for the group to continue down the wooded path before Hugo called her to his side. She relented after a few protest tugs.

"It's a fairy tree," Alice said.

"That's the founder's tree," Hugo responded.

"So, Newbury Grove's founder knew of the fairies?"

"No. Legend has it that a blue jay landed on the tree and caught the attention of the founder, Madeline Sinclair, as she was traveling through these woods. She took it as a sign, so she decided this was the best place to form the town. The tree is the town's symbol . . ." His words trailed off. "And it's the reason our high school mascot is a blue jay."

"Blue jays are associated with the otherworld, spirits, death, and rebirth. All signs pointing to a fairy tree." Alice's smile grew.

"I proposed"—Hugo glanced down the path—"I proposed to Elizabeth in front of that tree."

"Because it's a—"

He locked eyes with Alice again. "Well . . . how do you know it's a fairy tree?"

"The ring of stones around it. They're protecting the tree. It's in a small clearing. Late in dropping its leaves. They're all telltale signs of a fairy tree. Let me ask you this: has anyone ever disappeared?"

"Not that I recall . . ." Hugo's mouth dropped. "Wait. There was this twelve-year-old girl who disappeared when I was a sophomore in college. They never found her. They . . . still haven't found her twenty years later."

Alice raised her hands, confirming her suspicion. "Which means—"

"Huh. Looks like you're right. We have a fairy tree."

She moved closer to Hugo. The cedar and vanilla infused smell of his cologne tantalized her senses. The hair on her arms stood at the wicked thoughts racing through her mind. She leaned in to whisper into his ear, "Of course I'm right. And now you owe me tonight for doubting me."

"What do I owe you?" Hugo asked in a hushed response.

"You know the thing I like." She grinned.

He smiled and nodded. "Yes, ma'am."

"You have much to learn, Hugo Dodds."

"Now you're starting to sound like your reflect—"

Crack. The sound of branches snapping echoed throughout the woods.

Hugo whipped his head around to find the sound, and with his free hand, grabbed Alice's upper arm. "Look out," Hugo shouted as he whisked her and Max out of the way.

An enormous branch from a grim-looking ash tree fell with a thud and reverberated off the ground they once occupied before coming to a rest.

They stood in stunned silence, both enraptured by the branch laying in the pathway. Max moved to investigate her potential new chew toy.

"Are you hurt?" Hugo asked.

Alice shook her head as Hugo smiled back.

Hugo moved toward the tree. Fissures carved a path as the bark flecked to reveal the hardwood beneath.

"I think it's dead," Hugo said. "Ash borers, most likely. I'll call the park service tomorrow to let them know. Can't have more branches falling on people."

Alice knelt and rubbed her hands over the ash white tree limb. Her fingers traced the rough, gnarled grooves of the bark. A shiver ran down her spine. Alice glanced down the path for any stray eyes. They were alone.

She closed her eyes and murmured words in a forbidden language, which she knew Hugo wouldn't understand. A small bead of sweat flowed down the side of her face.

The branch twitched.

Alice's eyes snapped open. "This is it," she exclaimed.

Hugo turned around. "Are you sure?"

"This is the one. When a broom is ready to be found, it will present itself. It was meant for me to find it." She leaned closer and started an incantation. She snapped her fingers.

Minuscule ash borer larvae poured out of their holes in the tree and fell to the ground. They writhed in pain before shriveling up.

She bounced up and rushed over to the ash tree, placing both hands on the trunk. Her fingers filled in the gaps of the fractured bark and gaping holes. The invasive ash borers ravaged the tree and sucked the life essence out of it.

She leaned in. "It's okay. I'm here to help," she whispered to the tree. The breath of her words washed over the gnarled grooves of the tree trunk as she repeated the incantation. She snapped her fingers once more before backing away.

The parasitic infestation rained to the ground. They too writhed in pain before shriveling up amongst the fallen, decaying leaves.

Alice leaned in and whispered, "You're protected now."

"What did you do?" Hugo asked.

Alice peered into in his eyes before saying, "I saved it."

THE FIRST SONATA MOVEMENT

"ADAGIO SOSTENUTO"

CHAPTER 1
LA VIE EN VINO

Two wineglasses clinked together in the ethereal glow of the autumn moon. The whitish-blue hue bathed the trees of Wildgrove Park in light, fighting against the darkness of the night. It was still. Calm. Not a cloud in the sky. To Alice Primrose, it was perfect.

Alice and Hugo sat on a blanket in a clearing. A small picnic basket nestled between them. They each took a sip of their wine, sloshing it around in their mouths before drinking. Alice basked in the glow of the moon. She breathed in deeply. The smell of the crisp autumn air. The mustiness of the fallen leaves. It was heaven.

"So, Mr. Wine Connoisseur, what are your thoughts?" she asked Hugo.

"Well, it's bold and fruity," he replied.

"Bold and fruity, huh? You always say bold and fruity," Alice teased.

"Let me finish," Hugo responded with a sly smile. "It's bold and fruity—"

"We've established that," Alice interjected.

"With a hint of sweetness that conjures the image of passion. Sexiness," he said with a sultry gaze.

She lost herself in the gaze of his icy blue eyes. His eyebrows arched to complement his seductive smile. Alice bit her lips and blushed.

She averted her eyes, peering into her glass before asking, "Sexiness? Did you put it on the label?"

"No," Hugo replied. "But Oliver wanted to put it on the label. Right under your silhouette. He said it would sell more wine." Hugo took another sip.

"Did you? Please tell me you didn't."

"Carol wouldn't let us," Hugo said. "Are you sure you didn't add anything magical to this wine? It's making me feel something."

Alice took another sip. "Other than how it was made, nope. It's pure wine." Alice paused. With a hint of panic in her voice, she asked, "Why? Is something wrong? What are you feeling?"

Hugo finished his glass and set it in the picnic basket. He moved the basket back, removing all barriers between him and Alice. He leaned in. The smell of his vanilla and cedar cologne, combined with the worn leather of his jacket, tantalized Alice's senses. An unseen force emanated from Alice to Hugo, beckoning him to move closer to her, to touch her. He stopped short, teasing her, torturing her. She loved it.

"My stomach is twisted in knots. My heart beats uncontrollably. Madness runs through my mind. My soul aches for you. It's driving me crazy. Surely, you put a spell on me," Hugo proclaimed in a low, husky voice.

Alice leaned in, inviting, daring him to kiss her. Their lips hovered mere inches away, ready to remove the gap which separated them from their desires.

She whispered, "What if I did? Would that make me a bad witch? We're in the woods, after all. Don't bad witches live in the woods?"

Hugo removed Alice's wide-brimmed, curvy, pointed hat and tossed it onto the ground. "I don't think you're a bad witch."

"Be careful. I may lure you to my house," Alice whispered.

"And then what?"

"You'll just have to find out."

"I look forward to it," he replied.

His hand traced the contours of her jaw as it worked its way behind. His hand cradled the back of her head. His fingers entwined in her purple hair. He leaned in.

Their lips finally met in soft, tender embraces. Their tongues danced a familiar tango. A passionate union of two souls melded together by the fires of twin flames. Alice closed her eyes. The world faded away, leaving only the two of them behind. They lost themselves in all reality, time, and space. There was nothing else, only their love.

Alice leaned back to the ground and Hugo followed, never breaking their union. He caressed her head so it met the ground softly and safely. He leaned over her. Their hearts beat as one. His body shielded her from the night sky.

They broke their union. Alice's lips tingled, longing for more. She caught her breath, opened her emerald green eyes, and fixated onto his icy blues.

"So, am I a bad witch?" Alice asked.

He smirked. "What if I'm a witch hunter, secretly seducing you to bring you in?" Hugo playfully asked, staring down into her emerald green eyes.

"Then I'll sic my broomstick on you," Alice replied. Her voice grew louder. "Broomstick, attack Hugo."

They both peeped a glance toward the grayish-white, ash broomstick floating behind them. It continued floating there. Unmoving. Uncaring of the command.

Alice frowned. "Broomstick, help me. Get Hugo."

It didn't move.

"Is it okay?" Hugo asked as he rolled off Alice.

A sense of disappointment doused the internal flames of desire building up inside of her.

He sat up. "I mean, the process didn't like half work, did it?"

Alice sat up, keeping her eyes on the floating broomstick. "No, it . . . it worked. It has a different personality than Galahad did."

"Maybe he needs a name," Hugo said. "I named the last one. You have to name this one."

"That's the thing," Alice said. "I don't think it's a he. I think it's a she. When I conducted the creation ritual, I sensed an internal fury. A rage. A feminine rage. Hidden behind a poised facade. I know it too well."

"Okay, so it's a she. What are you naming her?"

"Well, since you named the last one after a knight of the round table, let's keep it an Arthurian name. What about Guinevere?" Alice glanced toward Hugo with a sly smile.

"I love it. Guinevere."

"Gwennie for short." Alice traced a finger along Hugo's chest. The black leather was soft to her touch. Her internal fires reignited. "Shall we continue?"

"After you lure me back to your house," Hugo said as he stood. "I have something I want to show you first."

Alice pouted. "Show me?"

"Yeah," he said as he sauntered over to Guinevere. He used two fingers to pet Guinevere on the end of the broomstick handle. His fingers traced the cracked grooves of her bark. "Nice to meet you, Guinevere. I look forward to many adventures together."

He flung his leg over the broomstick and sat on the brown leather saddle seat. He tapped the area behind him, inviting Alice to join him. "Hop on."

"Where are we going?" Alice asked.

"It's a surprise," Hugo answered.

"Tell me."

"Generally, surprises are left secret until you reveal them. Come on. Hop aboard."

"Fine." Alice stood and grabbed her witch's hat. She secured it on her head and took her place behind Hugo. With a snap of her fingers, the blanket folded neatly into a square. Another snap returned the blanket, bottle, and glasses to a basket. Once the contents returned, the basket lifted and flew to Alice. She tied the handle to a strap under the seat. "Where to?"

"As I said, it's a surprise. Hold tight."

Alice wrapped her arms around Hugo, holding him tightly. She rested her chin on his shoulder. Her breath teased at his ear.

He peeked back and smiled. "Ready?"

"Ready."

Hugo leaned forward and shouted, "Yaw!"

The broomstick took off. They flew out of Wildgrove Park, careful not to hit any of the tree branches attempting to strike them out of the night sky.

They raced toward the muted glow of Newbury Grove off in the distance. The trees were like blurry streaks beneath them. They passed above the town center. It was the witching hour, the time between 3 and 4 a.m. They were the only souls awake. Normally, they had a rule to stay away from the town center while flying to avoid a repeat of last March—back when Hugo flew across the sky, in front of a crowd of onlookers, as he raced to rescue Alice from the torment of the amulet of witch's fire.

Tonight was different. Alice allowed him to give her this view. This beautiful view of the turn of the twentieth-century buildings passing beneath them. Hugo pulled back to slow their speed, to not spoil this moment for Alice. She took it all in. The brightly colored awnings. Ornate light fixtures bathed the town center in an orangish glow. Neatly trimmed trees lined the street. This was her home. *Their* home.

Alice hugged Hugo tighter, wanting him to be as close to her as possible. She kissed him on the shoulder. He side-glanced back at her and smiled before banking to the left. They were following the streets below.

The building with the black-and-white striped awning came into view. The unmistakable, cursive black lettering. Raskin's Neighborhood Market.

Alice gave a curious look. "What are we doing here?"

"I told you it's a surprise," Hugo said.

Hugo maneuvered Guinevere to the back of the building. Alice snapped her fingers, and the area darkened to conceal their arrival from any onlookers. Their feet meet the ground with a cushioned touch as they landed. They disembarked and Hugo moved over to a door with an alarm.

"Are we breaking and entering?" Alice asked with a smile.

"Nah," Hugo said. "They trust me with the code. It's fine."

Hugo punched in a code on the security keypad. The door unlocked.

He opened it, holding and gesturing for her to go inside. "After you."

Alice smiled and said, "Gwennie, wait here." She entered the building with Hugo following behind her.

They were in the back loading area. Pallets of non-perishable items waited to be put on shelves. Hugo examined an electrical box on the wall. He flipped a few switches, and the entire store lit up.

"Follow me," Hugo commanded.

He proceeded through a swinging door. Alice followed.

They exited the loading area down a hallway leading to the main store. Alice followed Hugo as he forged a path through the lines of shelves. They passed by the deli counter, where only a year ago she told Hugo she would have said yes to a date if he had asked her out on the fateful night they first met. She was glad he had eventually asked her out.

"It's over here," Hugo said. "Wait. Close your eyes."

Alice stopped and did as commanded. "What is this?"

"It's your surprise. Trust me. Give me your hand," Hugo said.

Alice stuck out her hand, and he took it.

"Follow me." He led her down an aisle.

"I feel silly."

"That's okay. We can be silly together."

Alice tingled at his familiar phrase, conjuring images in her mind of when they stomped grapes together.

"Keep them closed."

"They're closed," she assured him.

"Okay, stop. Now open your eyes."

She did as instructed. Her mouth dropped with joyous glee. She covered the lower half of her face with her hands. The shock overwhelmed her. Tears formed in her eyes. She was motionless, frozen in time, not wanting to waste a second of the moment as it filled her soul.

Before her was a grand display. Multiple shelves of greenish-black bottles, neatly arranged in rows, glistened in the glow of the store lights. A cardboard cutout of Alice's silhouette stood next to the display. A banner hung above the shelves. An image of a witch riding a broom in front of the moon separated the two phrases "The Neighborhood Witch" and "Locally Brewed Wine" on the banner.

Alice approached the shelves. She dropped her hands and picked up a bottle. Her thumb traced the rectangular, dark purple label, exploring every bump and elevated line. In the center, there was a black silhouette of a witch from the waist up. She wore a curved, pointed, wide-brimmed hat and was snapping her fingers. A white line framed the image. The Neighborhood Witch was written across the bottom in a white font invoking the language of secret arcane knowledge.

Alice held the bottle, not wanting to let go. This was her bottle. This was her wine. This was her dream. Everything she ever wanted. She had her own wine in a store, not hidden away in some clandestine bar. Not anymore. She was on the store shelves. She made it.

"I helped them set up the display earlier today. Do you like it?" Hugo asked.

Alice pulled her eyes from the greenish-black bottle, tears running down her face.

Hugo's gleeful expression changed to one of worry. "If . . . if you don't like it, I can have the Raskins make a new label. This was only the first batch from the supplier."

"I love it. It's perfect."

Hugo breathed a sigh of relief. Alice put the bottle back on the shelf and hugged Hugo. He wrapped his arms around her as they embraced.

"Thank you. This means the world to me."

"I'm glad you like it," Hugo said.

"I love you, Hugo Dodds."

"I love you too, neighborhood witch."

They chuckled.

"It's the best Samhain present anyone could give me."

"Don't you mean Sauin?" he asked with a wink.

She let go of Hugo to glare at him with a coy smile.

"Come on. I'm going to show you what happens when I lure you back to my house." She grabbed Hugo's hand to lead him back home.

"Before we go, I have one more surprise," Hugo said.

Her face beamed with glee. "Oh. Another surprise?"

Hugo averted his gaze to the floor, biting his lower lip. He rocked back and forth, as if he was unsure of what to do next. Alice waited, her smile shrinking.

"I honestly didn't think I would ever be doing this again," Hugo said, never taking his eyes off the floor.

"Do what?" Alice asked.

"I thought things were over. Done. I was riding out time and waiting for . . . I don't know what. And then I met you. You changed everything. Thank you."

"Hugo . . . you're welcome." The smile faded from Alice as her joyful mood succumbed to Hugo's somber tone. "You've done more for me than anyone. You changed me too. This is possible because you helped me make it happen."

Hugo's gaze met hers. Tears in his eyes, he smiled and nodded. "I've struggled to find the right words because I didn't want to mess this up."

"You haven't messed anything up."

"Alice Primrose," Hugo said as he delved into his pocket. "You're the adventure of a lifetime, and I—"

Red and blue lights filled the grocery store. Banging noises against the front sliding doors echoed throughout the store. Hugo and Alice snapped their attention to the newfound commotion.

"I forgot to disarm the security alarm after we entered. Shit."

Hugo and Alice froze, checking with each other for clues on what to do next.

"Run?" Alice asked.

"No. I'll talk to them. The Raskins are going to be pissed tomorrow."

"You talk to them. I better get Gwennie in case they went around back." Alice took off, running for the back exit.

CHAPTER 2
OPENING DELAYS

The sun peeked through the light gray clouds that blanketed the midday sky. Hugo took Alice's hand as they approached the Raskin's Neighborhood Market. He rubbed his thumb in circles to send love messages he knew she wouldn't decipher, but her body would understand. Hugo risked a peek at Alice's face and smiled.

"Do you think they're still mad at you?" Alice asked with a returning grin.

"Nah," Hugo said. He thought for a moment. "I don't think so. It's all good. I explained to them what happened. I owe them for the cost of the false alarm . . . and maybe the late night wake-up call, but nothing major. I'm glad Gwennie took off and didn't get caught."

"Broomsticks tend to scatter when startled."

"Gally never scattered," Hugo said.

"Gally thought he was a dog," Alice replied. "He probably picked up some bad habits from Max."

Hugo chuckled. "Oh, no doubt. Luckily, Gwennie hid on the roof."

"She's a good broomstick. Young, but good," Alice said as she locked arms with Hugo. "I think the cop was more startled to see me."

They approached the front entrance. Shoppers came and went as they conducted their Saturday errands. Hugo and Alice passed through the automatic doors as a gush of air descended upon them. Alice quickly secured her curved witch's hat before it went flying off her head.

"One day, I'm going to lose my hat to that thing."

"It would be hilarious to watch you chase after your hat," he replied with a sly smile. "Unable to use your magick in front of everyone. Scrambling around the parking lot for it."

"Oh, there'd be magick," Alice replied with a Cheshire grin. "Believe that. I'm not chasing after this thing."

The store was bustling with activity, far busier than a typical Saturday crowd. There were candy stations setup through the store, so kids could trick-or-treat while their parents shopped for their weekly groceries. It was the Saturday before Halloween and, most importantly, the launch day for The Neighborhood Witch.

No one greeted them as they entered. Someone always welcomed customers into the store. Oliver wanted to welcome customers like an old friend returning for a visit.

Hugo focused on the registers as they continued past. Two were empty, very unusual for a Saturday. The other registers had lines stretching back into the aisles. The cashiers frantically hurried to get the customers through their lines as quickly as possible. They didn't have time for the usual pleasantries.

Hugo and Alice made their way through the store toward the deli counter. They were expecting Oliver to be holding court, but he was absent.

"Huh," Hugo said. "Oliver's usually hanging out here."

"Maybe he stepped away," Alice said.

Hugo smiled at Alice with a mischievous grin. "Let's go check out the display. Maybe they're over there."

They followed a familiar path to the wine section. There was a crowd of people checking out the new wine, holding and examining the bottle. Some people placed it back on the shelves. Others put the bottle in their carts. Alice turned to Hugo, a twinkle in her eye, grinning ear to ear.

"They're buying my wine. In a real store," she said in a hushed tone to Hugo.

"I'm so proud of you. Congratulations," Hugo said. He hugged her and gave her a quick kiss on top of her hat.

"You missed," she said.

"Did I?" he asked with a coy smile.

"Look, Mommy, it's the witch from the picture!" a small child belted out. "Are you a good witch or a bad witch?"

A small boy, standing next to Alice, caught her attention. She bent down to meet the child at his level. "What do you think? What kind of witch am I?"

The boy thought for a moment and said, "A good witch?"

Alice smiled. "And why am I a good witch?"

The boy paused for a moment. "Because your hair is purple. I like purple."

Hugo laughed. Alice side-glanced to him with a Cheshirish grin.

"I'm sorry," the boy's mother said. "He's five and says whatever is on his mind."

"It's okay," Alice said, turning her attention back to the boy.

"I like her hair too," Hugo said.

"Are you excited for Halloween?" Alice asked.

"Yep," he answered.

"Me too. Are you going to get lots of candy?"

"Yep," he answered once again.

"It's my favorite part. That and a bit of mischief," Alice replied.

The boy laughed.

Alice stood up, raising her arms above her head. "Now, my little minion, go forth and cause as much chaos and mischief as possible."

The boy giggled as he rushed behind his mom.

"Thank you," the mother said. "I love that they hired someone to dress up as a witch, especially with Halloween coming up."

"Oh, this isn't a—" Alice paused and nodded her head. "Thank you."

"She's the model for the wine label," Hugo added. "Doesn't she look the part?"

"Absolutely," the mother said. "Congratulations." She strolled off with her son.

Hugo draped his arm over Alice's shoulder. "So, is purple hair the difference between good and bad witches?"

"Hardly," Alice replied.

"There you two are," a voice said.

They turned around to see Carol Raskin standing behind them.

"So, how do you like the display?" Carol asked.

"I love it. It's far more than anything I could have asked for. Thank you," Alice said.

"Well, it was all Hugo's idea," Carol said as she gave Hugo a hug. "Speaking of which, if you're going to sneak in at night, next time remember the alarm code."

"It was all his idea, Mrs. Raskin," Alice said, pointing to Hugo.

"I smoothed things over with the police," Hugo said, smacking his hands together. "Mostly."

"Getting phone calls in the middle of the night isn't fun," Carol said.

"You should know better, Mr. Dodds," Alice said, moving next to Carol. She crossed her arms. "We're very disappointed in you."

"It won't happen again," Hugo said. "I promise."

"That's okay, sweetie," Carol said. "How did the other thing go?"

Hugo shook his head no and waved his hand to motion for Carol to stop asking.

"What other thing?" Alice asked.

"Max," Carol said. "How are things going with Max?"

"Max is Max. Still very much a puppy," Hugo said.

"How does she get along with your new . . . well, you know?" Carol asked.

"Max tries to get it to play, but—" Hugo started.

"It's not really in a playful mood," Alice finished.

"Well, you two be careful on that thing. It makes me nervous when you're are flying up there," Carol said. "Maybe wear a helmet or something."

"We're always careful," Hugo said. "Short staffed today?"

"It's the oddest thing," Carol said. "We've had so many people call off sick the past few days."

"Something's going around," Oliver said as he approached the group. "I think half the staff is sick."

"Sick?" Hugo said.

"They called in saying they felt tired and weak and wouldn't be able to make it in," Oliver explained. "They were perfectly fine the day before. It hit them all at once."

"Odd," Alice said.

Oliver turned his attention to Alice. "So, what do you think?"

"I love it," Alice said. "Thank you so much. It means the world to me."

"Well, thank you," Oliver said. "I think we're going to really move some wine."

"Being in the store is a dream come true for me," Alice said.

"Do you need any help?" Hugo asked. "I mean, it's been a few years, but I can jump behind a register if you need me."

"Don't worry about it, we're fine," Carol said.

"We don't do fine, Mrs. Raskin," Alice said. "We can help. Hugo can scan and I'll bag."

"Are you certain? I don't want to bother you two on your big day," Carol said.

"Nonsense," Hugo said. "You're not bothering us. We'd be glad to help."

"They want to help. Let them help," Oliver said. "Consider us even after last night's wake up call."

"I'm sorry about that," Hugo said. "It won't happen again."

"Besides, we'd have The Neighborhood Witch bagging groceries," Oliver added. "We can move even more product. Keep a couple bottles with you up at the register."

"Always thinking of some gimmick," Carol said. "Oh, okay."

Hugo turned to Alice. "Now you get to see me in action. I mean, it's been a *long* time, but it's just like riding a bike, right?"

"Didn't you take this job to spend time with Elizabeth only to quit a few weeks later?" Oliver asked.

Hugo turned to Oliver. "In my defense"—he raised his hands, trying to find a suitable answer—"our schedules didn't line up. I couldn't talk to her while doing the job, and I totally took the job because I wanted to talk to her. This will be different."

"Yeah," Alice said. "I'll be the one quitting early because I can't talk to Hugo while doing the job." She winked at him.

He rolled his eyes.

"Well, any help is appreciated," Carol said. "Thank you, sweetie."

"Here, I'll walk you up there and get a register going for you," Oliver said as he picked up a few bottles from the shelf.

Oliver and Alice headed toward the checkout.

"Hugo, sweetie, wait a moment," Carol said, touching his arm as if to hold him back.

"I'll meet you up front," Hugo said.

As soon as Oliver and Alice disappeared behind the corner, Carol asked, "Did she say no?"

Hugo chuckled. "I never got to ask. The police arrived as I started to ask her. I had my hand on the box when they knocked on the doors."

Carol smiled and shook her head. "I'm sorry, sweetie."

"It was the perfect moment, but there'll be another time, right? Besides, I felt like I was going to take away from her celebration, anyway."

"She would have loved it," Carol said.

"Her reflection told me so. She wasn't exactly happy it didn't happen," Hugo added. "She kept going on about how she can't wear her ring until I give it to Alice. She's threatening to spill the secret for me to hurry up."

"You're still going to ask her, right?" Carol asked.

"Of course. I would do it Halloween night, but we already have plans. We have dinner reservations for next Saturday to celebrate. So, I'll have to fall back on Plan B."

Carol smiled and gave Hugo a hug. "She'll love it. Trust me."

"I certainly hope so."

CHAPTER 3
UNDER NEW OWNERSHIP

I'm glad I wore the bigger pants this time.

A small box jostled around in Hugo's jacket pocket. He caressed the velvet covered lining, so it wouldn't bounce out on their way to dinner. A chill ran up his spine as the autumn wind swirled. A layer of dark, autumn clouds swirled in the night sky above.

I hope the rain holds off . . . Huh. Like last time.

He smiled at Alice. She returned the favor, beaming from ear to ear.

Hugo and Alice approached the town center hand in hand. It was bustling with activity as people finished their shopping. The ornate lampposts were in mid-holiday transition. Some were still decorated with pumpkins for Halloween a few days prior. Others were decorated in green wreaths for the upcoming Christmas season. The perfect mixture of Alice's favorite holidays welcomed them to their favorite restaurant. Hugo smiled.

This is going to be a magical night.

Hugo stopped. His eyes narrowed, and his mouth slightly dropped. Alice took a few more steps forward before stopping.

"What is it?" Alice asked.

"Look," he said.

Alice turned to see what stopped Hugo in his tracks. The awning for *Antonio's Italian Ristorante*—normally red, green, and white stripes—was now black with a single crimson stripe down the middle.

"Why would he change it?" Alice said.

"Let's ask him," Hugo replied.

They approached the door and stopped once more. They both focused on the gold lettering on the door. *Sylvia's Bistro.*

Hugo examined the front of the building, double checking the awnings along the strip. "This is the right place, right?"

"That's our table, but it's occupied," Alice said. "I thought you made reservations."

"I did."

A waitress handed a couple two menus as they sat down for their Saturday night dinner at their table. Their special table. He reexamined the gold lettering of the door. *Sylvia's.* He had passed through the door countless times before—it was unmistakable to him. This was the correct place, but not the right restaurant.

They checked with each other, a sense of foreboding in their eyes.

"Maybe Sylvia is his daughter or relative," Hugo said.

"It seems sudden," Alice replied. "Let's find out."

Hugo held the door as Alice entered. He hurried behind.

This was the same restaurant, only different. The walls were a darker, greenish-black paint. Crimson red curtains were pulled back in the windows. The white tablecloths were replaced with ones matching the curtains. The glass tea light candleholders, once on every table, had been replaced with black candlesticks holding melting red candles. The soft sounds of crooners entertaining guests was replaced by the symphonic melodies of classical piano.

"Welcome to Sylvia's. How many?" the hostess asked.

While he wasn't on a first-name basis with everyone, Hugo had spent enough time in Antonio's to recognize the faces of the employees. He scanned the restaurant, but didn't recognize a single face of the waitstaff.

"How many?"

"I believe we have a reservation," Alice said. "It should be under Dodds."

"Ah, yes. This way, please." The hostess picked up two menus and guided them around the corner to the back of the restaurant.

Alice followed, but Hugo didn't.

"Everything okay?" Alice whispered to Hugo.

"It feels . . . odd," Hugo whispered back.

"I'm sure it's fine. Let's go sit down," Alice said.

They followed the hostess.

The hostess placed the menus on the square table. "Enjoy," she said before returning to the front.

He pulled out Alice's chair, inviting her to sit.

"Still a gentleman," Alice said.

"Always."

Alice removed her hat and tailcoat, handing them both to Hugo before sitting down.

Hugo draped the coat over his arm and held onto her hat. Using them as a shield from Alice's prying eyes, he moved the velvet box from his jacket to his pant pocket. He moved to hang up their coats, but stopped. He searched, but couldn't find any coat racks. Unable to find any, he pulled out an empty chair, set her hat down in the seat, and draped the coats over the chairback.

He took his seat, picking up the menu. "This was Antonio's a few days ago, right?"

"Yeah," Alice said with hesitation in her voice. "At least, I think so."

A waitress approached. "Welcome to Sylvia's Bistro. Thank you for being part of our opening weekend. My name is Carmilla. May I start you off with something to drink?"

Alice greeted the young waitress with a smile. "Do you have a selection of wines?"

"Yes," Carmilla said, flipping Alice's menu over to the back. "We have a variety of selections on the back. The house specialty is a new blend from Red-Hearted Queen, exclusive to Sylvia's Bistro."

"NO!" Alice and Hugo shouted in unison as they both focused on Carmilla.

She took a step back at their reaction.

"Sorry. Uh, we'll start with water while we look over the list," Hugo said. His eyes checked Alice's reaction before nodding to Carmilla.

"I'll give you two a few minutes to look over the menu," Carmilla said. She turned to leave.

"Wait," Hugo said. "Wasn't this Antonio's?"

"Yes. Mr. Savino purchased the restaurant from Mr. Moretti. We've rebranded with all new offerings. Be careful touching the walls. The paint may still be wet in spots."

"What happened to Mr. Moretti?" Alice asked with a discerning expression.

"We're old friends, and he never mentioned he was selling," Hugo added.

"I'm not certain, but if you like, I can have Mr. Savino stop over. He may know," Carmilla suggested.

"That'd be great," Hugo said. "I'm curious about meeting Mr. Savino."

"Wonderful," Carmilla said. "I'll be right back with the water." She disappeared into the kitchen area.

Hugo turned to Alice and whispered, "I don't like this."

"What?" Alice asked.

"It takes more than a few days to rebrand and get a new restaurant up and running. Let alone hire new staff," Hugo replied.

"How do you know they hired a new staff?"

"I don't recognize anyone in here."

"Maybe they're very . . . efficient." Alice winked at him.

"Funny," Hugo said, picking up his menu. "Very funny."

"You don't like change," Alice said.

"I like change. I don't like surprises."

"Oh, really?" Alice set her menu down. "Every time we come here, you always get the same thing."

"I know what I like," Hugo said. "Now, I have to figure out my new thing."

"There's definitely a wide range on the menu."

Hugo read through the assortments of seafood and meat offerings. Each entrée had a wide assortment of fancy sounding sides glazed in sauces and expensive price tags. His eyes reread every option available multiple times, but he couldn't find what he really wanted—a helping of Antonio's world famous meatballs and spaghetti.

"I guess a steak for me." Hugo flipped the menu over, scanning the selection of wines.

"Oh, the salmon sounds wonderful. Glazed vegetables, roasted potatoes, and covered in a special sauce. Sold." Alice placed her menu down.

"These are all Red-Hearted Queen wines," Hugo said. His eyebrows furled with frustration.

"So, we skip the wine," Alice said.

"But I was looking forward to it." Hugo slapped the menu down. "Yet again, more surprises."

Alice tilted her head at him inquisitively with narrow eyes. "Everything okay?"

"Yeah. I want this to be a perfect night because I want to—" He paused, catching himself from revealing his secret. "I want to properly celebrate your release and a successful first week."

Alice smiled and blushed. She stretched across the table and took his hand. "It doesn't matter what we eat or drink. All that matters is that we're celebrating this together. That's all I really want."

"I guess you're right," Hugo said. "We'll have to toast to your success."

"*Our* success," Alice said. "This didn't happen without you. Remember that."

Hugo gazed into Alice's emerald green eyes.

"Two glasses of water," a man's voice said as he placed the glasses on the table.

Alice gulped as she examined the stranger standing next to them. Hugo broke his gaze from Alice to examine this mysterious man.

He was tall with black, wavy hair, parted long on top and tapered short on the sides. High cheekbones, a wide jaw, and a sharp jawline. His rough, stubbled beard masked his sunken face, as if he hadn't shaved for a few days.

He wore a black vest over a matching black dress shirt and red tie. His shirt was tailored fit and tight against his broad shoulders and muscular chest. Rolled-up sleeves to his elbow revealed a tattoo on his forearm—a red heart emerging from a crimson rose with a serpentine stem.

"Welcome to Sylvia's Bistro. Allow me to introduce myself. My name is Sebastian Savino. I'm the new owner of this establishment," he said in a low, gravelly voice. "I understand you have some questions about Mr. Moretti?"

Alice cleared her throat. "Yes, Mr. Moretti was a friend of ours. He never mentioned selling his beloved restaurant."

Sebastian smirked. "Ah, yes, Antonio. I'm new to town and wanted to open a restaurant of my own. I decided it would be easier to acquire this location instead of starting fresh, so I made an offer too good not to accept. He mentioned it would be nice to return to Italy. I learned all about his world-famous meatballs. I wanted to buy the recipe, but he refused. I guess I can't buy everything." He chuckled.

Hugo's eyes narrowed, studying Sebastian's reaction. "How did you get up and running so fast?"

"My methods are . . . efficient," Sebastian said, gazing directly into Hugo's eyes.

Hugo and Alice shared a glance.

"How efficient?" Alice asked as they both turned back to Sebastian.

Sebastian laughed. "This isn't my first establishment. I have multiple locations. I was able to make a few calls. I had my crew come in to redecorate quickly. I even brought in staff from other locations. As I said . . . efficient."

"You said you're new in town. It wouldn't be on Ravenhill Drive, would it?" Hugo asked.

"Why, yes. My wife, Sylvia, and I moved into a lovely house next to a very . . . eccentric one. It's a purple house."

"That's our purple house," Alice said.

He pressed his hands against his chest. "Oh, please forgive me. I meant no disrespect."

"None taken. I've heard worse," Alice replied.

"Ah, good. I don't want to start off on the wrong foot with our neighbors," Sebastian said with a hint of glee. "Since this is your first time here at Sylvia's and we're neighbors, your meal will be on the house."

"You don't have to do that on our account," Hugo said.

"No worries at all," Sebastian said. "It's my way of thanking you for visiting."

"That's very generous of you," Alice said.

"It's my pleasure," Sebastian said. "Would you like a bottle of wine? On the house, of course. We exclusively carry my wife's wine brand, Red Hearted-Queen. We even have a brand-new type we're testing out. I'll have one brought out to you."

"That's okay," Hugo said.

"I insist," Sebastian said.

"We've—" Hugo stated.

"We've had a few bad experiences with it," Alice finished.

Sebastian dropped his arms to his side and tilted his head. "A . . . reaction?"

"Yes," Alice said. "Last year, after it was first on sale."

"One right over there," Hugo added, pointing to his usual table. "It upset my . . . stomach." His mind dredged up memories of the ghoulish Elizabeth lurching toward him in an attempt to drag him into a deep, dark void. He shook his head to clear the memories of the horrible daymare.

"Ah, yes, we had a small production issue with the first few batches. It wasn't quite up to our standards of quality. I promise you, this one is much better. I'll have your waitress bring it out and take your orders," Sebastian said as he took a step away from the table and stopped. He turned back. "What are you two doing this evening?"

"Well, we did have a plan to go for a stroll after dinner," Hugo said.

"On a night like this? It could rain at any moment and ruin your wonderful evening," he said. "How would you like to go dancing?"

"I would love to go dancing," Alice said.

Hugo's heart sank. His perfectly planned evening with the perfect meal and the second-most perfect proposal were now in shambles. He couldn't say no to Alice's love of dancing. He should have proposed last Saturday. Or on Halloween. Or any other random time since then. The proposal would have to wait.

"Excellent. My wife owns a nightclub on High Street just north of campus in the city. I'll call and tell her to expect you two," he said. He pointed at Alice. "It's not a typical nightclub."

"We know of a rather unusual nightclub too," Hugo said with a wink to Alice.

"It's more of an . . . alternative nightclub," Sebastian said. He gestured to Alice with his open hand. "I think you'd fit right in there."

Alice gasped. Her face filled with glee. "We have to go. Do you know how long it's been since I went dancing? We're going."

"Perfect," Sebastian said. "I'll let her know to expect you. I'll go write down the address for you. It's called The Heart and Rose." He retreated into the kitchen.

A moment later, Carmilla returned with a bottle of Red-Hearted Queen. The familiar playing card logo with the card suits encircled a gold, multi-point crown. The heart was on top and the spade on the bottom. She poured the wine into two glasses.

Hugo and Alice took the glasses. They swirled the reddish-purple liquid in their glasses and took a sniff. The aroma of berries and earth tones filled Hugo's senses. He checked with Alice, tilting his head and giving a half-hearted smile, waiting for an excuse not to drink. Hugo didn't want to upset his new neighbor, but also didn't want another freak out in the restaurant.

Hugo's foot twitched. His heart raced. He tapped the table with his free index finger. His eyes darted back and forth from Alice to the glass, hoping to direct her attention, so she would say something. She raised an eyebrow and her glass. He smiled at Carmilla standing next to the table, holding the bottle. She smiled back. Hugo took one more sniff, pressed the glass against his lips, and drank.

He waited. Waited for anything to happen. Was the room going to melt away like last time? Would the ghoulish image of Elizabeth be replaced by Alice . . . or Johanna?

Nothing happened.

There was no odd aftertaste. It tasted . . . great. He shot a glance over to Alice with a pleasantly surprised expression. She took a sip.

"This is nice," Alice said. "Very smooth."

"Thank you," Carmilla said as she placed the bottle onto the table. "Now what would you like to order?"

CHAPTER 4
THE QUEEN'S COURT

"Did you bring any *Drink Me Juice*?" Hugo asked as he exited the black SUV.

"What's *Drink Me Juice*?" Alice asked as she exited the passenger side.

"You know, the blue liquid that sobers you up. You wrote *Drink Me* on it the night I passed out. I thought that's what it was called?"

"Oh, that," Alice said. "I never really gave it a name."

"Sounds like it has a name now."

"There's a box for Ez in the back. One should be in there. Why?"

"Well, it'll determine how much I drink tonight," Hugo replied as he opened the back gate. He rummaged through a box. "Yep. There's one here. Sounds like tonight is going to be fun."

The SUV beeped as he shut the gate and locked the doors. Alice held out her hand, and Hugo took it.

Alice smiled as they turned the corner. They parked on a side street away from the main traffic of High Street, which was hopping on a Saturday night. Cars drove up and down the street. People stumbled from bar to bar. College students reveled in the school's latest football victory. Some reveled too much as their friends helped them back home.

"So, tell me. How many times were you stumbling down this street heading back to the dorms?" Alice asked.

"You know what they say about us finance guys," he replied.

"Let me guess . . . Numbers by day. Party at night?"

"Something like that," Hugo replied.

Alice chuckled. "I never took you for a party animal."

"I was a much different man in college," Hugo said. "I can tell you were too."

"Oh, yeah? What can you tell about me?"

"I bet you were all kinds of trouble. *Fun* trouble," Hugo said with a sly smile.

"I resent that," Alice said as she lightly smacked him across the chest. "Even if it is true."

Hugo rubbed his black shirt where she struck him. "Two party animals, back on the town. Reliving their glory days."

"You might be, but this was a typical Saturday night for me," Alice said. "My friends and I would always go out for a night of dancing on the weekends."

Alice hadn't been out dancing since before her move to Newbury Grove. Not because she couldn't convince Hugo to go dancing, but there weren't the type of nightclubs she frequently visited. One catered more toward her aesthetic.

They approached The Heart and Rose in an older, rectangular building set on a street corner independent from other buildings. Two-story tall windows filled one side of the building overlooking the side street. A small, over capacity parking lot was on the other side.

The building appeared to cry black tears as a layer of dirt and grime dripped down the stone and brick facade. A black awning spanned the front of the building. A pole held the white, rectangular marquee high above the street, emblazoned with the same logo as Sebastian's forearm tattoo.

An electric mixture of music filled the street as the pounding beats seeped through the walls and doors. People were entering and leaving. All dressed in black.

Alice couldn't wait. She opened the door, instead of waiting for Hugo's chivalrous gesture.

The nightclub was a mixture of darkness and laser lights transitioning through an array of colors. The walls, flooring, and ceiling were painted black. Crimson red curtains covered the windows. A DJ booth stood in the corner to her left as she entered, and a dance stage was in the corner to her right. The bar lined the left wall with a storage room off to the side. A black and white checkerboard tiled dance floor dominated the center. A balcony overlooked the entire establishment, emitting a gentle glow from within its depths.

Alice could hardly contain her glee. She danced with the music in the entryway. Her low-cut, thick-soled shoes tapped the floor. Her hips swayed to the beats of the music, and her shoulders tried to keep up.

"Five-dollar entry fee," the doorman yelled over the sounds. He was dressed head to toe in black clothing, blending into the darkness. He was only highlighted by the soft glow of a lamp on top of a makeshift desk strewn with a money box, a hand stamp, a metal detector wand, and promotional ads for upcoming events.

Hugo took out his wallet and handed the doorman ten dollars.

He placed the money in the box and stamped their hands before waving the wand over them. "Enjoy."

They made their way into the crowd. Hugo strolled, while Alice bounced with the beats. An eclectic mix filled the dance floor. Some wore very revealing mesh and fishnet stockings. Others in leather and vinyl. Some, like Hugo, dressed in pants and long-sleeve shirts. Almost all dressed in all black. They blended seamlessly with the shadows, gracefully dancing in the darkness, their forms illuminated only by the vibrant lights swirling around the club.

Alice wore a mixture of everything. A black top with mesh sleeves with cut-outs for her thumbs. Fishnet stockings under a black leather skirt. Thick soled, low-cut shoes for dancing. She had left her hat and tailcoat at home as she planned to dance the night away unencumbered, letting her inhibitions run wild.

"Join me on the stage," Alice pleaded. "Please."

"That's your thing. I'll stand by the bar and watch."

"I thought party animal Hugo was coming out to play tonight." Alice made a pouty face.

He bowed his head to hide his smile. "Get enough drinks in me, and I'll consider it."

"Deal."

"Speaking of which, the usual?"

"Yep, but first, I dance." She was spellbound by the mixture of synthwave, industrial, and electronic beats enticing her as she danced her way to the stage.

Alice sprinted up the stage steps to join the other revelers. Her body exuded confidence and grace as she gyrated to the pulsating, electronic beats. A pinkish, red glow bathed her every move. Her presence and aura captivated the onlookers as they mimicked her movements.

She lost herself in the music, channeling her energy into a dazzling display of fluid movement. Her arms snaked and glided through the air like she was using unseen patterns to conjure forth a spell. A spell which enthralled anyone who beheld her movements. Each gesture more dynamic and daring than the last. Her body was an instrument for her soul to express pure joy.

Alice swayed her hips to the sensual beats. Each step purposeful, repositioning herself for the next improvised dance move. Her feet glided across the stage as she twisted, swirled, and stomped. Elegant and impeccable with every step. Her vibrant purple hair wildly swayed as it struggled to keep up with her movements.

She danced with a few people before breaking back out on her own. Song after song played. Her mind, body, and soul fused to become one. Time lost all meaning. There was only the moment.

Everyone was connected by the universal language of music and dance.

Alice lost track of how long she'd been on the stage. She searched for Hugo in the crowd. Her mind raced with thoughts of enticing him to join her on the stage. Alice's eyes adjusted to the darkness against the bright lights of the stage. Even in the darkness, she could find him. He was standing at the corner of the bar talking to a man. She could only make out his outline, but she recognized him from dinner earlier. Sebastian. Alice stopped dancing and strutted off the stage to meet them.

"I'm so glad you could make it," Sebastian said. "I see you're enjoying yourself."

"Very much so, thank you," Alice replied.

Hugo took a sip from his old fashioned as he handed Alice her vodka cranberry. "I was telling Sebastian I used to pass by this place when I was in college. I remember when it was a pool hall."

"I'd love for you to meet my wife, Sylvia. She's standing at the balcony railing right now," Sebastian said, pointing up and waving.

The silhouette of a woman against the backlight stood at the railing. One hand on the railing, another holding what appeared to be a wine goblet.

"She likes to hold court up there with the VIPs, but I think I can get you an audience with her highness." He chuckled.

Hugo and Alice waved up. The woman retreated from the railing.

"That'd be great," Alice said as she took a sip. "I'd love to meet her."

"Come along," Sebastian said as he led them toward a set of stairs.

Alice followed, but Hugo tapped her arm to stop her.

"Look." Hugo pointed to the bar and raised an eyebrow at Alice.

Bottles of Red-Hearted Queen stood amongst the other bottles of alcohol behind the bar.

"Don't see too many wines at a bar."

"Well, besides mine," Alice said.

"I guess if you're selling alcohol, you might as well sell yours too," Hugo said as they caught up to Sebastian.

He led them to a set of U-shaped stairs. A massive man blocked the stairs from unwelcome visitors.

"Evening, Mr. Savino." The man stepped aside.

"Good evening. They're with me," Sebastian said.

"Yes, sir."

Alice and Hugo followed Sebastian up the stairs.

The balcony was well decorated. Two crimson, high-back chairs were surrounded by couches and other assortments of furniture. The soft glow of lamps in the corners provided light in the otherwise dark space. An oversized fireplace dominated the middle of the back wall. A player piano was set against the wall. Sebastian moved around the high-back chairs.

"My love, our special guests are here," Sebastian said to the woman on the other side.

She set a wineglass on a table next to her. The dark, reddish liquid sloshed back and forth as she set it down. She stood and emerged from around the chair to greet them, staring Alice directly in the eyes.

Alice gasped, shocked at her exquisite beauty and enchanted by her presence. She was tall and slender like a fashion model. Strawberry blonde hair parted to her left and cascaded down below her shoulder in luscious waves. Her intense blue eyes were like sparkling sapphires enhanced by a touch of black mascara. Her face was sculpted to perfection with high cheekbones and a sharp jawline. Her pouty lips accentuated her natural beauty with a sense of strength and determination.

"Welcome to The Heart and Rose. I'm Sylvia Savino," she said, slightly bowing. "Please. Come sit." She motioned for them to sit on an adjoining couch.

Alice couldn't take her eyes off Sylvia, enthralled by her remarkable fashion sense. Her leather jacket fit snugly against her curvy frame—white with a red stripe across the shoulders, a modern take on an '80s design. The large lapels and a smooth texture accentuated her feminine magnetism. She wore a simple black top beneath her jacket that didn't distract Alice's eyes from her natural beauty. The black leather pants complementing her look hugged the curves of her hips and left nothing to the imagination.

Alice's heart fluttered as she was hypnotized and captivated by her beauty.

"It's not polite to stare," Hugo whispered to Alice.

Hugo's words broke her trance. Alice blushed and followed him to the couches. Sebastian sat next to Sylvia in the other high-back chair.

Sylvia picked up her wineglass and took a drink. "Sebastian told me we're neighbors," Sylvia said over the pulsating beats below.

"We live in the purple house. You can't miss it." Hugo chuckled.

"I love what you did with the house," Sylvia said. "It's so unique and . . . interesting."

"I can't take credit for it. She painted it before I moved in." Hugo motioned to Alice with his head.

Alice sat frozen, only to take the occasional sip from her vodka cranberry, unable to pull her eyes off Sylvia.

Hugo continued, "Your house actually used to be mine."

"How interesting," Sylvia said. "It's a quaint little house. You took care of it well."

Hugo glanced to his empty ring finger. "Thank you. It was a great home, but I have a better one now." He placed his hand on Alice's leg.

Hugo's touch broke Alice's gaze from Sylvia. The room swirled as she became lightheaded. Her heart raced.

Hugo leaned in and whispered, "Everything okay?"

Alice brought her drink up to shield her mouth from the Savinos' view. "I'm fine. Just got lightheaded for a moment. Drinking and dancing." She took a sip.

"Ah," Hugo replied.

"Are you enjoying yourselves?" Sylvia asked.

"It's been great," Alice replied. "I could see myself here every Saturday night."

"Well, I hope so," Sylvia replied. "I was watching you. You're a great dancer."

"Thank you," Alice said.

"So, what brought you to Newbury Grove?" Hugo asked.

Sylvia took a drink and set it down. "We wanted a quieter life. A smaller place to unwind. We run a small restaurant and nightclub empire. A few establishments in a few cities. Nothing much. It's easy to get lost in the hustle and bustle. We wanted some place quiet and disconnected from everything else. Where we could relax and be ourselves."

"Well, Ravenhill Drive is just that—quiet," Hugo said.

The pulsating beats echoed off the walls.

"It's fairly loud in here and not exactly the best place to introduce ourselves," Sylvia said. The oppressive sounds grew louder and louder. "We would love to get together and get to know each other in a more intimate setting."

"Yeah, that would be great," Alice said.

"Perfect. We tend to work late, and we're not exactly morning people. How about tomorrow night?" Sylvia asked. "We'd love to have you over for dinner."

Hugo and Alice nodded at each other.

"That'd be wonderful," Alice replied.

"Prefect. Let's say . . . seven tomorrow. I look forward to our conversations," Sylvia said with a smile. "Now, go enjoy yourselves. Tell the bartender Sylvia said your tab was covered."

"You don't have to do that," Alice protested.

"Please. Consider it us being neighborly," Sebastian replied.

"Thank you," Hugo said. "We look forward to tomorrow."

"As do we," Sylvia said with a smile.

Alice stood up and took Hugo's hand. "Come on. You owe me that dance."

CHAPTER 5

DINNER AND UNUSUAL DRINKS

"Should we bring a bottle?" Alice asked as she peeked into the bathroom. The thought of bringing a gift raced through her mind all day. Rarely was she invited as a guest to someone's new home, and she didn't want to seem like she was imposing. "I can grab one from downstairs."

Hugo finished buttoning up his dark blue shirt. "I don't know. Maybe?" He turned to the mirror. "What do you two think?"

Alice and Hugo's reflections were in the heat of an intense, passionate kiss. They ignored the question.

Alice whistled. "You two. Knock it off for a moment."

They stopped; their eyebrows arched in annoyance at their non-reflective selves.

"I don't care," Alice's reflection said.

"Does it matter? They probably have a bunch of wine there, anyway. It'd be like giving air as a present," Hugo's reflection said. "Kind of useless."

"He's right," Alice's reflection said. "Useless."

"Do you know what's not useless?" Hugo's reflection whispered to Alice's reflection, staring her in the eyes.

Alice's reflection locked eyes with Hugo's reflection. She whispered back, "What?"

"Every waking moment with you," he responded in a low growl. "My heart burns for you. I can't stand it. Every moment we spend apart is torturous."

"Wait. When are you two ever apart? You're together all the time. All you do is make out," Hugo said.

They glared daggers at Hugo.

"Hey! You're ruining the mood," Hugo's reflection said.

"Out. Now," Alice's reflection commanded as she pointed to the door.

"Lights off," Hugo's reflection added.

"No," Alice's reflection corrected. "Leave them on. I want to stare into your eyes."

"Oh, I love you," Hugo's reflection said.

"I loved you first," Alice's reflection replied.

He lifted her up, and she wrapped her arms and legs around him. They renewed their sensual conquest.

"You two have fun," Alice said.

Alice's reflection waved for her to go away. Alice moved back into the bedroom, and Hugo followed.

"Have you considered getting a normal mirror? Hang that other one off to the side, so I don't have to guess at how I look." He tugged on his sleeves and fixed his shirt collar.

"Where's the fun in that?" Alice said with a smile. "You look fine."

They exited the bedroom and descended the stairs. Loud whines, playful growls, and the occasional dog toy squeaker echoed from the living room. Hugo and Alice removed their coats from the rack and slipped them on. They glanced into the living room at the noise.

Max held her toy cauldron in her mouth, a gift from Alice last Christmas, shaking it back and forth. She bent down in a downward dog position, ready to jump and play, except her partner was unwilling. Guinevere hovered in the air, unfazed by the playful advances of the golden retriever.

"I don't think she wants to play with you, buddy," Hugo said.

Max stopped and focused on him, her tail wagging with excitement. She trotted over to Hugo and Alice, excited at the prospect of leaving.

He continued, "You have to stay. We'll be back."

Alice bent down and rubbed Max's head. "You be good while we're gone. Keep Gwennie company. We'll see you later."

Max stood there, thrashing her golden tail back and forth in a manipulative attempt to get them to take her with them. It didn't work.

They opened the door and exited.

"Be good. See you later," Hugo said as he closed the black door behind him.

Darkness engulfed Ravenhill Drive. Nighttime crept in earlier and earlier in the chilly November air. Only the light from porch lamps fought back. A car or two drove down the street. Children played and protested as they were called inside for the evening.

"Are you ready?" Alice asked.

"Yep," Hugo replied.

"I mean, are you ready to go in there?"

Hugo paused, focusing on his former white, folk Victorian home. He flexed his hand and then nodded. "Yeah."

"Are you certain? We can call it off if you don't want to go."

"I'm good. It was my home. It's not any longer." He tapped the purple siding of their house with the back of his hand. "This is my home now. I'm good."

Alice smiled and took his hand.

"You're not going to stare at her all night, are you?" Hugo teased.

"For the last time, I think I was dehydrated or something. I got lightheaded and was kind of out of it for a while," Alice replied.

Hugo arched his eyebrow and smiled to give her a playful, discerning look.

"Honest."

"Let's go," he said with a smile.

Hand in hand, Alice and Hugo headed down the gray porch steps. They crossed the yard and up the steps to the front door. Even though the porch light was off and the darkness filled the void, the crimson red paint on the door was unmistakable. Alice squeezed Hugo's hand at the first sign of change to his old family home.

"Their home, not mine," he said before knocking on the door.

The crimson door opened. Sylvia stood in the door, shadowed by the backlight behind her.

"Good evening and welcome," she said, backing away from the doorway. "Please enter and make yourselves at home."

Alice and Hugo entered. Sylvia shut the door behind them.

Hugo stood in the hallway, taking in the new decorations. The walls were painted a dark, blackish-green color. A sharp contrast from the lighter, beige color when Hugo lived there. Crimson red curtains were drawn over the windows in the living room. Chesterfield style furniture, all in black leather, filled the room. The walls were filled with various picture frames and old family relics.

The shelves and mantle of the fireplace, once white, were now the same blackish-green as the walls. Each shelf was filled with an assortment of books. Some new, but mostly old, as if they were original copies. Their canvas bindings were frayed and well worn. The leather-bound books had an inviting appearance as if the soft, supple leather beckoned Alice to open them to discover their secrets. The light throughout the house was dim and flickering, simulating candlelight.

The once bright and cheerful happy home was steeped in an eerie darkness.

"I love your hair," Sylvia said. "It's so unique and vibrant. Your hat too."

"Thank you," Alice responded as she removed her hat and tousled her hair.

"You can hang up your coats in the closet if you'd like. Sebastian should be finishing up dinner in a moment," Sylvia said as she retreated down the hallway toward the kitchen. Her backless red dress swayed with every step as the hem glided above the hardwood floor.

Sylvia disappeared into the kitchen. When she was gone, Alice and Hugo glanced at each other.

"I think I'm underdressed." Alice gestured to her outfit. She wore a long sleeve, black, tunic blouse which flared out at the bottom like the skirt of a dress paired with a blackish-gray pair of jeans.

"Me too," Hugo said. He wore a blue button-up shirt and dark blue jeans.

Hugo opened the closet door and hung up their outerwear. They proceeded down the hallway to the dining area.

A crimson red tablecloth covered a rectangular table. There were four place settings—two on each side—with gold silverware and black napkins. Wine goblets were placed behind every plate. A black candelabra with red candlesticks melted away in the center of the table. Alice glanced at Hugo, raising an eyebrow.

He leaned in and whispered, "Need I remind you, you're the one with purple hair and a purple house?"

"Fair point," Alice replied.

Sebastian entered carrying a large plate of pasta in one hand and a bowl of sausage, peppers, and onions in a tomato sauce in the other. He set them down, one on each side of the candelabra.

"I hope you're hungry. I made my favorite dish—a family specialty from back home in Italy. Sweet Italian sausage with peppers and onions in homemade red sauce," he said. "I hope you like garlic. We Savinos have been known to add a little too much to our sauce."

"Are you from Italy?" Hugo said. "Not to offend, but I don't hear an accent."

"Sí." Sebastian brushed off his white apron. "And no offense taken. I lost my accent with age. I was much younger when I came over. Although my family was originally from Italy, I grew up on the

French side of the border. So, I'm a bit of Italian and French. It's also why I wanted Antonio's secret recipe; although he wouldn't give it to me, no matter the price." He chuckled.

Alice's mouth watered at the as the sweet aromas filled her senses. "It smells wonderful."

"Thank you. Please sit," he said. "Sylvia went downstairs to grab a bottle of wine from the wine cellar."

"You have a wine cellar downstairs?" Hugo asked.

"More like racks. A modest, personal collection I don't sell in my restaurant," Sebastian said. He rolled down his red sleeves, adjusted his black tie, and straightened his black vest before taking his seat.

Alice and Hugo sat down as well.

Sylvia entered carrying a bottle of wine and set it on the table. "It took me awhile to find it. It's an older vintage," she said.

Sylvia collected Hugo's and Alice's goblets and began filling them. The reddish-purple liquid sloshed around before coming to a rest. She filled hers and Sebastian's as well. "We love wine. Are you two big wine drinkers?"

"More than you know," Alice responded.

Sylvia smiled and set the bottle down. She tilted her head as if she knew a secret. "Are you The Neighborhood Witch?"

Alice blushed and shied away from Sylvia's question. Hugo glanced at Alice.

"You look very similar to the woman on the bottle at the store. I thought maybe the wine was yours," Sylvia added as she took her seat.

"No. Well . . . yes, but it's not—" Alice stumbled over her words, trying to find an answer.

"We work in distribution," Hugo said. "A partner asked Alice to pose for their label considering her witchy appearance."

"We're in distribution too," Sebastian said. "We own Red Heart Distribution. It's the top distributor in the state. Who do you work for?"

"Umm . . ." Hugo was at a loss for words.

"We work for an independent distributor. A small one. Very small. Brand new, even," Alice said.

"A micro-brewery? How wonderful. What's the name?" Sylvia asked with a smile.

"Moonlight Brewers," Hugo said with a wink to Alice.

"Moonlight Brewers . . . I've never heard of them," Sylvia said.

"They're very small," Alice said. "The Neighborhood Witch is their first offering."

"Getting in on the ground floor. I admire your entrepreneurial spirit," Sebastian said. "We started offering our own brand as well."

"Red-Hearted Queen," Sylvia said.

"Sebastian mentioned it at the restaurant," Alice said.

"Have you tried it?" Sylvia asked.

Hugo and Alice glanced at each other as if they were telepathically negotiating what to say next. They negotiated with facial expressions, which Alice interrupted to take the polite path. Alice wanted to tell them there was something in their wine, but didn't want to disrespect them, especially as guests in their home. Alice turned her attention back to Sylvia.

"Oh, we've had it three times," Alice replied. "Twice when it first came out and again recently at your restaurant."

"How was it?" Sylvia asked.

"Well . . . "Alice answered, breaking eye contact as she struggled to find the right words. "There was something in the wine the first two times. Something about it didn't quite taste right. Hugo had a bad reaction to it."

"Two reactions," Hugo added.

Inquisitively, Alice leaned to Hugo and whispered, "When was the second one?"

"Halloween night when we had too much to drink, and you helped me home. I'll tell you about it later," he replied under his breath.

"See." Sylvia tapped Sebastian's arm. "There was something wrong with the first batch."

"We had a . . . production error with the first batch. We weren't aware of it until it was too late. We think we have it perfected now. We had to cycle a year of the vintage first," Sebastian said.

"The most recent batch at your restaurant was much better," Hugo said.

"We can give you a few bottles to take home if you'd like," Sylvia offered.

"That's very generous, but—" Hugo started.

"We insist," Sebastian said. "It's a new batch. Much better. Very dream-like, if I do say so myself."

"Thank you," Alice replied.

"Please dig in before it gets cold. I'm going to play some music if you don't mind," Sebastian said.

"No, music would be great," Alice said as she picked up the bowl of food and dished it out on her plate.

Sebastian went into the living room. The melodic tones of Beethoven's "Moonlight Sonata" filled the house. Sebastian returned in time for Sylvia to hand him the bowl of Italian sausage.

"'Moonlight Sonata' is my all-time favorite song," Sebastian said. "It helps me unwind after a busy, stressful day."

"I love all things moon related—" Alice began as she poked a piece of sausage with her fork. "But "Clair de Lune" is my favorite moon song."

"'Clair de Lune" is a flirt. It's a tease," Sebastian said. He picked up his wineglass and took a sip. Sebastian focused his gaze on Sylvia, never wavering, and smiled. "'Moonlight Sonata' is a lover. It's more romantic. It commands and builds anticipation in a way that forces the listener to surrender to its beauty. It relishes in your vulnerability, yet makes you feel safe and secure. It tugs at your heart strings and leaves you wanting more, but you know it won't last forever. That's what makes it wonderful. It's the sad beauty of a lost love."

Sebastian's eyes narrowed as he peered into Sylvia's sapphire blue eyes. He never took his eyes off of her. Sylvia traced the top of the wineglass with her finger, never breaking her gaze, as if she was entranced by him. An uncomfortable silence, backed by the piano notes, filled the room. Sylvia took a sip.

"'Can't Help Falling In Love,'" Hugo broke the silence. "That song would probably be my favorite. I danced to it at my wedding."

"How long have you two been married?" Sylvia asked, breaking her intimate moment with Sebastian.

"No, we're not married," Alice answered.

"I was married before, but she passed away," Hugo said. "It was our song."

"I'm sorry," Sylvia said.

"Thank you," Hugo replied.

"Life is so precious. It's a shame we can't hold on to it forever," Sylvia said.

"Very true," Hugo said. He paused and took Alice's hand. "I have Alice now, and she means the world to me. I'd do anything for her."

They smiled at each other before taking a bite of the food. The mixture of spicy and savory flavors excited her senses and enraptured her imagination. This was the creation of an expert chef.

"This is exquisite," Alice said.

"Thank you," Sebastian said with a near mouthful.

"You should try the wine," Sylvia said.

Hugo lifted his glass and smelled the inside. "It smells heavenly." He took a sip and sloshed it around in his mouth before drinking. "Tastes great too. Very sweet. Did you make this?"

"No," Sylvia said. "But it did serve as inspiration for our wine."

Alice picked up her glass. She swirled the wine and smelled it, breathing in the earthly aroma. She held it up to her lips and took a sip. The acidic, reddish-purple liquid washed over her tongue. The sweet taste enticed her taste buds. There was something else, something hidden within the wine—a foreign taste. A taste she couldn't conjure in her mind, but it seemed familiar. It wasn't as bitter as the Red-Hearted Queen taste.

Hugo took another generous sip. Alice did as well. The Savinos joined in. Hugo refilled his glass.

"Enjoying the wine?" Sylvia fixated onto Hugo's eyes.

"Very much. Thank you," Hugo said.

Alice's eyes narrowed; her right eyebrow arched. This wasn't a stare she would give someone when paying attention to them speak. It wasn't a flirtatious look. It was something else. It was a look of purpose. A look of determination. A look of . . . intensity.

Alice took another sip, holding the glass to her lips. She sloshed it around in her mouth. There was that taste. That familiar taste. She couldn't quite place it. She had tasted it before, but rarely. It wasn't any ingredient she ever used when making her wine. No, it was—

Alice spit the wine back into the glass without making too much noise. She didn't want to alert the Savinos of her action. Alice darted her eyes over to Sylvia, who was still focused on Hugo. A quick glance over to Sebastian, and he was staring back at her. They bent in closer, almost leaning into the food on their plates.

Alice set the glass back down. A distraction so she could slide her other hand below the table. She gulped. "Where is this from?"

"Europe. Near the French and Italian boarder," Sebastian said. "Close to my old home."

Sylvia never acknowledged Alice. She intently focused on Hugo as he picked up the glass.

Before he could take a sip, Alice snapped her fingers. The wine spilled all over his shirt. He backed away in his chair and stood up, breaking Sylvia's concentration on Hugo.

Hugo picked up the napkins. "I'm sorry. It just slipped out of my hand."

Alice jolted up and grabbed Hugo's arm. "Thank you for dinner, but we better go soak his shirt before it stains."

"Nonsense," Sebastian said. "Please sit and finish your meal. I can take your shirt and soak it for you."

Alice tugged on Hugo's arm, attempting to drag him back down the hallway.

He resisted.

"If they're offering, I don't want to be rude."

She glared at Hugo and pointed to the door with her head. "We need to *soak* your shirt," she said in a raised voice.

"Why don't you get a new shirt and come right back?" Sylvia offered.

"I can go get a new one," Hugo said. "Stay and I'll be right back." He started past Alice.

"I'll come with you," Alice said as she followed him.

Sebastian and Sylvia stood and followed them.

Alice quickened her pace, never taking her eyes off the Savinos. The darkness of the hallway enveloped them. She frantically searched for the closet doorknob behind her, only finding the wood door with the back of her hand. She didn't want to turn away and lose track of the Savinos. Her hand landed on the brass knob, but slipped. She tapped around a few times and found the knob once again.

The Savinos lurched down the hall, their eyes focused on Hugo and Alice with the unsettling intensity of predators hunting their prey. As they moved deeper into the darkened hallway, their eyes glowed a bright red. They never broke eye contact, moving at a methodical, even pace.

A force pulled Alice toward them. She wanted to break eye contact with Sebastian, but something held her in place. The longer she peered into his eyes, the stronger the pull. She struggled to move her head, but some unseen restraint held her gaze.

She turned the knob and flung the closet door open. The wooden barrier broke her connection, and she was free to move her head. She put on her hat and removed their coats from the closet. She left the door open and ducked her head down. She dragged Hugo toward the front door.

"Thank you for a wonderful evening," Alice said.

"You should return," Sylvia commanded as she pushed the closet door closed.

Alice averted her eyes from Sylvia to avoid falling under her sway.

"We'll be right back," Hugo said.

"Open the door," Alice whispered to him.

Hugo opened the door and exited. Alice avoided the Savinos, only keeping their feet in the corner of her eye.

"Again, thank you. It was lovely." Alice left, shutting the door behind her.

Hugo and Alice rushed down the steps toward their house.

"What was that about? I can get a new shirt on my own," he said.

She squeezed his arm, still carrying their coats. "We need to get inside now!" She headed to their porch, dragging Hugo along.

"Why? What's happening?"

"I'll tell you inside," Alice said.

They hurried their pace across the lawns and up toward their front door. Alice kept glancing over her shoulder to see if they were being followed. They raced up the steps. Alice removed the brass key from her pocket. She opened the door. They hurried inside, and she locked the door shut behind them.

An excited Max wagged her tail as they returned home. Hugo petted Max on the head.

"So, do you want to let me in on what's happening?" he asked.

Alice tossed the coats onto the landing step. She pulled back the sheer black curtain to look outside. There was no one.

"Alice! What's going on?" Hugo asked.

She turned around. "There was something in the wine," Alice said. "Something similar to Red-Hearted Queen."

"It didn't taste the same. Are you sure?"

"Yes. I tasted it before. You said you had another reaction on Halloween night. What happened?"

"It was a dream. A very real dream. After I passed out, I woke up in my bed. I was laying with someone who I thought was Elizabeth, only it turned out to be you. I swear . . . for a moment, it was real. You were there. We were in bed together. It was as if everything before was the dream and what I was experiencing was reality. I wouldn't have snapped out of it if Max didn't wake me up."

Alice leaned back against the wall in deep thought. "It was real . . . at least to your mind. It probably would have kept going until something snapped you out of it. You were in a trance-like state, reflecting what your mind wanted you to see. Similar to how the ghoulish Elizabeth appeared before you in the restaurant until my voice brought you back. The same with Max."

"Were they trying to poison us?"

"Worse. It was blood wine. They were using it to make it easier to enthrall us."

Hugo reared back and titled his head. A perplexed smirk on his face. "What do you mean blood wine? What do you mean enthrall?"

The ornate, diamond shape doorknob jiggled, filling the hallway with the sounds of brass against brass. Alice and Hugo snapped their focus to the origin of the sound. Alice flicked her right hand, producing a flaming purple ball of arcane energy.

"They can't get through, right?"

"Still have your key?"

"Yep."

"Then they're not getting through."

The doorknob stopped jostling. Scratching, like the sound of fingernails against wood, came from the door as someone traced the wood frame on the other side of the door. Alice gingerly approached the door. Her heart pounded. She gulped.

Max came to her aid by barking at the would-be intruders. The scratching stopped. Max growled at the door, not fully satisfied they were gone.

Alice moved her free hand to the black curtain over the window of the door. She sought conformation from Hugo before progressing. His face was pale, eyebrows furled, and he was clearly holding his breath. However, he clenched his fist and stood ready to strike. He nodded. She pulled the curtain back to reveal the would-be intruder.

No one was there.

Alice moved closer to get a full view of the porch. No sign of

Sylvia, Sebastian, or anyone else. Alice put the curtain back and dissipated her arcane flame. She turned back to Hugo.

"They didn't have us over for dinner to be neighborly," Alice said. "We were going to be their dessert."

Hugo shook his head in shock. "What are you talking about?"

"They're vampires."

CHAPTER 6
THE KING'S QUEEN

"It's her." Sylvia slammed the door behind her. "We found her."

Sebastian sat at the dining room table finishing his meal. He never let his good food go to waste. He took another bite. "Are you certain?"

"Positive," Sylvia said with a gleeful smile on her face. Her shoulders pulled back and chin up, she strode down the hall with a sense of confidence. "There were markings on her door exactly as *she* said there would be."

"She must have figured out what was in the wine," Sebastian said. "I knew it wouldn't work. Not with her."

"It was worth a shot," Sylvia responded. "Besides, now we know. It's right next door."

Sebastian took another bite and sat in silence as he chewed. Sylvia loved silence. She reveled in it. She especially enjoyed when Sebastian drew out the silent moments in their conversations as if he was playfully teasing her. It was their game—their love language. A game of who could draw the other to speak first.

He fixated on her, peering through her eyes and straight to her soul. A rush coursed through her body, as if every nerve ending ignited at once. Sylvia never broke eye contact. It would mean admitting he won, and she hated to lose. She took in a deep breath to steady herself. Sylvia placed her hands on the table and bent over so the view from her low-cut red dress would entice him to speak.

Sebastian smiled and set his fork on the plate. He shoved the plate to the side, never breaking his gaze. He placed his elbow on the table and interlocked his fingers together. He formed a shelf to rest his chin on with his thumbs. He leaned in closer, inches from her.

His presence overwhelmed her. His aura. His controlled, drawn-out breathing. His scent. A wonderful, woodsy aromatic fragrance captivated her senses. It set her desire ablaze. She wanted him. She grinned at him before blowing him a kiss. He remained unfazed. She leaned forward, pushing her arms in closer to her chest.

His breath washed over her like a silent siren song, provoking her emotions, her desires.

Sebastian leaned back, holding his captivating stare over her. A possible sign of surrender in their little game. He untied his tie and let it dangle over his chest. She couldn't help but imagine the tie dangling and brushing against his muscular chest. The temptation to peek was too great, but couldn't let him win.

He stood up, never taking his eyes off of Sylvia. Her eyes still locked onto his with his every movement. He sashayed around the table. She didn't move. She wanted him to see her low-cut dress hugging the curves of her ass as it flowed from the small of her back to the floor.

He didn't take the bait. He never broke his gaze. Their tango dance of the eyes continued.

She stood as Sebastian towered over her. They nearly touched, separated only by the tension between them. She wanted to win so badly. She had to win. She thought of something, anything, to break his gaze and the silence. She raised both of her hands, and with the gentle touch of her fingers, ran them down his chest toward his stomach.

He pulled out his tie and fashioned it into a fireman's knot. With one swift move, he stepped back, placed her hands into the knot, and tightened. He pulled on the tie, raising her hands above her head. The momentum pushed her backward, pinning her against the wall. She gasped and blinked, caught off guard by the movement.

He leaned in with a mischievous smile. "I win," Sebastian said in a low growl.

"No fair," Sylvia responded in low, hushed tones. "You can't use props."

"My game, my rules."

He moved in as if to kiss her. His lips lingered over hers, letting her suffer in the wait, the anticipation. Sylvia bit her lip. Her chest rose and fell with every deep breath. She squirmed back and forth, awaiting his next move. The tension was like ambrosia to her.

"Can you sense it?" Sebastian growled. "Can you feel how close we are?"

She could. Every teasing breath he took, caused her body to tighten and grow more tense. She craved the touch of his lips, hoping it would ease the suffering within her soul. He held his lips back as if to let the tension linger. It was torturous. It was insufferable. It was exquisite.

"After years of searching, years of wanting, years of waiting . . ." he whispered. "It's right there for the taking. So close. Can you feel it?"

"I can feel it," she moaned. "I want it. I must have it. I need it. Now!" She raised her eyebrows with excitement.

He pulled back. "Not yet. In due time."

"It's right there. Right next door," Sylvia said. "The Lovers' Kiss. It's so close. I can sense it. I can taste it. I want it *now*."

Sylvia had searched for hundreds of years for the spell. She was close so many times, but never this close. Never close enough where the spell was right next door to her. Hidden away inside a witch's purple house. The only thing she wanted more than going next door and taking the house apart, piece by piece, was for Sebastian to take her upstairs and ravage her in pure bliss.

Sebastian raised his free hand. He placed his fingers under her chin. His thumb traced an invisible line over her lips and down her chin. "Patience, my love," he whispered. "We continue with our plan. We'll squeeze them. We'll torture them. We'll make them suffer. They'll have no choice but to hand it over. And when they do, we'll bleed them dry."

She narrowed her eyes and pouted her lips, exhaling at the thought. Sylvia squirmed in her restraints. Her body was now aflame with passion and desire. She could easily loosen herself from the restraint, but she relished in it. She loved it. Sebastian was the one man, the one person, who could temper her controlling desires. She surrendered to his every whim.

"Let's follow the plan," Sylvia whispered. "Let's wait."

"That's my good girl." He leaned in and kissed her.

Sebastian was in full control. Their lips met in soft, slow, deliberate gentle touches. She wanted him to press further, to end the glorious, painful suffering of desire in her passionate soul. Their lips brushed against each other as he savored the exploration of her supple, red lips.

She clenched her fists, wanting to break free from her restraints, so she could wrap them around his body to draw him closer. Her heart raced and her body yearned for his touch. Her soul was alive.

Their kiss deepened, the softness replaced by intensity and urgency. He gave into his wild desires, and she was the recipient of those pleasures. The world faded as they became lost in each other. Time lost all meaning. There was nothing else. For a moment, all longing for the spell disappeared. There was only the two of them. A shiver ran down her body as passion coursed through her veins.

Sebastian stopped. He pulled back and lowered his hands. Her hands followed, still caught in his necktie. He tightened her restraints, tugging on the tie. They gazed into each other's eyes once more. Her soul still yearned for his touch, his body.

"I love you," Sylvia said.

He said nothing in return. Sylvia squirmed in the uncomfortable silence as moments passed.

She gulped before asking, "Will you not profess your love for me as I have for you?"

He yanked on the necktie to guide her down the hallway. She followed without protest. They proceeded up the winding staircase. Sylvia's heart raced with every step. Her breath was short and shallow with anticipation. Each step was one step closer to her release from the blissful excitement.

They entered the bedroom, and he shut the door. Thick, crimson red curtains blocked out the rest of the world. There was only the two of them.

Sebastian led her to the edge of their bed. He pulled back the matching crimson red bedcovers and black bedsheets. He loosened the necktie, freeing her hands from their restraints. Sylvia dropped them to her sides.

Sebastian lifted one of his hands to her face. His fingers grazed her cheek before he drew them over her jaw, under her chin, and down her neck to meet her shoulder. Her body twinged. His touch fueled her burning desires.

He grinned.

Sebastian raised his other hand and pushed the straps of her dress over her shoulders. It slipped down her arms, past her hips, and fell to the floor. She was left exposed to the nighttime air as she stepped out of the dress.

She shivered with anticipation and smiled.

"I love you against all reason and wisdom. You are the only light I need in the darkness. I want to see you elevated as the rightful queen that you are. There is no one else I'd spend an undying eternity with. That is my profession of love," Sebastian growled as he placed his thumb on her chin. "And now it's time for my reward."

CHAPTER 7

DAYLIGHT PLOTTING TIME

Hugo removed boxes from the spare bedroom closet, stacking them neatly behind him. The spare bedroom was less of a bedroom and more of a museum to the past. He peeled back layers of historical artifacts and documents—items they didn't want to throw away, yet had no place to display them.

He uncovered the treasure he sought—a wooden box with metal handles on the side. He pulled on the handle to free it from its hidden location. The stack behind it wavered as he pulled. He braced the boxes with his hand, but they tumbled to the ground.

The two hat boxes spilled their contents onto the floor. Max was quick to investigate, worming her way in between the items and Hugo to get a better look.

"Max, back up," Hugo said.

She didn't listen. She continued her exploration. She smelled each item on the floor. First, an old witch's hat. It was black with an oversized wide brim and a tall point. The end was bent over with age. The second was an old, black cowboy hat. Two playing cards spilled out from the hat—an Ace and Eight of Spades. Their once white color now yellowed with age.

Hugo pushed the adventurous pup back. "Watch out, Max."

She backed away.

Hugo removed the wooden box from the closet, setting it next to him, where Max once stood. He used it to block her from coming closer. He gathered up the playing cards and placed them back in the cowboy hat. He placed both hats in their respective boxes and returned all the items.

He lifted the wooden box and kicked the closet door closed. He carried his treasure out of the bedroom. Max followed. They went down the stairs and into the dining room, where he set it on the table. Max raised her nose above the table to smell the wooden box. Unsatisfied, she jumped up and placed her front paws on the table to look.

"Get down, Max," Hugo said as he pushed her down.

Max whined in frustration.

Hugo turned his attention to Alice, who was clutching a cup of tea and looking out the bay window.

"What are they doing now?"

"Nothing," Alice replied. "They're shuffling around, acting like they're doing yard work."

Hugo peered out the bay window. Four male figures, all wearing matching white canvas coveralls, meandered in the Savinos' backyard. One of the playing card symbols—a black club, a black spade, a red diamond, or a red heart—was painted below their left shoulders. They each held rakes, sweeping the backyard without any real purpose. Their eyes scanned every inch of the fence and occasionally focused back on Alice and Hugo's purple house.

One, the red heart, appeared to make eye contact with Hugo.

"They can't see us, right?" Hugo asked.

"Of course not," Alice said.

"Then why does it feel like he's looking at me?"

The worker's eyes moved to another location.

"He can't," Alice assured him.

"Positive?"

Alice arched her eyebrows and tilted her head toward Hugo. "Did you ever see me?"

"So, you were spying on me. *I knew it,*" Hugo said with a smirk. "What's in the box?"

They turned their attention to the old wooden box sitting on the table. Alice set her cup on the table.

"This is my vampire hunter's kit," Alice said.

She flipped open the lid and removed a wooden tray. It contained an assortment of items—a pistol next to a gunpowder pouch, six silver musket balls, and a flask of holy water. She set it on the table.

"Why do you have a vampire hunter's kit?"

"Remember last Halloween when I joked about dating a vampire?"

"Vaguely."

"Well, I dated a vampire, and he really did suck."

"Witches, fairies, and now vampires. Anything else exist I should know about?" Hugo asked with a sarcastic tone.

"All myths, legends, and fairytales are rooted in some truth. A lot of misconceptions, but some truth," Alice replied.

Hugo picked up the pistol. "Why don't we shoot them in the heart with this?"

"If you want to piss them off, go right ahead. Most of the items in here don't work. There's only one."

Below the tray were more items to hunt the creatures of the night —a Bible, a crucifix, a mallet, and a wooden stake.

"This is the only thing that can hurt a vampire."

Alice withdrew the wooden stake and presented it to Hugo. He placed the pistol back on the tray and took the weapon. It was over a foot long and narrowed to a point on one end. The stake was smooth and well sanded. The top was flattened, and the edges frayed from repeated strikes of the mallet.

"What about garlic?"

"He cooked with garlic," she said, pointing to the house next door. "Again, it's a lie told to people, so they won't be frightened . . .

sort of like a safety blanket. If they think it works, they'll stay calm."

"Well, they can't get in unless invited, right?"

Alice pointed to the front door behind Hugo.

"They tend to leave out the part about witches protecting the door, so vampires can't enter unless invited in."

Hugo raised an eyebrow into a flabbergasted expression. "So, all of those vampire myths are a load of crap?"

"Pretty much. The only way to take them out is a wooden stake through the heart or taking off their head," Alice said. "Sunlight too. That's real."

Hugo held up the wooden stake. "It's the middle of the day. Let's get the jump on them and go storm their castle."

Alice was momentarily silent as she surveyed the house next door. "I thought of that. They have those four spies. What if there are more? We only saw what they wanted to show us last night. We don't know how many are in there. We'd be walking right into a trap."

Something in Alice's front yard drew the attention of the four workers. They moved to the fence, standing shoulder to shoulder to peer over.

"I think she's here," Hugo said.

Max followed Alice to the front door. Her tail wagged with excitement at the prospect of either going on a walk or greeting a new visitor. Alice pulled back the black curtain to look out, her hand on the ornate diamond doorknob. She turned it and let in their visitor—Esmerelda Honeydew.

"That's a little unsettling," Ez said as she entered.

Alice quickly closed the door behind her.

Ez continued, "Have they been out there all morning?"

"Yes. Just watching us," Alice replied.

Max whined and clacked her paws against the hardwood floors. Her tail thrashed about, smacking the walls as she greeted the new house guest.

Ez patted Max on the head with a series of small taps. "Good to see you too," Ez greeted her four-legged friend.

Ez took off her overcoat and handed it to Alice. Her emerald green, knee length dress and yellow belt commanded attention and contrasted against the dark interior walls of the home.

Ez glanced up the stairs. "Where's the other one?"

Alice pointed to the living room.

Ez peeked in from the hallway. "It's not moving."

"It doesn't really react to anyone. Only when called. It's very stoic," Alice said.

"I'm sure it will in due time. How are you doing, kiddo?" Ez said.

Alice exhaled. "We got lucky last night. One tried to enter too. Now, we're watching their workers."

"Show me," Ez said.

Alice led Ez down the hallway to the dining table. Max followed closely behind, trying to worm her way to the front of the pack, but was thwarted by the console tables blocking her ability to pass them.

"How was the trip down?" Hugo asked.

"Feels like it gets longer and longer," she replied. "Maybe I should rethink the location."

"We can always reconnect the rooms again. It'll save on gas money," Alice said.

"Let's deal with your vampire problem first," Ez responded. She stepped to where Alice was earlier and surveyed the scene outside the bay window.

"We've only seen the four so far," Hugo said. "We didn't see any last night."

"You're absolutely sure you tasted blood wine?" Ez asked.

"Definitely," Alice replied as she stood behind Ez, peeking over her beehive hairdo to the four workers outside. "I'd recognize the taste anywhere."

The workers continued their robotic like actions in the backyard. Scanning and searching the fence, they occasionally turned back to the bay window.

"You're positive they can't see us?" Hugo asked again.

Alice paused. "I'm positive . . . ninety-nine percent positive."

"They're ghouls," Ez said. "Not living, not dead. Husks of their former selves. Puppets for the vampires. They're commanded and compelled to repeat those actions. They can't see us."

Hugo sighed. "Well, that's good."

Ez turned to Alice. "Can you be a dear and put on a pot of tea?"

"Already made," Alice said. She went into the kitchen.

Ez examined the wooden box and then the stake clutched in his hand. "Don't lose that," Ez said as she sat down.

Max rested her head on Ez's lap, who then scratched the manipulative golden retriever behind the ears.

"Yeah, Alice already told me it's the only thing that will work," Hugo said as he sat down. He placed the wooden stake next to him. "That and sunlight."

"A good beheading will work too," Ez added.

Alice returned with a teapot and two additional cups floating behind her, as if held up by magical hands. The cups floated to their proper places on the table. Alice poured the tea into each cup.

"Thank you, kiddo," Ez said as she took a sip.

"Thanks, babe," Hugo said as she poured some into his cup. He took a sip. Heated to perfection, the liquid was a warm welcome on the cold autumn day.

Alice topped off her cup, set the teapot down, and took a seat. She joined in and took a sip.

Ez lowered her cup, cradling it with both hands below her nose. The steam rose into her face. "So, tell me what happened."

"They invited us to dinner and offered us some old wine. They were entertaining us, keeping the conversation going and the wine flowing. There was a distinct taste to it. It was definitely blood wine. They even claimed Red-Hearted Queen was based on the wine they offered us. As the conversation went on, they leaned in, trying to enthrall us. They would have succeeded if not for the distinct taste," Alice said.

Ez glared into her tea for a moment and then took a sip.

"I'd like to circle back to blood wine," Hugo said. "Were we drinking blood?"

"No," Alice said.

Hugo sighed. "That's a relief."

"It's a magical wine that can attune to blood types and make it easier for them to enthrall, to hypnotize their victims," Alice explained. "They're doing it with Red-Hearted Queen. Except on a larger scale."

"So, we take out the wine, and it stops them, right?" Hugo asked.

"They can still enthrall people. It's what they do to feed, but the process can take a lot out of them. If they can make it easier to hypnotize someone"—Alice took a sip of tea—"then they can do more than feed."

"And if they have access to someone's blood, they can compel them to do practically whatever they want," Ez added.

"Are they magick users too?" Hugo asked.

"No," Ez said. "The vampiric transformation will strip anyone of the ability to call forth the arcane. Spells, however, can be attuned so anyone can cast them if they follow the exact process and know the arcane words."

"Fantastic," Hugo said in a sarcastic tone. He took a sip. "So, what do we do?"

"Have they done anything?" Ez asked.

"I'm not sure yet," Alice replied.

"What about all of those sick employees at the market?" Hugo asked. "It's kind of strange so many have come down sick recently."

"Hearsay . . . unless you can prove it. Until they do something, you can't do anything," Ez said. "Or else you'll risk all-out war."

Hugo sat back in his chair, narrowing his eyes. "War?"

"Witches and vampires haven't always gotten along," Alice said.

Ez took one more sip and set her cup down. "Witches and vampires have been fighting for centuries. Thousands of years, to be exact. The last all-out conflict, The Great Vampire-Witch War, lasted decades and took many lives. Peace wasn't declared until the losses were too much on both sides. An uneasy peace has lasted for over five hundred years."

"What did they fight over?" Hugo asked.

Hugo followed Ez's finger as she pointed to Alice. An uneasy smile came across Alice's face.

"What?" Hugo asked.

Alice took a sip. "They fought over the spell."

"Your spell?" Hugo asked.

"*Our* spell," Alice corrected. "The vampires were determined to find it. The witches and wizards did their best to hide it."

"Why?"

"They sought immortality," Ez said. "They thought the spell could prevent them from dying to anything. If they couldn't die, then they could rule over everything and everyone forever, with nothing to stop them."

"That's not true, right?" Hugo asked.

"We don't know," Alice said. "We don't want to find out either."

"So, why not destroy it if the spell is so powerful?"

"Can't. I tried. I didn't want the responsibility. I threw it in a fire right after I acquired it from my grandmother. It wouldn't burn. I tried to rip it, cut it, destroy it. Nothing worked. Not even magick. The spell is protected, which is why I hide it. I figured it's better to keep it hidden than let it fall into the wrong hands," Alice said.

"I thought vampires were already undead. Why seek immortality?"

"Thousands of years ago, there was a king who wanted to rule forever. He sought out a witch to create a spell that would grant him immortality. The witch refused. This angered the king. No one told him no," Ez said before taking another sip of tea.

She continued, "The king imprisoned the witch. He tortured her until she would agree to his demands. She refused, and the torture continued until she was left in a bloody, bruised mess. She was near death when she relented and decided to create his special spell."

"That's horrible," Hugo said.

"It gets worse," Alice said.

"She created a spell and gave it to the king in the form of wine. His transformation began after drinking the wine. The witch wanted to punish him for the bloody torture he put her through. She laced it with her blood and told the king his bloodlust would never be quenched. His pursuit of immortality would be his undoing," Ez continued.

She took another sip and finished, "He craved blood. He needed it, or else he would frenzy until his thirst was quenched. His incisors grew into fangs. The king was forced into the darkness as sunlight would boil his blood from the inside. It drove him mad. She designed the spell so his only relief would be something that once bled piercing his dark heart."

"Trees bleed, hence the stake," Hugo said.

"Correct," Alice said. "But there's more. The king ordered the witch be burned for condemning him to this life of torture. She called for other witches to help, but none did. They remained hidden in the shadows out of fear of reprisal. Abandoned by her own kind. Her final act would be her ultimate vengeance."

"The witch activated a part of the spell that allowed the king to create an army of vampires. He could choose to pass on his curse, so the entire kingdom would suffer the same fate. She gave him the power to hypnotize victims, enthrall them to do whatever he commanded, such as willingly allow him to drink their blood," Ez finished.

"It's been the burden, *the guilt,* of every witch and wizard since then. Protect the world from being overrun by vampires," Alice said before taking a sip. "Even if they persecute us. It's our duty . . . our burden."

Hugo sat in stunned silence. He didn't know what to say or how to respond. His silence became uncomfortable as it filled the dining area.

Max whined, breaking the silence as she commanded attention. Ez scratched her under the chin.

"I think there's a bigger problem," Alice said. She placed the cup on the table. "They know about The Neighborhood Witch."

Ez nearly dropped her cup, pulling her other hand away from Max to steady it. "How?"

"Sylvia called out Alice yesterday. Asked her point-blank if she was The Neighborhood Witch on the wine label," Hugo answered.

"What did you tell her?" Ez inquired.

"That we worked for the distribution company and they asked me to pose for the label," Alice answered. "Unfortunately, they're in distribution too, and it's a matter of time before they figure it out."

"So what?" Hugo asked. "They already knew we had the magical barrier at the door. They already know you're a witch. What are they going to do?"

"Hopefully, nothing," Alice said. "I hope they're not looking for something more." Her face turned expressionless as she focused on a spot on the table.

"They couldn't know," Hugo reassured her. He extended his hands across the table and grabbed her hands. "There's no way they know."

"We have to assume they do know," Ez said.

"What if they don't?" Hugo asked. "We treat everything like normal. There are a lot of witches and wizards, right? For all they know, someone else could have it."

"Are you trying to make me feel better?" Alice asked.

"Possibly," Hugo responded.

"We should still be cautious," Ez added.

"Look, we'll keep an eye on them. Besides, you had a vampire boyfriend before. Maybe they're just looking for a quiet place to live," Hugo said.

"Honestly, I should have staked him while I had the chance," Alice said.

"What did he do?" Hugo asked.

"Cheated on me," Alice replied. "I already know what I'm going to do to you if you cheat." She picked up her cup and winked at him.

Hugo sat upright. He held his breath, astonished at her remarks.

"I'm joking. I know you won't cheat on me," Alice said.

"Honestly, I'm offended that you think I would," Hugo said as he relaxed into a smile. He winked back.

Ez set her cup down. "If you two are done flirting, you can take me to lunch."

"I know where we shouldn't go for—" Hugo trailed off.

He paused. A thought occurred to him. If those ghouls were spying on them and people mysteriously became sick, they might be overlooking Sylvia and Sebastian's next move. The one place where, if the Savinos were to strike, they would immediately attack.

The Raskins.

"We have to go see the Raskins," Hugo said.

"Why?" Alice said.

"If they were to do something, and they can't get in here, what's their next move? The Raskins," Hugo said. "They know about the wine. They know where it's sold. If they wanted to do anything, they'd apply pressure there. We need to tell them. We have to at least put the magical barrier on their house."

"I agree," Ez said. "It's better to be prepared than caught off guard."

Hugo and Ez glanced toward Alice.

She nodded. "I'll get my stuff." Alice stood from the table and headed for the basement door.

"We can stop there on the way to lunch," Ez said. "Besides, I want to see your display in person."

CHAPTER 8
PUBLIC SECRETS

"We had a contract," Mr. White said. "It brings me no pleasure to do this. You'll have to forgive my lateness, but my employer wanted to give you a few extra days to see if events unfolded differently. Clearly, they did not."

"What is he talking about?" Carol Raskin asked Oliver.

Oliver scratched his head, not knowing what to say next. Men in black coveralls removed wine bottles from the shelves and carefully placed them into cardboard boxes. They removed bottles of Red-Hearted Queen and other wine selections, leaving the shelves barren.

"I informed your husband pursuant to the terms with Red Heart Distribution and our partners, you must prominently display bottles of Red-Hearted Queen in your store or you'd be in breach of your contractual obligations. Considering you still have a display of The Neighborhood Witch in our rightful spot, you are failing to meet those obligations," Mr. White said as he handed a piece of paper to Carol. "This letter spells out every violation in our contract and why we are taking the proper steps to remedy the situation."

Carol read through the multi-page document, flipping through the stapled pages at a hurried pace. Oliver wrapped his arm around her shoulders.

"Per the contract, you won't be compensated for your purchase price, and henceforth, all distribution agreements are considered null and void," Mr. White said, picking up his briefcase. He pulled two business cards from the inner pocket of his navy suit jacket. He handed cards to Carol and Oliver. "If you have any questions, if you lawyer up to fight us, or want to sign a new distribution contract, you can contact me at this number. I bid you good day."

He moved over to the men loading up the wine. After a brief conversation, he left. The men followed behind, pushing a dolly full of crated wine bottles. The shoppers, with confused expressions, murmured to themselves at what had transpired.

"Oliver . . ." Carol said. "Oliver, what do we do?"

Oliver's face sunk as he took in his once proud and beautiful displays of wine. A kaleidoscope of offerings gone. Only barren shelves left behind. Oliver rubbed his hands together, staring past the empty shelves into a void only he could see. There was only the nothingness. White flashes of light engulfed the world around him until only the empty shelves were left.

What do we do? This will ruin us.

All ambient sound was gone—the voices of the shoppers, the background noise of commerce—all gone. He could only hear the raspy sound of his breathing in and out. The ever-accelerating pounding of his heart.

A hand touched his arm. Not any hand, but his calming influence. Oliver's rock. His partner. The hand of his beloved Carol.

It pulled him out of the enthralling trance of his void. The world came back into focus as the white light faded back into the depleted shelving. His heart slowed. His breathing returned to normal.

"Oliver, what do we do?"

He gave her a hug, tapping her on the shoulder. "We'll be okay. We'll think of something." He turned toward the untouched shelves featuring bottles of The Neighborhood Witch wine. “We’ll just have to sell more of their wine. We can do it.”

More eyes focused their attention on the Raskins as they stood amongst the empty shelves.

He turned Carol toward the direction of the office. “Let’s go someplace quiet and talk,” Oliver said.

Oliver’s arm still hugged Carol as they sulked toward the hallway in the back of the store.

“Oliver,” Hugo’s voice called out. “We need to speak with you.”

The Raskins stopped.

Hugo, Alice, and Ez rushed down the aisle at a quick pace. Esmerelda lagged, struggling to match the longer strides of Hugo and Alice.

“Hugo, what’s wrong?” Carol asked.

“We need to go talk in private,” he responded.

“It’s about the wine,” Alice said. She spun around, marching backward, as if she was searching for something. She was on guard, but Oliver had no idea what she was guarding against.

Oliver arched his eyebrows, shocked at Alice’s statement. He asked, “How did you know?”

“Know what?” Hugo asked.

“They were just here,” Carol replied. She handed Hugo the multi-page document. He frantically flipped through the pages.

Oliver rubbed his hands together. He added, “They took everything. We couldn’t do anything. It’s all gone.”

“Who took what?” Alice asked. “What’s all gone?”

“Let me show you,” Oliver replied.

He led them to the wine and liquor section. Aisle after aisle. Shelf after shelf. All empty. Hugo and Alice touched the empty shelves where the blackish-green bottles once stood. Their fingers dragged over the aluminum shelves before their eyes met each other with a flabbergasted expression.

“It’s all gone. Everything. The wine. The liquor. The beer. Everything," Oliver explained. "Every distributor pulled their items from the shelves."

Hugo turned to Oliver, his face sunken in disbelief. "Why?"

Oliver gulped. He averted his gaze, holding onto his answer. He couldn't. He couldn't tell them why. He knew it would devastate them both, especially Alice.

"Why did they take everything?" Alice asked.

Oliver couldn't say it. The truth would crush Alice's spirit. His eyes watered, overcome with guilt. He couldn't utter the words, so the burden fell onto his body. Hugo and Alice followed his finger as he pointed to Alice's wine display.

"My wine did this?" Alice asked.

Oliver nodded.

Ez examined the display. "They're making a move."

Alice hugged Oliver. "Why didn't you tell me?"

"I couldn't . . ." Oliver said. "I couldn't take away your dream. Not after you worked so hard."

"We need to talk in private," Ez said.

"We can talk in our office in the back," Carol offered.

Ez took off, not waiting for the others to join her. They all followed her down the hallway and into the Raskins' office. Ez shut the door behind everyone.

"First, the restaurant, and now the market," Hugo said. "They're moving pieces on the chessboard, and we don't even know it."

"Who is doing what?" Oliver asked.

"You might want to sit down for this," Hugo suggested.

The Raskins sat down.

"This is going to sound strange, but our neighbors are vampires," Alice said.

"*Vampires*?" Carol asked.

"Like fangs and capes and turning into bats?" Oliver asked.

"Fangs, yes. Capes and bats, not so much," Hugo said. "But yeah, those bloodsucking monsters."

"We believe they're targeting us," Alice said.

"How do you know?" Oliver asked.

"Because they tried to get us last night," Hugo said. "They invited us over for dinner and tried to hypnotize us."

Oliver sat back in his chair. *Vampires?*

Memories of taking Carol to see the old Christopher Lee *Dracula* movies in their youth raced through his mind.

"So, do we need a lot of garlic or something?" Oliver asked.

"It won't work," Hugo said.

"It's a myth," Ez said. "It's something you tell someone to calm them down."

Oliver shifted his focus from Ez to Hugo, then to Alice, then back to Hugo, trying to find who would break first. The one to give away the prank.

Yes. This is all a prank. They'll bring everything back, and we'll all laugh.

He turned to Carol, his rock. She clenched her hand into a tight fist and pressed it against her lips. She glanced off into the distance, lost in thought. He wasn't being pranked. This was real. They were dealing with vampires like in the old movies.

"Let's think this through," Ez said. "We don't know if they're targeting everyone in this room. I work in the beverage business. It's a tough business. There are business disputes all the time. It could be a coincidence."

Oliver pulled the business card out of his pocket and handed it to Hugo. "This is their card. Maybe you can call them and work something out.

Hugo took the card and flipped it over. He gasped. "Oh, shit," he said as he slumped his head and drooped his shoulders.

"What is it?" Alice asked.

He handed the card to her. Her face turned pale and lost all expression.

Alice focused back on Oliver with narrowed eyes and a curled lip. Her solemn face now showed a hint of anger. "When did they first contact you?"

"Over a week ago," he replied. "Their representative was in here a day before the launch. He gave me an ultimatum. Take down the display or lose everything. I called his bluff."

"This logo is tattooed on Sebastian's forearm." Alice handed the card to Ez.

She took the card and flipped it over a few times to examine every corner.

"It's them." Alice ran a hand through her hair.

Oliver focused on a stack of papers, so he didn't have to see the disappointment on Alice's face. He couldn't let her down, even though he risked it all and lost.

Oliver glanced over to Carol. Her face expressionless. Her hand still in front of her mouth. Carol's eyes glazed over as she was enveloped in the shock. He tapped her forearm a few times before his hand came to a rest in hopes of comforting her. Carol snapped out of her haze and returned the glance to him, tears in her eyes.

"It's all my fault. I'm sorry I put you through this," Alice said. "I'm really sorry. If you had told me, I would have pulled every bottle from your store."

"It's not your fault, sweetie," Carol reassured her. She placed both hands in her lap and sat up. "None of us are to blame."

"No, it's my fault," Oliver said. "I told him no one comes in here and threatens me in my store. I can deal with this. I can fix it."

"It doesn't matter," Ez said. "If they were going to target you, then they would have found anything. It was an easy target."

Her words were like a warm blanket to soothe his frayed, anxiety ridden nerves.

"Ez is right," Hugo said. "They would have found anything. They must have been spying on us for weeks. They knew about the restaurant and took it over. They knew about our connection here and acted. If not the wine, it could have been anything. How has the staff been?"

"We're still understaffed," Carol said. "They've been calling in sick."

"Some kind of illness . . ." Oliver said. He paused for a moment, then dragged his eyes toward Hugo. "Do you think . . . ?"

"As I said, they would have found any weakness," Ez answered.

"So, what do we do?" Oliver asked.

"We need to go to your house right now," Hugo said.

"I'll put a protection spell on your house, so no one can enter without a special key," Alice said. "They can't get inside, and you'll be protected."

"You'll have to close the store early," Ez said.

"We can't close early," Oliver said. "Our weekday traffic is higher in the evenings."

"You'll be vulnerable at night," Ez said. "They can only move at night and may try to strike. It's the only way to protect yourselves and your employees. Close before sunset."

"We can't—" Oliver began.

"You must. No excuses," Ez commanded as she slapped her hands on his desk.

Her short stature towered over Oliver in his well-worn office chair. Oliver had worked in the business for over fifty years. He had dealt with a lot of personalities and always stood his ground. With Esmerelda Honeydew, however, she was the only one who could slap his desk and command his attention.

She glared at him. "If you care for your staff and yourselves, you'll close before sunset," she continued.

"We'll close before sunset," he said.

Ez pulled back from the desk. "Kiddo, you put the protection spell on their house. I'm going to head back to my place and make some calls. Maybe I can convince the vampiric conclave to intervene."

"Vampiric conclave?" Oliver asked. "You mean there's more of them?"

"It's comprised of the heads of the different vampire factions. Most of the vampires swear an allegiance to one of the different courts. It's how they keep themselves in line without one vampire overtaking the rest. They tend to look down on lone wolfs, regardless of rank, and squash them to keep the rest in order. They may offer a sit-down with the Savinos and tell them to back off," Ez said.

"You could tell them any further action against us could escalate the situation, and neither side would want that," Alice offered.

"Good point," Ez said.

"You mean, a sit-down like in the mob movies?" Oliver asked. "Why don't you have a sit-down yourselves?"

"I'd highly advise against it. You don't know what could happen," Ez said.

"Oliver's right," Hugo said.

"Out of the question," Ez responded.

"We've been playing catch up, while they're maneuvering around in the shadows. If we go on the offensive, it could catch them off guard," Hugo said.

"We'll know their exact demands," Alice added. "Then we can figure out our next steps."

"You'll be going in alone," Ez said.

"Not if that vampiric conclave knows about it," Hugo said.

"If anything happens to me, then it would be considered an act of war," Alice added.

"Besides, we'll be armed," Hugo said. "I'll have the stake and Alice has her magick."

Alice glanced at Hugo. "I should face them alone. If you bring a stake, then it could escalate. If it escalates and goes sideways—"

Hugo faced Alice, his eyebrows arched. "I can't let you confront them alone. We do it together or neither of us do it. I'll be armed. You'll be armed. We'll be fine. Trust me."

Alice lowered her eyes for a moment. She nodded her head. "Okay. We do it together."

Ez was silent. She rubbed her forehead, careful not to smear any of her blue eyeshadow and drawn on eyebrows. Her silence spread to the rest of the small office space. Everyone else stared at each other, unsure of what to do or say next.

"I can't believe I'm going to say this again," Ez said. "Oliver does have a good point. The sit-down might be our next best action."

Oliver turned to Carol. "See, I'm good for more than one idea."

"Stop it." Carol tapped him on the arm. "You've had at least two before this. One was marrying me."

Oliver winked at her.

Alice stood upright, pulling back on her witch's hat. "Then it's settled. We'll contact them to get a sit-down in the next few days. Ez, you'll contact the conclave and let them know. In the meantime, I'll put the protection on your house," Alice said.

"How are we going to contact them without knocking on the front door?" Hugo asked.

Ez handed him the business card. "Call their representative. I'm sure he'll pass along the good word," she said.

"This will work. I believe in this," Alice said.

"Before I go, I wanted to let you know that it's a wonderful display," Ez said. "I'm really proud of everyone in here."

Alice smiled. "Thank you. That means a lot to me."

Oliver stood up and Carol followed. "Let's go show them no one comes into our town and pushes us around."

Esmerelda took a deep breath and exhaled. "Be smart. Be vigilant. Be ready. Follow the plan, and don't do anything you'll regret." She checked her watch. "It's getting late. The sun will be going down soon. We need to move now."

CHAPTER 9
THE SIT-DOWN

"Do you think they'll show?" Hugo asked. He tapped the wooden stake in his palm as he paced around the empty front entrance of Raskin's Neighborhood Market. The store was deserted of the evening shoppers. He checked his phone. "They're late."

"They're not late. They're pulling a power play," Alice said. She leaned back against the checkout counter with her arms crossed and eyes focused on the door.

Hugo stopped. He turned to Alice and smiled. "Hockey lingo?"

She smiled back. "Thought you'd enjoy it."

"Wrong term, but I'll let it slip," Hugo said.

"What term, then?"

Hugo shrugged. "More like delay of game." He continued tapping the wooden stake in his palm and pacing around like he was on patrol.

Alice focused through the automatic doors, into the darkness outside and the empty parking lot. She checked her phone. It was only 8:00 p.m. This store should be bustling with activity, a haven to commerce. Yet, it was desolate. Quiet. Empty.

Her fingers tapped her arms like they were playing invisible piano keys, striking with purpose and building speed. Anything to keep her mind off what was about to transpire. Her heart raced and anxiety flowed through her like it was the source of life. Every nerve was on edge.

Something in the parking lot caught Alice's eye. "They're here."

Two headlights cut through the darkness as an SUV pulled into the parking lot. The two yellow balls of light grew larger as the car approached the entrance. The vehicle pulled in front of the door. Two ghouls exited the front of the SUV wearing black suits and white shirts. One with a red tie and one with a black one.

"Now it's a power play," Alice said.

They opened the back passenger doors, and Sebastian and Sylvia emerged from the SUV. They wore matching outfits—a further attempt at intimidation. He was in an all-red suit and black shirt. She wore a fashionable red leather jacket, red pants that accentuated her figure, and a simple black top. Their hair was immaculate. They strode with confidence with their shoulders pulled back and chins high, wearing black sunglasses covering their eyes. They took their time as they approached the automatic doors.

Alice straightened her posture—shoulders pulled back, head tilted up, and no longer leaning against the counter. Eyes focused on their every move.

Hugo stood next to her in a show of support. "Sunglasses might be a tad much, don't you think?"

Alice didn't reply. She pulled down on the brim of her hat. Her eyes peeked out from under the black brim. Hugo unzipped his black leather jacket and pulled back his shoulders. It was a stalemate of body language, a precursor to the verbal and mental battle about to commence.

The automatic doors opened, and the Savinos entered with the ghouls following behind.

"They have to remain outside," Alice said. "It's only the four of us."

Sebastian and Sylvia checked with each other in silence. It lingered for more than a moment as if they were communicating with each other in an unspoken language. Only the occasional eyebrow twitch or lip curl gave insight to their conversation.

Alice's finger twitched. She gulped, holding her breath.

Sebastian turned away from Sylvia, and with two fingers, pointed to the SUV. The two ghouls spun around and went back to the car.

"Satisfied?" Sylvia asked.

"Yes," Alice responded.

Sylvia removed her sunglasses. She tilted her head, staring at the object Hugo held in his hand. "I'm flattered you'd bring a stake to a sit-down. Are we that big of a threat to you?"

"Consider it protection," Hugo said.

"We had our protection too, and you sent them away." Sylvia brought her hands up to her chest as if feigning being the victim. "As a sign of good faith, we'd expect you to return the gesture."

Alice glanced over toward Hugo. He gripped the wooden stake with both hands. His eyes focused on Sylvia and Sebastian.

She turned her attention back to the Savinos. "We offer to stash it behind this counter," she said, tapping the side panel. "Your men outside. Our wooden stake here. That's the best offer."

"Deal," Sylvia said without hesitation.

Alice nodded to Hugo. He went the long way around the counter, avoiding getting close to the Savinos. He placed the wooden stake on a shelf.

"Satisfied?" Alice asked.

"Tremendously," Sylvia said with a wicked grin.

"Are we to conduct business here in the entryway or do you have someplace more comfortable for your guests?" Sebastian asked.

"I'll take you there," Hugo said as he marched off into the store.

"After you." Alice gestured with her hands.

"I'm loving the hospitality," Sylvia said. "So welcoming."

"*So* welcoming," Sebastian said as he removed his sunglasses.

They followed Hugo with Alice following behind, keeping an eye on the Savinos.

Hugo led them through the store and past the empty shelves of the wine section. Alice and Hugo had set up a folding table in front of The Neighborhood Witch display. Hugo and Alice took chairs, so the Savinos had to stare directly at the display.

"Sold out of wine?" Sebastian asked.

"Or are you having problems stocking it in?" Sylvia added.

Alice and Hugo didn't answer. Their faces remained solemn and focused on the Savinos. Alice's blood boiled at their comments. Adrenaline pulsated through her veins. She wanted to lay into the Savinos, but used every fiber of her arcane being to hold herself back.

"Please, sit." Alice pointed to the chairs.

The Savinos joined Hugo and Alice at the table. Sylvia tilted her head to the side. Her wavy, strawberry blonde hair cascaded down her side. She crossed her legs and placed her hands on her knee. Sebastian placed his elbows on the table and interlocked his hands.

Hugo remained motionless, focused on their every move. Alice constantly scanned around the store, waiting for some trick, some ambush they had planned for them. There was nothing. It was quiet. No one said a word.

Time stood still. It could have been minutes or hours or only a few seconds. She didn't know. The silence was unbearable. The only sound was the reverberating noise in Alice's head of her breathing in and out. Her stomach churned.

"This is the part where the first to speak loses, right?" Hugo asked. "So, why don't we cut to the chase and stop wasting everyone's time?"

Sylvia leaned back in her chair. "You're no fun." She winked at him.

"So, what do you have to offer us?" Sebastian asked.

"We want you to leave the Raskins alone. Restore all of their inventory and lay off their employees," Alice commanded. "This town is under the protection of the Coven of the Moon. Any further action taken against this town will be in direct violation of the Vampire-Witch Accords."

Sylvia and Sebastian beheld each other with shocked, knowing expressions. They smirked at each other.

"We aren't in any direct violation of any accords," Sylvia said. "I'm sure they explained fully to you what occurred."

"This is a business dispute," Sebastian said. He pointed to the bottles behind her. "That has more to do with these empty shelves than anything we did."

Alice gulped.

"As for the employees . . . we had no knowledge of who worked here and who didn't. I believe the accords state we're free to feed as long as no one dies. The last time I checked, no one died, so we aren't in violation of anything."

"We know you tried to enthrall us," Hugo said.

"Enthrall you?" Sebastian asked with a knowing grin. "We would never."

Sylvia once again placed her hand over her heart. "We merely invited you into our home, cooked a good meal, and offered you some of our finest wine. You were the ones who left in a hurry. How are we the ones at fault for anything?"

Hugo peered toward Alice as if searching for what to do next. Alice had nothing. Her mind erased all thoughts as they unraveled before her.

"We know you tried to get in the house after we left," Hugo said.

"Was that us?" Sylvia asked.

"Are you sure?" Sebastian added. "Did you see us? How do we know you aren't making it up?"

"It seems to us, it is you who violated the Vampire-Witch accords," Sylvia said. "We're merely business owners trying to eke out a living. Harassed and tormented by a witch. Thank you for confirming, by the way."

"Confirming what?" Alice asked.

"You're the witch of Newbury Grove. That you were the one

caught riding a broomstick—in daylight—in front of a crowd of people," Sylvia said. "Shame on you."

Hugo slumped back in his chair.

Sylvia uncrossed her legs, placed both of her arms on the table, and leaned forward. She continued, "We've been looking for a witch. Someone who is on the run. Someone who is hiding. Someone we'd like to make a deal with."

"Imagine our surprise when we came across the news headline. Well, we figured we should investigate. Maybe she was the witch we sought," Sebastian said.

"Lo and behold, we found out there was a new wine being distributed and marketed with a witch on the label. The witch we were after loved to make wine. Isn't that right, my love?" Sylvia asked.

"You're correct," Sebastian answered.

Sylvia continued, "And then there was a house for sale. A nice, lovely house that happened to be right next door to a purple house. Love, what was the witch's favorite color?"

"Purple," Sebastian answered.

"Well, we thought this was surely the witch we sought. We thought what a perfect place to move our operations. I had my doubts, but well, you confirmed it." Sylvia sat back in her chair and grinned.

Alice's heart sank. Each word, each answer, like daggers to the chest. She had been so foolish. Of course, she had to be herself. She couldn't lie low. It nearly cost her life, and now . . . now the very people she was on the run from sat across the table from her. Her reflection was right, and she was never going to let Alice hear the end of it.

Alice's eyes darted to Hugo. His elbows rested on the table with his head in his hands. A passing thought surged through her mind toward the devastation Hugo must be experiencing, knowing he led the Savinos here. There wasn't time to dwell on the past. She needed a plan, something to turn the tide. Maybe they didn't know about the spell.

No. They had to know. They had to know about the spell. They were teasing and toying with her. Waiting. Making her suffer before they mentioned it. Their ultimate bargaining chip. Don't mention the spell.

She glared at Sylvia. "So, what do you want?"

"Immortality," Sylvia answered, never breaking eye contact with Alice. "A decent return on my investment isn't bad either."

"It seems we hold all the cards. There is nothing you can offer us," Sebastian said. "We're very generous. Your friends, the Raskins, are free to renegotiate a new contract with us. Of course, their rates will be slightly higher. But their shelves will be fully stocked."

"Or there is another way," Sylvia said. "We want you to work for us."

Alice gulped, holding her breath. Her body tightened. Her head pounded as her ears rang. Rage, anger, fear, hatred—a cocktail of mixed emotions surged through her.

"Why would I work for you?"

"You're the best. You'd be a great asset," Sylvia said. "We could give you everything you ever wanted. Why be in a local regional grocery when you could be worldwide? Your wine all over the world. You'd be like a princess in our empire. All you have to do is work for us."

A shiver ran down Alice's back at the thought. Her wine . . . sold worldwide.

"You'd be a bridge to a better future. A brighter future. Vampires and witches working together. Just think about it. All because of you."

Sebastian's words flowed over her ears like a siren-song—tempting, teasing, and compelling her to choose their offer. She had already achieved her goal. Her wine was in stores, not hidden away in a clandestine nightclub. This was her chance to go to the next level. *Worldwide.*

Alice studied her wine display. Her eyes inspected greenish-black bottles glistening in the store lights. She imagined shelves and shelves full of those bottles—her wine—all over the world.

"There is a catch, though," Sylvia said. Alice fixed her gaze on Sylvia. "You have to give us something in return. We want *The Lovers' Kiss*. We know you have it. A friend of yours told us you had it. Her name slips my tongue, but not the taste of her blood. Very sweet, I recall. She wore a lovely red hat."

Alice clenched her fists beneath the table. There was only one person she knew who wore a red hat. Sam. Alice's inhales became pronounced. Her emotions were a mixture of anger and concern for her former lover.

"Is she still alive?" Alice asked.

Sylvia smiled and tilted her head.

"Is she?" Alice pressed. Her nose snarled.

"Why would I kill a valuable asset? She helped to lead me to you, didn't she?" Sylvia asked.

Alice released her clenched fists.

Sylvia continued, "We know you have it. We want it."

Alice couldn't hand it over. Not after promising her grandmother to guard and hide it. Not after all the people who died to prevent it from falling into the wrong hands. It was her duty—her obligation—to protect it, and at the moment, she was failing.

Why shouldn't I hand it over? It's brought me nothing but pain and suffering since I've had it. I wouldn't have had to move and uproot my life if not for that stupid spell. I didn't want it, anyway. Give it to them, and end this stupid war.

"Everything you ever wanted. Right there. For the taking," Sebastian teased.

His words pulled her ever closer to blurting out the word yes.

"Let's make a deal. What do you say?"

What about Hugo? If not for that spell, that wonderful spell, I would have never met Hugo. The love of my life. He'd still be lost and broken. I'd be miserable with Sam. I can't give it up now.

Alice turned to Hugo, hoping for a confirmation to take the deal and live out her dreams. He lifted his head, his eyes watery as if they were holding back tears. He swung his head left and right as if to beg her to turn down the offer. Alice shook her head, wiping away the temptation. She couldn't do it. She couldn't do it to her grandmother, her family, Ez, and Hugo. This was her burden. Her responsibility. Her legacy. She knew what she had to do.

Alice raised up to look at both Sylvia and Sebastian from under the bottom brim of her hat.

"Why would I want to be a princess when I'm already a witch?" she asked.

Sylvia slammed her hands down on the table.

Alice jolted in her seat.

"This is your last chance. Give us the spell and join us, or else face the consequences," Sylvia shouted.

Sebastian placed his hand on hers.

"Or what?" Alice growled in a low voice. She ignited a purple flame of arcane energy in her hand.

Sylvia cowered back in her seat.

"Whoa, whoa, whoa," Sebastian said as he threw himself against Sylvia's body, attempting to shield her. "Let's not do anything hasty."

Sylvia snarled at Alice. "If you walk away or run or do anything else, we'll find you." She displayed her elongated fangs. "That's a promise."

"How about we all calm down?" Hugo said. "Maybe we should walk away for now and think about this later."

"I think that's a good idea," Sebastian said.

Alice lowered her arm and dissipated the flame.

Sebastian stood. "We'll give you some time to think it over. Until you decide, we won't do anything to anyone. You have our word."

Sylvia glared at Alice, never taking her eyes off her. She stood and joined her husband. "You have our card. We expect to hear from you shortly."

They turned and strutted toward the entrance.

Alice and Hugo stood and followed them, never letting them out of their sight. The Savinos left the store and entered their SUV, taking off.

"What do you plan on doing?" Hugo asked.

Alice paused. "I don't know." She turned to Hugo, locking eyes with him. "But I do know they'll never get the spell as long as I live."

CHAPTER 10
CHECK

Alice stood alone in her wine cellar with her arms crossed and a hand placed on her chin. She was lost in thought, staring off at the stone wall behind her workstation. Shadows from the candlelight danced on the stone wall. The room was dim, as if she didn't want any spirits to see what she was doing.

Thoughts raced through her mind. The emotions of the past few days had finally caught up to her. She wanted to run. She wanted to hide. She wanted to fight. She wanted to take out the Savinos.

Alice couldn't act or speak. She was lost in a sea of confusion and anxiety as she contemplated her next move. The pieces on the chessboard had been in motion without her knowledge, and now it was finally her turn to make a move. She was at a loss of what to do.

Alice's eyes focused on a single stone in the wall. The only stone in the wall holding a secret. It was more than a secret—it was a curse. It had ruined many lives. It had caused devastation and destruction. So many lives lost. She only wished she could have destroyed it.

Why did she have to carry the burden? She never asked for it. She didn't want it. It was thrust upon her. Her grandmother knew its history. Her grandmother knew what it meant for her to carry this throughout her life. Why did her grandmother give it to her?

Alice sighed.

She approached her workstation and snapped her fingers. The stone in the wall opened. Inside the wooden box was her terrible curse. She pulled out the box and set it amongst the mortars and pestles neatly organized on her workstation. She opened the lid and pulled out the spell scroll.

It was worn and yellowed with age. No one knew how old it was. Its architect was lost to time. Its ultimate power remained unknown. All Alice knew was a portion of the spell worked.

She wouldn't be standing there if not for her desire to make the spell with Hugo. If not for his quick thinking, she would have died at the hands of Johanna Newes.

Alice unfurled the scroll, reading its components over and over. She tried to commit them to memory, but as soon as she removed her eyes from the arcane words, all knowledge of them were gone. The spells protection so it couldn't fall into the wrong hands . . . or be made with the wrong individual.

Her memories slipped back to a time when she first made a promise, when she swore her oath of protection.

~

"My sweet, Allie, let me look at you," the old woman said. "You're all grown up. Give your old grandma a hug."

"Hi, Grandma Bee," an eighteen-year-old Alice Primrose said as she wrapped her arms around the flowing dress of the woman.

Beatrice 'Bee' Hawthorn was tall and slender. The colorful, floral print dress brushed against the ground. A sharp contrast to Alice's tight-fitting, black clothes. She was in her late 60s with wild, naturally gray hair. Her fingers were filled with various colorful rings, and her wrists were wrapped in beaded bracelets.

"I love what you've done with your hair," Bee said as she ran her fingers through Alice's hair. "It's so vibrant."

"Thank you. Purple is my favorite color, so I thought, 'why not?'"

"What does your mom think?"

Alice hesitated, her eyes drifting as if she was trying to find a diplomatic answer. "She doesn't like it. She wants to know why I would ruin my perfectly good black hair."

"Don't listen to her. You keep being you, no matter what," Bee said. "Got me?"

"Yep. I'll always be me."

"That's my girl."

Alice hesitated. "It's also kind of permanent."

"Oh?"

"I used a spell to do it, and well . . ." Alice paused. "It's not exactly a dye job."

Beatrice laughed as she patted Alice's shoulders. "You'll get better. Come. I have the tea ready."

She led Alice through her home. An eclectic mishmash of furniture and items with no central theme were scattered throughout her living room. In her cozy kitchen, green vines hung from baskets. An assortment of herbs grew in small pots in a window above the sink. There were a few glass vials and baking utensils haphazardly placed on the kitchen counter.

They pulled out their chairs and sat at the square table. A mint-colored teapot sat in the middle of the table with two matching cups.

Beatrice snapped her fingers. The teapot rose to fill each cup before floating back to its original position. "So, tell me all about your plans for school."

Alice picked up the cup. She held it aloft with both hands, her elbows on the table. She took a sip; its refreshing liquid warmed her throat. "I'm going to focus on my apothecary skills. I want to be a witch who brews potions and makes people feel good."

"Oh," Beatrice said as she took a sip. She focused on Alice. "What does your mother think?"

"She doesn't want me to. She said I should be something else, a kitchen witch or a green herbal witch like her. I'm sorry, but cottagecore isn't exactly my aesthetic." Alice pointed to her black, mesh sleeves. "I want to be an apothecary witch."

Beatrice took another sip and set her cup on the table. She placed her hand on Alice's elbow. "You are you and not anyone else. You get to define who you are—not your mom, not me, not anyone. If your passion is in apothecary, then go be an apothecary witch."

Alice nodded and took a sip.

"I think I might know why your mom was so apprehensive about you wanting to focus on apothecary," Beatrice said as she rose from the table. "I think it's time you learned your family secrets."

"Secrets?"

Beatrice exited the kitchen. Alice turned to follow her with her eyes. She disappeared back into the living room and onward down the hall to her bedroom. Alice took another sip from her cup and placed it onto the table.

A moment passed.

Beatrice returned carrying a large hat box. She placed it on the table. She removed the lid and pulled out a black witch's hat with an oversized brim. A leather band with a brass buckle wrapped around the tall point. The tip was bent over with age.

"If you're going to tell me I'm a witch, I'm already aware," Alice said with a slight chuckle.

"Funny," Beatrice replied. "But this is more than a witch's hat. This is our family legacy. It's why your mother doesn't want you to be an apothecary witch. I was going to wait to show you, but now is as good of a time as any."

"Does the hat have special powers?" Alice asked.

"It's not the hat, but what's inside," Beatrice answered. She stuck her hand into the hat. "There is a secret pocket inside. The pocket contains one of the most valuable, sought after spells in the world." She pulled out a weathered scroll and handed it to Alice.

"What does it do?" Alice asked as she unfurled it. She read the spell, memorizing the ingredients. "The Lovers' Kiss?"

"No one knows," Beatrice said. "It's rumored to have the power to grant great strength, give you whatever your heart desires, or even bring someone back from the dead."

Alice tore her eyes away from the spell. Every ingredient and method vanished from her mind. "I- I completely forgot what I read."

"You must maintain eye contact, or you forget. It's the reason there is only one."

"Have you ever tried to make it?"

"Once, with your grandfather, God rest his soul," Beatrice said. She bowed her head and placed her hands over her heart. She paused for a moment before lifting her head back up. "We tried, but nothing happened. They said it only works after an expression of love."

"By love, do you mean . . .?" Alice's words trailed off.

Beatrice placed her hands on her hips. "There is more than one way to express your love for someone. But it must be shared together."

"How did you get it?"

"This hat belonged to your great-great grandmother—my grandmother. She passed it down to me right before she passed. This was her witch's hat. She kept it safe in there. It was passed down through generations. We've kept it hidden and safe."

"Why?"

"People have fought and died over it. My grandfather and grandmother defended an entire town to keep it safe. There are those who seek it to use it for nefarious purposes. It's been that way for ages. And now, the responsibility falls onto you."

Alice shook her head and handed it back. "I don't want it."

Beatrice cupped Alice's hands with hers. She gazed into Alice's eyes. "Your mother didn't want it either. If you don't take it, there will be no one left. I'm an old woman. I can't keep it forever. It could easily fall into the wrong hands, and then who will stop them?"

Alice leered at the scroll. Her eyes lingered on the weathered paper.

"I don't know if I can handle the responsibility," Alice said.

"I know it won't be easy, but I believe in you," Beatrice assured her. Alice raised up to meet Beatrice's eyes. "Keep it hidden. Don't tell anyone. And when the time is right, you'll know when to try it for yourself."

"How are you doing?" Hugo's voice jolted Alice out of her memory.

A shiver ran down her spine.

"I didn't mean to startle you."

"You didn't startle me," Alice said as she rolled up the scroll and placed it back into the wooden box. She snapped her fingers. The box rose, entered its clandestine hiding spot, and the stone closed behind it. "I was only thinking."

"What are you going to do?" Hugo asked.

Alice placed her hands on the workstation. She leaned her head forward, hiding behind the purple hair cascading down around her. "Can I ask you a question?"

"Of course."

"Will you answer me truthfully?"

"Always."

She stood up, brushing her hair back behind her ears. She turned to face Hugo, tears in her eyes. "Why do you love me?"

"Why do I love you?" Hugo took a step back His head tilted and eyebrows scrunched like a curious puppy. "Is this a trick?"

"Please . . . please just answer."

"Okay," Hugo said as he took her hand.

She lost herself in his icy blues as they locked with her emerald greens. A glint in his eye.

"I love you because you're kind, compassionate, caring, understanding, and patient."

Alice smiled, holding back tears. She let go of Hugo's hand to wipe away a tear and immediately took it again.

Hugo continued, "I've been in love with you since the moment you leaned over my fence promising to accept me for who I am. Ultimately, that's why I love you. You accept me for who I am, and I accept you for who you are. Everything about you. Your witchy powers. Your love of wine making. I can't imagine my life without you."

"Thank you," Alice said. "I love you because you accept me. I've loved you since I first met you in the backyard. I knew you caught me flying, and yet, you said nothing. That's why I kept following you until you asked me out."

Hugo smiled. "What brought this on?"

Alice slumped her shoulders. "I was thinking about what brought me here. How the spell turned my life upside down and led me here. How I've hated the spell since it was first given to me. How I never wanted it."

"I'm sorry," Hugo said. "I'm sorry you had to go through that."

"But if not for the spell, I would have never met you," she said. Alice let go of Hugo's hands and fixated on the ground. "I've been thinking it over. The spell has put more than just me in danger. It's caused trouble for Ez and now the Raskins. All because of me. I can't ask them to stay in harm's way."

"What are you getting at?"

"I've decided the best thing to do is run again," Alice said, returning to Hugo's eyes. "I'll understand if you don't want to follow me."

Hugo took her hands again and leaned closer. He fixed his gaze on her, never taking his icy blue eyes away. Her soul set ablaze by their connection. A connection deeper than anything spoken. Something not born out of infatuation or lust—a connection born out of love.

"I'll do whatever it takes to keep you safe," Hugo said. "If you think it's best to move, then let's move."

A tear rolled down Alice's cheek. "You don't have to—"

Hugo let go of one hand to cup her face and used his thumb to wipe away the tear. She placed her hand on top of his. He gently lifted her chin.

"I love you. Your very essence has bewitched my soul. I'll follow you to the ends of the earth to make sure you're safe. Whatever it takes. You have my word. Everything will be okay. I promise," Hugo said.

"Thank you," Alice mouthed; no words spoken.

They wrapped their arms around each other, connecting their hearts and souls together. Alice wanted this moment to last forever, safe and secure within Hugo's arms in their wine cellar.

"It's almost sundown," Alice said. "We should get going if we're going to Ez's place."

They relinquished their hug, much to the dismay of Alice's soul. They left the wine cellar. The candles extinguished as the door closed shut behind them. They made their way up the creaky basement stairs to an awaiting Max. Her tail wagged as she welcomed them back from the basement.

"So, will Ez take us some place tonight?" Hugo asked as they made their way to the front door. "Do we need to bring Max and Gwennie?"

Alice pulled her black and purple tailcoat from the coat rack. She slipped her arms into the sleeves and pulled it tight around her body.

"Probably not," Alice said. "But we can begin preparations."

"Why not call her?" Hugo asked.

"Because she'll say no. This is going to require showing up in person."

"If it won't be tonight, then maybe I should stay behind," Hugo said. Alice tilted her head in confusion. "If they see us both leave, what if they try to do something to the Raskins or someone else in the town? No doubt they're tracking our movements with their ghouls. It's a little suspicious if we both leave."

Alice grabbed her curved witch's hat. "I see your point. I don't like it, but you have a point. Stay inside until I get back."

"If they make a move?"

Her fingers crumpled the black brim as she nervously rotated the hat in her hands. "Don't do anything unless you absolutely must. Call the Raskins to let them know our plan. Tell them not to leave under any circumstances. If they move on the town, then we'll have to let them."

"I can do that," Hugo said.

She gave him another hug, laying her head on his chest. She squeezed him tightly, not wanting to let him go. He leaned his head against hers.

"Be safe," Hugo said.

"You too," Alice replied. She kissed him on the cheek. She placed her hat on her head, tugging on the brim to ensure a snug fit. She pulled back the black curtain. It was clear. She opened the door. "I love you."

"Of course you do," Hugo said with a wink. He blew her a kiss.

Alice smiled. She acted as if she caught it in the air and put her hand in the coat pocket. "I'll save it for later." She gave him a wink and left, shutting the door behind her.

CHAPTER 11
VAMPIRE HUNTERS

"I'm going to stake the Savinos tonight," Hugo said.

He stood before the bathroom mirror. His arms were crossed and his lips pulled in. He waited for the reaction of his fellow vampire hunting consultants.

"That's the dumbest fucking thing I've ever heard," Alice's reflection yelled toward Hugo. "Do you know how utterly . . . You want to take on two vampires at once?"

"To be fair," Hugo's reflection said. "I agree with him."

She snapped her attention to Hugo's reflection, her eyes filled with a fiery glare as if she were ready to rip him apart. "You stay out of this." With a single motion, she backhanded him across his chest, folded her arms, and turned away from the mirror. "I'm done talking with both of you."

Hugo rubbed the sides of his head. "I need your help," he said. "You're the only one who can help me. I'm begging you. Please. Help."

"I don't want to be a part of this," Alice's reflection said.

"Babe, we need your help." Hugo's reflection rubbed his chest over his tight-fitting, long-sleeve, black T-shirt. "You know how to deal with them. We don't. Please."

"Why should I help?" She turned around to stare Hugo directly in the eyes. "Why should I help you storm off and get yourself killed? Get *him* killed." She pointed to Hugo's reflection.

Alice's reflection glared at Hugo with the eyes of a scorned lover. Without breaking her gaze, she raised her left hand and pointed to her ring finger. "What about this?"

"What about it?" Hugo asked.

"When are you going to ask her?" Alice's reflection asked. "I want my ring. He can't give me my ring without you giving it to her first."

"It didn't seem like a very appropriate thing to do the past couple of days," Hugo replied.

"So what?" Alice's reflection said. "I want my ring. Give it to her."

"This is all playing out entirely how I envisioned it in my head. 'Oh, hey. While we're fighting off this vampire attack that could destroy everything, here's a ring. Let's get married,'" Hugo said with a sarcastic tone.

Alice's reflection stood in silence with her still unrelenting gaze. "Then why are you running off to get yourself killed?"

"I have to do this," Hugo yelled.

"Why?" Alice's reflection yelled back as she furled her eyebrows.

Hugo lowered his head and placed a hand on his hip. He slumped forward, bracing himself with one arm against the wall.

"Because this is all my fault," he said in a hushed tone. He raised his head to meet Alice's reflection. "If I didn't lose . . . If I didn't lose my temper, none of this would have happened."

"It's not your fault," Alice's reflection said. Her eyes finally broke his gaze. "Don't take responsibility for her past."

"How is it not my fault?" Hugo asked, standing up. He pointed to himself. "I was the one who lost control of my temper. I was the one who yelled at her. I was the one who almost got her killed."

"And she was the one who lost control of her emotions and blew her cover," Alice's reflection answered.

"But I was on the broomstick . . . on Galahad. I was the one in the news article. I was the one who brought the vampires here," Hugo responded, as tears formed in his eyes. "I'm the reason the Raskins could lose their store. I'm the reason Alice has to move again. I'm the reason all of this happened. Please. Please help me fix this."

Alice's reflection buried her face into her hands, muffling growls as she screamed into clenched teeth and an unseen void. As they subsided, she reemerged from behind her temporary sanctum. She locked eyes with Hugo. Her eyes weren't full of rage or contempt or scorn, but a single emotion Hugo had known many times before. The same emotion he experienced every time Elizabeth went for treatments or doctor visits or when exhaustion engulfed her—fear.

"Babe," Hugo's reflection said in a soothing tone as he wrapped his arms around her shoulders. "It's not an ideal situation. And you know you wouldn't allow it. Sometimes we have to play the hand we're dealt. It's a really shitty hand, but I think it could work. *We* think it could work, but we need your help."

Alice's reflection closed her eyes and took in a deep breath. She held it for a moment before finally releasing it—a sign she accepted Hugo's decision. She opened her eyes once again; they turned bloodshot as she held back tears. "What's your plan, lover boy?"

Lover boy? The first name she called Hugo when they met.

He stood upright. "Okay, here's the play. We get them alone, just them and me. It has to be in a familiar setting. Some place I know like the back of my hand in case anything goes wrong."

"It can't be the old house. Too many unknowns," Hugo's reflection added.

"Well, it's not going to be here," Alice's reflection said. "The front door remains closed."

"The Neighborhood Market is too open," Hugo said. He paused, losing himself in thought. "It has to be the restaurant."

Hugo's reflection snapped his fingers and pointed at Hugo. "The restaurant could work. Familiar territory. It's small enough. It's on their turf. They'd gladly accept a meeting."

"It would have to be after they close for the evening. Tonight," Hugo said.

"You have the place," Alice's reflection said. "How are you going to do it?"

"The round tables are off to the side and only seat two, so we'll be seated at a square table. I'll keep Sylvia in front of me and Sebastian to the side. I can control the placement."

"What if they jump you as soon as you enter?" Hugo's reflection said.

"Tell them I would level the building if you don't walk out," Alice's reflection answered. "Tell them I sent you to negotiate for me and ease the tension."

"Okay. That keeps you safe," Hugo's reflection said. "Now how are you going to take them out?"

"I can't walk in with a stake, so I'll have to hide it," Hugo answered.

"Where would you hide it?" Alice's reflection asked.

"Up my arm sleeve," Hugo replied. "The one from the kit is too large. It would be noticeable. I need something . . . something I could conceal. Something smaller."

Hugo paused. He rotated his right forearm back and forth, deep in thought.

"Oh. Ohhhh," Hugo's reflection blurted out. "That could work!"

"What? What could work?" Alice's reflection asked.

"Anything that once bled, right, regardless of size? That's what I need?" Hugo asked.

"Yeah, but what is it?" Alice's reflection asked. "Tell me."

"Control the sweater . . ." Hugo said.

"Control the fight," Hugo's reflection finished.

Hugo rushed out of the bathroom and past a waiting Max, fearful of a possible bath should she enter the bathroom. Hugo flung open the closet door and dropped to his knees. He rummaged through boxes piled up, Alice and Hugo's many pairs of shoes, and other items flung inside the closet. He pulled out a box labeled *Hockey Stuff*, tucked away in the back of their bedroom closet.

He opened the cardboard box and rummaged through the contents—old pictures of his playing days, his used high school game sweater, giveaways from professional hockey games, commemorative pucks. There, laying across the bottom of the box, was his newfound vampire hunting weapon—a wooden mini hockey stick, longer than a foot, emblazoned with the logo of Columbus' professional hockey team.

Hugo shoved the contents back into the box and rose to his feet. He flung the box into the closet and shut the door. He bounded with excitement into the bathroom, nearly slipping on the checkerboard tile floor. Max still resisted entering the bathroom, tapping her paws on the ground, out of fear it was a ploy to get her in the bathtub. She wagged her tail at the excitement. Hugo held his new weapon high in the air for the reflections to see.

"With this!" Hugo shouted.

"You're going to do what . . . scratch their back with it?" Alice's reflection said.

"No, I'll trim it down and turn one end into a spike. I can tape it to my forearm. I'll wear a dark shirt. They'll never see it. Then when I'm ready to strike, I'll use the chair leg to dislodge it and slide it down into my hand. It's perfect," Hugo said.

Hugo's reflection turned to Alice's. "It's the best option we have."

Alice's reflection crossed her arms and turned her back to Hugo's reflection. "I don't like this. Not one bit."

"What other option is there? Move again? Then they keep coming after us until they get what they want," Hugo pleaded. "We make a stand. We make it tonight."

"Run me through it." Alice's reflection turned toward Hugo. "Every little detail."

"Okay, imagine the table is here." He motioned with his hands. "I'm sitting here, and Sylvia is across from me. Now, ideally, I want

Sebastian to be to my right. It gives me a direct shot at his heart. I can stab him right here." He pointed to a spot on his chest.

"And if he doesn't?" Alice's reflection asked.

"Then we control the sweater," Hugo's reflection stated.

"What does that even mean?" Alice's reflection asked.

"With my left hand, I grab his shirt, pull on it, and force him closer to me. Just like in a hockey fight," Hugo replied.

"He'll be off balance," his reflection added. "Then we strike."

Hugo made the motion with the mini wooden hockey stick. "Poof, cloud of dust."

"Well, that's one," Alice's reflection said. "What about his wife, who you mostly likely sent into a frenzied rage?"

"I'm not going to lie, it's a fifty-fifty shot," Hugo said.

"You expect me to agree to those odds?" she asked.

"No. No, I don't," Hugo said. "I need him." He pointed to his reflection, who was lost in deep thought.

Hugo's reflection rubbed his chin and scratched his beard. He focused on the tile floor below him, working out the situation in his head.

"The only advantage we have is the table will be between us and her. It will give us time to react. She'll probably leap across it in the heat of the moment," Hugo's reflection stated.

"If she leaps across it, I could grab her and force her down. Then stab from behind," Hugo said.

"What if she doesn't?" Alice's reflection asked.

"Then it's a hockey fight. I can grab her clothing and yank and pull her in a direction where I can get in a good strike at her heart," Hugo replied.

"And if she gets you first? There's no skating away to stick taps after it's over," Alice's reflection said.

"So . . . you do know hockey lingo," Hugo's reflection said.

She smacked him across the chest. "I've been to hockey games with you, you doofus. Of course, I've picked up a few things."

"You know, this could be my last night," his reflection stated.

He wrapped his arms around her waist, pulling her close to him. She wrapped her arms around his torso. They pressed against each other, holding each other tightly.

Alice's reflection met her gaze to his. She batted her eyes a few times. Her eyes hid a sense of sadness masquerading as lust.

"I know," she said. She lowered her head.

He placed a finger under her chin and lifted her head to stare into her emerald green eyes once more. "I was thinking—"

"What?" Alice's reflection asked as her puppy dog eyes met his icy blues.

He let go of her chin and slipped his hand around her back. His finger tips grazed the curves of her body before they settled onto her spine. Alice's reflection closed her eyes and bit her lip. Her body shivered slightly as his finger tips traced an invisible line down to the small of her back. She let out a small, audible moan. He continued further, his fingers now tracing the curve of her ass.

"What were you thinking?" Alice's reflection whispered into his ear. "Could it be what I'm thinking?"

"Are you two seriously flirting right now?" Hugo asked.

Alice's reflection glared at him. "Shut up. Don't ruin this for me." She turned her attention back to Hugo's reflection.

Hugo's reflection grabbed a handful of her ass and pulled her closer. "I might not be coming back. Maybe, one last time, we could play hockey player and figure skater. You know, as a last request."

She buried her head into his chest. "I hate how much I love you right now," Alice's reflection said in muffled tones.

Hugo's reflection chuckled. "Yeah, but at least you love me."

She pulled her head back. He tilted his, leaning in to meet and embraced with a kiss. Their lips pressed against each other in long, drawn out kisses. They only relinquished to take in a gulp of air and reposition their heads.

"Both of you do know I'm still here, right?" Hugo asked.

They paid no attention to him. Their hands explored each other's backs with gentle, sensuous touches, as if discovering something new. Hugo's reflection slid both of his hands below her ass and lifted her up. She wrapped her legs around his waist, interlocking their bodies as one. He pressed her against the wall of their reflected bathroom.

She stopped kissing him for a moment to smile a Cheshirish grin. Devious, illicit thoughts no doubt running through her mind. She shook her head a few times to allow her purple hair to go wild. Her eyes filled with a fiery passion of hunger and lust.

Hugo's reflection titled his head forward, his eyes never breaking from hers. "Tell me all about your triple axel."

She bit her lip as her Cheshire grin grew larger. She held it for a moment before her expression turned into a smolder with pursed lips. "Tell me all about how you'd score in the five hole."

Hugo smacked the mirror frame with the back of his hand. "Can you two stop for like five seconds?" Hugo broke their intimate moment.

They both glared at him.

He continued, "Are we doing this or not?"

"Fine," Alice said with a disapproving stare. She turned her attention back to Hugo's reflection. "If anything happens to you, I swear I'll raise you from the dead to kill you myself."

"Deal," Hugo's reflection answered.

Their lips familiarized themselves once again.

"So . . . I'll make the call?" Hugo asked.

The reflections ignored Hugo's question and continued their sexual exploits.

"I'll make the call." He turned and proceeded out of the bathroom, wooden hockey stick in hand.

"Turn out the lights," both reflections yelled.

Hugo stretched back in and flicked the switch.

"Wait," Alice's reflection said. "Leave it on. I want to melt into those icy blues."

Without looking, Hugo once more flicked the lights on.

Max stood up, her tail wagging, as Hugo returned from the bathroom—no bath time for her this evening.

Hugo left the bedroom and whistled. "Come on, Max. Give them their privacy."

Max followed Hugo into the hallway, and Hugo shut the door.

Max bounded down the stairs in her usual unannounced race against Hugo to be the first one to arrive at the bottom. Hugo followed, but not in his usual bouncy stride. Each step was deliberate and slow. The harsh reality of the situation weighed on him like a suffocating blanket. He paused when he landed on the bottom step. His eyes focused on the wooden hockey stick clutched in his right hand.

This is the dumbest thing you've ever done.

Max's bark from the living room shook him from his trance. He went to investigate. Max turned in circles, trying to get the attention of Guinevere. The broomstick floated there, not fazed by the golden retriever's attempt for attention. Max, still very much an impish puppy, maneuvered and danced around, trying to get the broomstick to play with her. It didn't move.

Guinevere was quite different from Galahad's childlike disposition. *Galahad.* The name drew Hugo's attention to the top of Alice's memory shrine bookcase. The remains of Galahad—Alice's faithful horse, dog, broomstick—rested on a stand, giving it the appearance of being in mid-flight. Hugo's breath quickened. Vivid images of the fateful evening flooded his mind, replaying the events leading to the broomstick's demise at the hand of the anti-magick wand. Hugo closed his eyes and dropped his head, hoping to end the guilt for Galahad's death.

This is all your fault. Galahad. The vampires. Having to move. It's all your fault. You have to do it. You have to fix this.

Hugo opened his eyes and knelt. "Come here, Max. Come here, girl."

Max, not finding a playing partner in the broomstick, gleefully nestled herself into the waiting arms of Hugo. She sat in front of him, her tail sweeping the hardwood floor, and tried to kiss Hugo. Hugo resisted a little, but allowed her to get in a few licks on his face. He hugged Max and squeezed her tightly.

"I love you, Max. Thank you for everything you've done for me," he said. She continued to wag her tail, her face smiling at the affection Hugo was showing her. "If I don't come back, you be good for Alice."

Max continued to wag her tail in excitement.

"Know that I love you." He gave her a few scratches behind the ears and stood up.

His eyes bloodshot, he wiped away a tear rolling down his cheek. His somber expression turned to furious determination as he found his phone sitting on the end table. He picked it up, unlocked it, and searched online for the phone number to Sylvia's Bistro. He pressed the entry.

The pause between each ring was an eternity. Thoughts raced through his mind. He wanted to hang up. He wanted to continue. He wished Alice was here to help.

A woman answered. "Thank you for calling Sylvia's. How may I help you?"

"Is Sebastian available?"

"I'm sorry. Mr. Savino is unavailable at the moment," she replied.

"I really need to speak to Sebastian. When will he be available?" Hugo asked.

"I can relay a message for him," she answered.

"Tell him Hugo Dodds is calling. He'll know what it's about."

There was a pause.

The silence was excruciating. Hugo glanced at his phone's screen to make sure he didn't lose connection. He continued to wait. Each doubting thought ran through his mind the longer he waited.

"Hello?" Hugo asked.

"One moment," the woman said, breaking the silence. "What would you like to tell Mr. Savino?"

"Tell him I'll be at the restaurant tonight after closing. Just us. No one else. Let's make a deal."

The silence returned. Hugo tapped the wooden hockey stick against his thigh.

Come on. Come on.

"You're in luck. Mr. Savino informed me the restaurant will be closing an hour early tonight," the woman's voice said.

"Good. Tell him I'll be there a half hour after."

"Wonderful. He looks—"

Hugo hung up the phone. He continued tapping the stick against his thigh. Hugo focused on the red velvet couch. The memory of his first night together with Alice drinking wine drifted through his mind, when he unknowingly messed with her magical hourglass and slowed time. The memory of the same hourglass saving Alice the night he rushed her lifeless body home. How he was able to revive her with The Lovers' Kiss. The silly little spell. That stupid spell.

Alice's words rushed back to him. *Some have died trying to obtain it.*

He marched out of the living room, opened the basement door, and descended the stairs. On this night, two more names would join the list. Sebastian and Sylvia Savino. Hugo would make certain of it.

THE SECOND SONATA MOVEMENT

"ALLEGRETTO"

CHAPTER 12
TABLE STAKES

The night was dark, the moon mostly engulfed by a layer of dense clouds. Porch lights and the orangish glow of the street lamps lining the Newbury Grove town center provided relief from the darkness creeping over the land. It was quiet. Shops had closed for the evening. People were at home, staying warm and secure in the late autumn cold. The occasional car drove by, winding their way through the town toward their destination.

Ghostly vapor trails were like momentary bread crumbs as Hugo marched toward the town center. His pulse increased with each step. His heart thumped louder and louder in reverberations only his body could hear. His hand twitched. His exhale lingered, trying to calm and steady himself.

Relax. You have to relax.

He paused.

He closed his eyes and took a few more inhales, breathing deeply to fill his lungs. The ghostly vapor trails materialized once again in the frigid air. He opened his eyes and basked in the glow of the moon. The moon was Alice's anchor, providing her with a sense of joy and comfort. Hugo hoped it would do the same for him. Its whitish-blue glow disappeared behind the clouds, leaving only darkness in the night sky.

He turned his attention to the black and red crimson awning above what was once Antonio's Italian Ristorante. The restaurant was dark. No light seeped through the glass in the door. The crimson curtains concealed the interior from prying eyes.

This is the dumbest thing you've ever done.

Hugo's eyes lingered on the gold lettering of the door: Sylvia's Bistro. That name. That wretched name. He lingered for an eternity, yet it was only a moment. The time had come. It was now or never. He pulled his black leather jacket tight and continued forth.

He opened the door and peered in. Candles scattered across the various tables illuminated the room with a flickering orange glow. There was no movement. There was no one to greet him.

"Come in," Sylvia's unseen voice said. "Don't be afraid. We won't bite." She laughed, joined in by Sebastian.

Welcome to my parlor, said the spider to the fly.

"Before I enter, I want to set some ground rules," Hugo replied.

"Name them," Sylvia responded.

"First, I'm entering by myself. Alice is outside. We thought it would ease the tension," Hugo said.

"So, the witch refuses to meet with her queen face-to-face?" Sylvia responded.

You're not her queen.

"She sent me to negotiate on her behalf," Hugo said.

"Fine," Sylvia answered. "Hopefully, negotiations will go smoother than the last time."

"Second, if I don't walk out of here, Alice will level this entire building without hesitation."

"I already told you, we don't bite," Sylvia said.

"Do you accept these terms?" Hugo asked. "It's the only way I'm walking through this door."

"How do we know you aren't armed yourself?" Sebastian asked.

"How do we know you aren't setting us up? We haven't forgotten about last time."

"That's why I'm alone," Hugo responded. "I'll show you I'm unarmed. Do you accept?"

"Deal," Sylvia said.

Hugo entered the restaurant. Each step was thoughtful and deliberate. He held his arms out waist high. He turned the corner, and sitting in the center of the restaurant at a square table was Sylvia Savino, as he had hoped.

She wore a crimson, Victorian style frock jacket—a far cry from her usual trendy fashion. The collar, lapel, and cuffs were outlined in black with embroidered patterns. The room was too dark to see their ornate details. It hugged tightly against her frame. Three silver buttons adorned both sides of the jacket. The crimson red didn't close fully; instead, there was a patch of black material which zipped all the way up and hugged her neck.

Sebastian positioned himself behind her. He rested a hand on her shoulder and leaned in to whisper something into her ear. They laughed. He wore his usual tight black dress shirt, vest, and dress pants with a bloodred tie. If not for the red tie, he could have blended into the background. He smiled at Hugo.

Hmm. Must not have had time to change into matching outfits.

"I'm unarmed," Hugo said.

"Remove your jacket," Sylvia commanded. "Spin around and show me."

Hugo unzipped his black leather jacket. He held it in his right hand, hoping the flowing leather would conceal the makeshift stake taped to his forearm as he moved his arms around. The long sleeve of his black Henley shirt was loose enough to hide it, but twirling around the jacket was even better. He turned around, revealing nothing besides his shirt tucked into the waistband.

He faced Sylvia again. "Satisfied?"

"For now," she answered in a hushed tone. "Please. Have a seat."

Hugo hesitated. *Is Sebastian going to sit?*

Sebastian stepped to the side of the table—Hugo's right—and pulled out the chair to sit down.

Perfect.

Sylvia motioned for Hugo to take his place. He placed his leather jacket on the back of the chair and sat down. He laid his left arm on the table, while keeping his right at his side.

"Nice jacket. Seems a little over the top, don't you think?" Hugo asked.

"When I hold court, I expect everyone to be properly dressed. You'll have to forgive my husband as the quickness of your meeting caught him off guard. I have my tailors standing by, ready to make an outfit for your witchy girlfriend when she finally agrees to join us. I could make one for you as well." Sylvia picked up a wine bottle resting on the table. "I hope you don't mind if we eat in front of you. You're free to join in if you wish."

Four wineglasses were set on the table, two in front of Sylvia and two in front of Hugo. The dark, blackish-red liquid poured out into her two glasses. Not as viscous as wine, it was thicker. He had poured enough glasses of wine in his lifetime; he knew it wasn't wine they were drinking.

She presented Hugo with the bottle. "Care for some? It's the mana of life."

The Savinos laughed. They picked up their glasses, swirled their drinks around, smelled it, and held it up to their mouths. They tilted their heads back and drank.

Now. Do it. Now!

Hugo rubbed his arm against the chair leg. The tape peeled itself from Hugo's skin. He kept pushing. The stake was freed from one side of the tape, but the other side remained. The stake was almost completely freed when Sylvia returned her half empty glass to the table. She let out an exhale of pleasure as she used her finger to lap up any trailing blood on her lips. She licked her finger, locked eyes with Hugo, and smiled.

"I almost forgot." Sylvia turned her attention to Sebastian. "Please, my dear, go get our gesture of goodwill."

Sebastian set his glass down and rose from the table.

No!

He disappeared behind the swinging doors leading into the kitchen. Hugo stopped rubbing the stake against the chair leg.

"We wanted to give you something. Something we hope shows our good faith during the negotiations," she continued.

Hugo's eyes shifted back and forth between Sylvia and the kitchen door. There were no other entrances to the restaurant. Nothing Sebastian could use to sneak up on him. He glanced back at the entrance and then to Sylvia.

She once again picked up her glass and offered it to Hugo. Her steel-blue, malevolent eyes locked onto Hugo. "Are you sure you don't want some? It's a little stronger than we offer in Red-Hearted Queen."

"I'm fine," Hugo replied. "Should we get down to business?"

"All business and no talk with you." She took a sip of her glass and moaned. "It's so good. You don't know what you're missing."

"Anyone I know?"

"An old friend."

Hugo's eyes narrowed. "Who?"

She placed her elbow on the table, rested her chin in her free hand, and smiled. She swirled the glass with her other hand. There was a moment of eerie silence which Hugo didn't enjoy.

"We want you gone," Hugo said. "Leave Newbury Grove and never return."

Sylvia sat up. "You're no fun." Sylvia set her glass down and raised a finger to her mouth.

In the flickering candlelight, she displayed one of her fangs. She rubbed her finger against the point, no doubt wanting to intimidate Hugo further.

His heart raced. The beating traveled up his body. His breath quickened. He tapped the chair leg with his right hand. His left foot shook. He breathed deeply through his nose to help relax.

Calm down.

"Okay. What are your terms?" Sylvia asked.

"We want you gone—" Hugo started.

"You already mentioned that," Sylvia said with a flourished hand gesture. "Is there more?"

"No. We want you to never return. To leave the people of Newbury Grove alone. We want you to restore all distribution contracts with Raskin's Neighborhood Market. No more disruptions."

"That's it?"

He's been gone too long.

"Where did he go?" Hugo asked.

"Don't worry about him," Sylvia said. "I told you, it's in good faith. I'm many things, but I'm also honest. Now . . . my counter offer. I'll accept your offer, plus the spell, but I want your witchy girlfriend to work for me."

Hugo's heart sank at the very thought of Alice working for this monster. "How long?"

"For as long as she's useful to me. Her skills are exquisite, and I plan on expanding my little empire with her as the backbone. My resources. Her skills. That spell. We'd be unstoppable. We'd have worldwide distribution. It's the perfect union of vampires and witches," Sylvia said as she interlocked her hands together. "Together. Peacefully. With me at the helm."

"Peace as long as you're in charge?"

"What is peace, but others' acceptance of defeat."

"It was never about the spell, was it?" Hugo asked.

"Oh . . . Oh, no," Sylvia said. "The spell is more powerful than you can imagine. I've spent multiple lifetimes searching for it. I almost had it if not for that blundering idiot, Alabaster Sinclair. It was tracked out west. Alabaster sent one of his hired goons to retrieve it before my people could get to the spell. If you want something done right, do it yourself."

"How do you know that name?"

"You don't know your history very well, do you, Hugo Dodds? The Sinclair family's motivations were . . . well, less than altruistic. If I'm not mistaken, this town was founded by a Sinclair. She thought it held a special tree of some sort."

The fairy tree! Alice was right.

Hugo jolted at the sound of the kitchen door swinging open.

Sebastian returned holding a red paper gift bag. "It took me a little longer to find it. It was moved."

"We'll deal with the staff member tomorrow," Sylvia replied. "Besides, it allowed me to give our friend Hugo here a brief history lesson."

Sebastian moved to the closest chair, to Hugo's left, and sat down. He placed the bag in front of Hugo. "Your gift."

Why did he move? Does he know?

With his left hand, Hugo grasped the bag, while his right hand remained still by his side. Hesitantly, he peered inside. The soft glow of the candlelight cast an air of mystery, leaving the contents shrouded in secrecy. It resembled a tangled mess of yarn, all knotted together.

"Please take it out," Sylvia said.

Leave. Leave now! While you can.

Hugo delved into the bag. He gripped the cotton fibers of something knitted and withdrew it. Awestruck, he examined the red knit hat held in his grasp. While he hadn't seen it, he knew exactly who wore such a hat—Sam.

"I was hoping to give it to Alice personally, but since she decided to skip out on negotiations, you'll have to deliver to it her yourself," Sylvia said.

Hugo shot a glance to Sebastian and then Sylvia with malice in his eyes. "Where did you get this?"

Sebastian replied, "An old friend of Alice's. She wanted her to have it as a reminder of a life long gone. She begged us to give it to her before . . . What was her name again?"

"It was short for something. Hmm." Sylvia tapped a finger against her lips, deep in thought. "Ah, I remember. Her name was Sam."

Hugo lowered the hat back into the bag. He never took his eyes off Sylvia. His eyebrows furled. "What if we call off all deals?"

Sylvia sat upright. She placed both hands on the table and leaned forward with her head tilted down. Her eyes narrowed, and she raised her right eyebrow. Her strawberry blonde, wavy hair, parted to the left, obscured part of her face from the flickering candlelight and cast it into darkness. Her sharp jawline was much more pronounced against the flickering light. She asserted her dominance over the negotiations.

"I would advise against calling off this deal. We can make life, not only for you, but all of Newbury Grove miserable," she answered. "We're allowing your friends to live. We only take the blood we need, instead of leaving them bone dry."

She leaned forward. "We will ruin your friends, the Raskins. They'll suffer as they watch their life's work go up in flames. And when it's complete, I'll personally rip their heads off," Sylvia threatened. "But I won't stop there. The streets will run red with blood as my colony of vampires descends on this town. And I'll make both of you watch."

Hugo's breathing quickened, and his heart raced. The thud, thud, thud, of his heart beats pulsed through his ears, trying to drown out Sylvia's threats. His eyes darted to Sebastian, whose wicked, ear-to-ear grin sent a shiver down his spine, and then back to Sylvia.

You have to do it.

"And when all is said and done, and you two are the remaining survivors, you'll watch in horror as the other one bleeds out," Sylvia added.

Control the sweater . . .

"A toast." Sebastian stretched out across the table for his glass. He raised it aloft.

Sylvia raised her glass and matched him.

"To our new empire!" Sebastian shouted.

"To our new empire!" Sylvia answered. "You can either join us or be destroyed by us."

Sylvia and Sebastian leaned their heads back and took a drink.

Control the fight!

Hugo flicked his arm against the chair leg, releasing the last bit of tape. The stake slid down into his waiting hand. He lunged for Sebastian's black dress shirt. It was tight against Sebastian's muscular chest, and his fingers struggled to securely grab onto the material. Hugo's hand slid across the shirt, but he managed to snare Sebastian's suit vest. With a singular motion, Hugo yanked Sebastian toward him and stabbed him in the chest with the stake.

"Die, you fucker!" Hugo shouted.

Sebastian dropped his wineglass and focused on the wooden mini hockey stick planted directly in his chest. Sebastian glanced up at Hugo in shocked disbelief. Hugo growled at him and pushed deeper with the makeshift stake. It wouldn't budge. He hit something.

Hugo leaned in, trying to drive it deeper into his chest and nick his heart. The wooden hockey stick cracked and broke in half. Part of it jutted out of Sebastian's chest. Sebastian's shock faded into rage. His eyes narrowed. His nose snarled. His fangs jetted out to their fully elongated position.

Sylvia shrieked in anger. She stood up and pushed the table toward Hugo; its remaining contents rained down as the table knocked him and his chair backward. He landed with a thud onto the ground, the ribbed chair back smashing into Hugo's back. Sylvia pushed on the table to pin him down.

The force of the table edge pressed against his abdomen, trying to cut him in half. Hugo cried out in agony as sharp pains cut across his stomach and back. He tried to push the table off, but the chair held him at a decline, so he couldn't get leverage. He squirmed, but the table dug deeper.

Sebastian leapt from his chair and grabbed the table, forcing it down harder onto Hugo, who roared in anguish.

"Check the door," Sebastian growled.

"Are you okay, my love?" Sylvia asked.

"I'm fine. Check the door," he answered as he ripped the broken stake from his chest. His black dress shirt was damp as he bled from his wound.

Sylvia sprinted to the front door. Hugo could hear the door opening and closing moments later. The audible click of the door lock echoed through the restaurant.

"It's clear. I don't see anything," she responded as she returned.

"Where is she?" Sebastian yelled. "Are you alone?"

Hugo struggled to breathe as the weight of Sebastian drove the table further into his stomach. He tried to respond, but could only muster more sounds of torment.

Sylvia moved like a stalking predator at an even, methodical pace, ready to pounce on injured prey. "Would you like to do the honors, my dear?" she asked Sebastian.

"While I'd like nothing more, I think it would be more meaningful coming from you," Sebastian responded. "Grab the table. I'll get his arms."

Sylvia put her weight on the table, and Sebastian let go. He rushed behind the vulnerable Hugo, trying to restrain both of his arms, but Hugo fought back.

"Fuck you," Hugo said as his arms flared to strike back.

Hugo took hold of Sebastian's pant leg, yanking, and trying to trip him. Sebastian kicked his leg back, yanking his pant leg from Hugo's grasp. He reared his leg back, and Hugo winced as Sebastian kicked him in his side.

Hugo let his guard down, and Sebastian trapped both of his wrists. He pulled them back over Hugo's head and down to the ground. Sebastian kneeled on them, pinning his hands under him. He placed his forearm on Hugo's head to keep him in place.

Sylvia threw the table to the side, providing Hugo a sense of relief. The relief was momentary, as she yanked the chair out from under him, scraping his back in the process. He howled. She stood over Hugo, her high heels on both sides of his chest, looking down on him. Her black leather pants squeaked as she knelt, straddling his torso. She lowered her body weight on the spot where the table was trying to cut him in half.

Hugo grimaced. His legs kicked and flailed, trying to escape. Sylvia used her hips to grind on his stomach, extruding as much pain as possible. He screamed in agony.

She leaned forward, pushing her left hand into his right shoulder, her face mere inches from his. Her breath washed over his lips as if she were leaning in to kiss him. Although, her kiss wouldn't be on the lips. Sylvia traced under his jawline to his chin using the lightest touch of her finger. A shiver of both excitement and despair ran down Hugo's body.

She shifted back and forth on his torso. Hugo winced with each swaying motion of her hips.

She smiled. "Does this excite you?" she whispered as her breath washed over Hugo's ear.

"She'll tear your world down, so help me, she'll destroy you," Hugo yelled.

She sat up with a pouting scowl on her face. "You really are no fun. I always like to have a little bit of fun before dinner."

Hugo squirmed and kicked, but couldn't dislodge her. "Go to hell!"

Sylvia lightly smacked him on both cheeks, batting him like a cat with a small toy. "You know, I've beheaded people for a lesser offense than trying to stake me and my husband. It makes it easier to bleed them dry. But today is your lucky day," Sylvia said, raising her hands in the air in celebration. "You're more valuable to me undead than beheaded."

Sebastian turned Hugo's head, exposing his neck. Sylvia leaned in and licked it. Hugo tightened at the sensation of her rough tongue dragging across his neck. His heart beat faster and faster. He let out a yell, hoping someone passing by would hear him.

"I can hear your heart beating. I can smell the blood coursing through your veins. It's exquisite. In time, you'll learn to appreciate my generous gift I'm giving you. In time, she'll learn to appreciate it as well," Sylvia said.

I'm sorry, Alice.

Sylvia's fangs elongated. She turned to Sebastian. "Darling, please be a dear, and go get a bottle. I don't want to waste any of this." She lurched forward and clamped down on Hugo's neck, piercing his skin with a fiery sting.

It was like a plastic straw pushing into a lid as the fangs slid deeper to find his blood. His blood bubbled and boiled under the skin. His body was on fire, ravaged by what was transpiring. He called out for help, but it never came.

Sylvia moaned with excitement and ecstasy.

Sylvia. Sebastian. The restaurant. They all faded into black as he slipped from his mortal coil. He gave a final thought before disappearing into nothingness.

Alice, please forgive me.

CHAPTER 13
WHICH WITCH ARE YOU?

Alice sat alone at the bar of Ez's new club, The Coven Club, located in a different city far away from their original home. The Coven Club was fancier than the original. It was designed from the ground up, not shoved into an existing building like the one before. Everything was top of the line and spewed elegance. The walls were exposed brick. The bar top was made of a polished, black onyx and lined one side. The center was filled with square tables a few steps down from the rest of the bar. Gold railings surrounded them with more tables on the outside.

Gold and crystal light fixtures hung over every table, providing a dim spotlight on the occupants below. A curved stage filled the back wall. Thick, navy curtains were drawn back to reveal the floating instruments bathed in a blue and purple light. The entire floor was covered in a red velvet like carpet—a far cry from the black, wood floor of the original. If Ez had to start over, at least she went big this time.

"She'll be right out," a man's voice said from behind the bar. "Can I get you anything to drink?"

Alice shook her head. "No, I'm fine. Thank you."

"Let me know if you need anything," he said before returning to his prep for the night. His sleeves were rolled up to his elbows.

Alice chuckled. Time was circular. This seemed all too familiar as her mind slipped back to that fateful evening.

~

Soft jazz music filled the room as instruments floated above the stage. Unseen arcane hands plucked the strings, tapped the drums, and pressed the brass valves to conjure the melodic sounds. The room was dimly lit, smokey, and full of energy. A clandestine place for those empowered with arcane abilities to meet and mingle.

Alice Primrose sat alone at the bar with her head tilted and witch's hat off-kilter. She held the left side of her head in her hand. Her elbow was propped up on top of the bar. She swirled her drink with her other hand. A cocktail mixture of cranberry juice and vodka —extra vodka—over ice in a rocks glass. She paused her twirling and took a sip. She set the glass back down and glanced at the rows of alcohol bottles stacked in front of her. A few were the wine bottles she had supplied.

"Not drinking the usual, I see," a woman's voice said from behind the bar.

A blonde woman captured Alice's attention, her hands diligently scrubbing glasses in a sink. She placed the glasses down, one by one, on rubber mats to let them dry.

"Let me guess. Relationship troubles?"

"Good guess," Alice said as she took another sip. "I needed something a little stronger tonight."

Sam wiped her hands on a clean bar rag and moved closer to Alice. "Want me to deal with him? Or is it a her?"

Alice snickered. "No, I don't need him to be dealt with, even if it is an enticing thought."

Sam placed her hands on her hips and tilted her head. "Are you sure? I can be very forceful if need be."

Alice's gaze surveyed Sam, carefully noting each delicate feature. Ez had a very strict dress policy for her clubs, and Sam was known for skirting as close to the line as possible. She wore a tartan style vest—which was probably a size too small—that hugged and highlighted her hourglass frame. She left a few of the top buttons on her white, collar shirt unbuttoned to give the patrons an eyeful . . . and Alice appreciated the view.

Her sleeves were rolled up to her elbows. Ez preferred the sleeves all the way down, but Sam protested. She claimed they got wet when washing glasses. Alice knew Sam wanted to show off her colorful forearm tattoos.

Alice's eyes lingered over every inch of her body. The way her wavy blonde hair fell on her shoulders as she tilted her head. Her hands placed on her curvy hips. The too tight vest. The tattoos.

I bet she'd be fun to date. A jolt ran down Alice's spine at the thought. Maybe someday, but not now. Not after being recently scorned by her former lover, The Cheating Bastard.

"I don't think it's necessary. I'm just going to drown my sorrows in this vodka cranberry," Alice said.

"Want an ear to listen?"

Alice sat upright on the barstool. "All right. I have a new rule. Never date a vampire. They suck. Literally *and* figuratively."

"Why, Ms. Primrose, didn't your mother ever tell you to stay away from those vampire boys?" Sam asked with a sly smile. "Or was it a vampire girl?" She batted her eyes.

"Boy. His name is now *The Cheating Bastard.*"

"Of course." Sam crossed her arms, pushing her chest higher.

Either the vodka was getting to Alice or Sam was trying to flirt with her. Either way, it was bliss.

"He had this look that made me melt," Alice said.

"Are you sure he didn't try to enthrall you?"

"He didn't need to. Curly hair. Sharp cheekbones. Tall. Muscles. I fell head over heels for him. It was all such a whirlwind. He told me he loved me. He said he cared for me. That I was special. All lies."

"How did you find out?"

"He forgot his phone, and text messages started appearing saying, 'The door's unlocked. I'll be upstairs waiting for you,'" Alice said with a slight slurring of her words. "I found out he took one of my Luck bottles. When he returned, I confronted him. He said it was a misunderstanding, but like I said, lies. I told him if I ever saw him again, I'd have my broomstick stab him right in the heart. And he left, and now I'm here . . . alone."

Alice took another sip and continued, "Always alone. Never appreciated."

Sam cupped Alice's hand with her own. "Maybe you just haven't found the right guy . . . or gal."

Alice gazed into Sam's eyes. Her stomach fluttered, and a tingle pulsed up her arm. Sam's touch was electric. Maybe it was the vodka coursing through her or something else, but Alice didn't want her to let go.

Sam continued, "I get off in a half-hour. Want to go do something fun?"

Alice smiled. "Yeah. I could use fun."

"Great. It's a date," Sam said as she let go of Alice's hand.

"How was the drive, kiddo?" Ez asked, interrupting Alice's memory.

It was a two-hour drive from her home to The Coven Club. Ez wanted to be close to Alice, yet not too close to attract attention. They had decided Alice would move to central Ohio, and Ez would move to the northeast.

"Long, but fine," Alice replied.

"So, what's the urgent thing you wanted to see me about?" Ez asked.

"I need a favor."

"A good favor or a . . . special favor?"

"Let's go in the back and talk. Away from other ears."

"A special favor it is," Ez said. "Follow me."

Alice moved around the bar and followed Ez through a doorway. They proceeded down a hallway, passing a few of the offices. At the end of the hallway was a wooden door covered in ornate iron fixtures. Very similar to the one in Alice's basement. Ez pulled a key from her pocket and unlocked the door. She pulled it open to reveal a massive library.

Rows and rows of books and sacred scrolls containing arcane text. Stained mahogany bookcases stretched from the floor to the ceiling. Ladders on railings allowed those who wanted to ascend to the top to peruse various works. The colorful spines worn with age. Many old texts and some new ones. The smell of old paper overwhelmed Alice's senses. A yellowish-orange glow emanated from vintage lamps hanging from the ceiling.

Ez was a coven witch, a keeper of the knowledge. She preserved ancient history, spells, rituals, and other things for witches and wizards to use. This was her sanctuary. If they needed a more secluded place to talk business, then Alice knew this was the place to be.

"So, talk, kiddo. What do you need?" Ez asked.

"How did the meeting with the Vampiric Conclave go?" Alice asked with a crack in her voice.

"They won't intervene. They're claiming it's a business dispute. We're on our own," Ez said. "You didn't come all the way up to ask me that question, did you?"

Alice hung her head. Her hands pressed together in front of her mouth. Thoughts raced through her mind. She knew what she wanted to ask, but was afraid of Ez's answer. She parsed the words carefully, making sure they were crafted so Ez wouldn't freak out.

Alice dropped her hands, breathed deep, and pulled back her shoulders to conjure the confidence needed for her next words. "We need to move again."

"Out of the question," Ez said as she flailed her arms in exasperation. "I finally got this place settled. I'm not moving again."

"You don't have to move. Just Hugo and myself."

"Why?" Ez placed her hands on her hips.

"They know." Alice took a deep breath. "The vampires know I have the spell."

Ez dropped her hands to her side. "Are you certain?"

"Yes. They told me. They know. They tracked us down. They . . . they found out about the news article where people spotted Hugo. They know about my wine. They put two and two together and figured—" Alice's voice cracked. "This is my fault. Again, everything is my fault." Tears formed in Alice's eyes.

"It's not your fault, kiddo."

"Yes, it is. The Savinos promised to make our lives miserable if I don't give them what they want. They'll make sure the Raskins lose their store. They threatened to pick the town apart piece by piece until they get their way. Until they have the spell."

Ez lowered her head. "I'm sorry, kiddo. I'm truly sorry."

"That's not all. They don't just want the spell. They want me to join them. They talked about how we'd be perfect for each other," Alice said.

"What did you tell them?"

"I told them to go to hell. I work for me and me alone."

"That's my girl. Stand your ground."

"They told me to reconsider. If I don't join them, they'll make life difficult. They didn't elaborate, but I can guess. If I stay there, I'm a threat to the town. If I leave, they'll leave too, trying to find me again." A tear fell down Alice's cheek.

Ez breathed deeply. "What if they don't?"

"They'd try to follow me . . . wouldn't they?"

"What if they don't leave and use the town against you? They'll do more than make people sick. The'll put pressure on you to return. They know you've taken a liking to the town. What if they destroy the town, piece by piece, until nothing is left?"

Alice shook her head in disbelief. "They wouldn't. They'd . . . they'd try to follow me."

"Kiddo, they wouldn't. They'd destroy everything and everyone, including your friends, the Raskins. And who would stop them? I can't move an entire town. I can't send witches and wizards to fight vampires. It would escalate into another war. You're the only one standing between them and the place you call home. The people you love."

Alice pursed her lips and sniffled to hold back tears. "Nope. There has to be someone else. I can't do it. I should run and draw them away."

Esmerelda tapped the hardwood flooring with her shoe and crossed her arms. She glared at Alice. "Who are you?"

Alice was taken aback by the question. She scrunched her eyebrows, narrowing her eyes. "What kind of question is that?"

"I want to know who you are. Which witch are you?" Ez asked.

Alice stood in stunned silence.

Ez continued, "Are you a witch who runs from her troubles? You ran from Sam."

Alice broke her gaze from Ez. Her mouth gaped open. Her mind blank.

"Or are you a witch that turns around and fights? Who upholds the promise you made to your grandmother? Who honors the legacy of your great-great grandmother? She guarded the spell and defended an entire town when faced with overwhelming odds. The same great-great grandmother who wasn't willing to abandon the people she loved."

Alice surveyed the room for answers, but found none. Her breath shortened, constricted by an unseen force collapsing her throat. She struggled to breathe. She shook her head, not wanting to answer.

"So, which witch are you?"

Alice's phone dinged from an incoming text message. She withdrew her phone from her pocket, glancing at the screen. Alice let out a blood-curdling scream.

"No," she yelled before covering her mouth.

"What is it?" Ez asked.

She read the words over and over as fast as she could.

FROM HUGO:

Looks like I now have a key - Sylvia

Alice beheld the horror of the picture that accompanied the text. It was a picture of her front door. Hugo slumped in the corner unconscious. Blood dripped down his neck.

"They got Hugo!" Alice shouted as she showed Ez the picture. "I have to go."

"Oh, kiddo, get out of here. Go. Let me know what you need," Ez said.

Alice sprinted toward the entrance. She leaned her shoulder into the door to push it open and disappeared into the hallway.

CHAPTER 14
SPECIAL DELIVERY

Alice smashed the gas pedal to the floor. Her black SUV revved and pushed well beyond the speed limit for US 33. The highway was dark, except for the occasional car light traveling in the opposite direction, as it approached the witching hour. She was well beyond the lights of the Columbus city limits and into developing farmland. She let off the gas momentarily to pass a straggling car before pressing the accelerator again as the car revved forward.

"Hugo, what did you do?" Alice asked. "What did you do?"

She was tormented by the agony of the hours long drive. Uncontrollable thoughts raced through her mind. Was he dead? Was he still alive? Was it worse?

Alice gripped the wheel tighter as she approached the exit for Newbury Grove. She slowed and, without stopping, turned on to US 42 and once again pushed the SUV to its limits as she raced for home. The darkness of the less populated highway enveloped the car; only the headlights fought back to light the path.

She passed Wildgrove Park and entered the Newbury Grove town center. The tires screeched as she turned through traffic signs without stopping. After a few more turns, she was home on Ravenhill Drive. She slammed on the brakes as she approached her purple house. The tires jumped the curb. She didn't care. She only thought of one thing: Hugo.

She exited the SUV, sprinting up the walkway and porch stairs. She froze. Laying against the front door, face nestled into the corner and covered by his black leather jacket, was Hugo.

"Hugo!" Alice shouted before covering her mouth in abject terror.

He was in the same spot as the picture and wasn't moving. She rushed to his side, throwing off the leather jacket. His neck and shirt were covered in blood. *His blood.*

"Hugo, can you hear me?"

He didn't move.

She shook him. "Hugo, please wake up."

He was lifeless.

Tears welled in her eyes. "No. No, no, no, no."

She tried the door. It was locked.

The defenses held.

Max's muffled bark came from inside. She pulled a brass key from her pocket, unlocked the door, and opened it. Hugo slumped forward as the door gave way. Max rushed to see who was entering the house. She tried to nestle against the slumping Hugo.

"Not now, Max," Alice said as she pushed her back.

Alice threw Hugo's arm over her shoulder, snapped her fingers, and as if some unseen force assisted her, she lifted Hugo off the ground. His limp legs and Chelsea boots dragged along the hardwood floor as Alice brought Hugo to the living room. She snapped her fingers, and the door slammed shut.

Shrieks of terror came from her reflection in the upstairs bathroom. "Hey, you, help me. He's not responding," her reflection yelled.

"I'm working on it," Alice yelled back up. "Give me a moment."

She dragged him into the living room and plopped him onto the red velvet, Victorian couch. He collapsed onto the cushions, properly exposing his wounds. Two trails of blood flowed like dried riverbeds from healed wounds on his neck down to his shirt.

Max sniffed Hugo and placed her head on the couch. She let out a low whimper. The reality of the situation washed over Alice. Tears flowed down her cheeks.

"Hugo, what did you do?"

She peered over to the hourglass sitting on the end table. Her sadness turned to a fleeting moment of joyous eureka.

"The Lovers' Kiss!" Alice shouted.

She ran out of the living and opened the basement door. With a snap of her fingers, the lights turned on. She stumbled down the creaky wooden stairs into the basement. She rushed to the wine cellar door and flung it open without the assistance of the arcane. The candles in the wall sconces roared to life as she entered.

She rushed to her work bench, frantically pulling open her apothecary cabinet drawers. She opened a few, not able to find what she was searching for until she found a vial filled with blue liquid. She clutched the bottle and hurried past wine racks filled with various bottles waiting for their trip to Ez's nightclub.

A special rack stood in the corner of the wine cellar filled with more than a dozen blackish-green bottles. Each with a special label marked *The Lovers' Kiss Hugo & Alice*. She grabbed a bottle and raced out of the cellar, not even stopping to shut the door. She charged up the stairs and back into the living room.

"Glass!" she shouted.

She set the bottle and vial on the end table. She darted out of the far entryway, through the hallway, and into the kitchen. She flung open cabinet doors with a snap of her fingers to expose the hidden wineglass. With her prize in hand, she returned to the living room.

Max still held her gaze on Hugo's unresponsive face. Her tail wagged, not with excitement, but low swipes of concern. Alice set the glass down, and with the same movement, palmed the vial filled with blue liquid. She took hold of Hugo's shoulders and jostled him, so he was upright, leaning his head back against the couch.

"I hope this works, Max," Alice said. "I've only used it on passed out drunks. I have no idea about vampire bites."

She snapped her fingers, and the cork flew out. She placed the vial over Hugo's open lips and poured the contents into his mouth. She wiped away some of the liquid that escaped through the side of his mouth.

Time stood still as she held her breath, the world around her frozen in fear. Hugo didn't move. She ran her fingers through his coifed hair to the back of his head. She held him steady and fixated on his closed eyes.

"Hugo, honey, can you hear me?" Alice pleaded. "Please wake up. I need you. Please." A tear trickled off her face.

Max whimpered. Alice waited. Hugo wasn't moving.

Alice set his head back down and picked up the wine bottle. She bit down on the cork and yanked it from the bottle. There was no time for magical theatrics. The cork bounced as she spit it onto the hardwood floor. She poured the purplish-red liquid into the awaiting glass. When nearly full, she swapped holding the bottle for the glass. She poured the entire glass into Hugo's mouth. Alice backed away and waited.

He didn't move.

"Hugo, can you hear me?"

He didn't respond.

Alice tensed up, and her body shook. She cupped her hands around her mouth and nose in disbelief.

"Oh, no. Please no."

She glanced over to the hourglass. She twisted the ring of the hourglass to speed up time, but only a little.

Hugo's hand twitched, and he made a gurgling noise. She normalized the ring.

"Hugo," Alice said. "Hugo, can you hear me?"

Air rushed into his lungs as his chest rose and fell. He lifted his right hand and rubbed where he was bitten. Alice let out a joyous giggle. Hugo was alive.

He moaned as he continued to rub his neck. He shifted around in his seat, opened his eyes, and locked his icy blue eyes with Alice's emerald greens.

"Hey," Hugo mustered. "Please forgive me."

Alice collapsed on top of him, burying her head into his shoulder. "Of course, you doofus," Alice's muffled voice said. "Just don't let me think you died again."

"I'll try not to. Consider us even." He wrapped his free arm around her back. Hugo ran his fingers through her purple hair, massaging the back of her head.

Alice and Hugo held each other. Sobbed together. Breathed as one. They didn't want to let go.

Max barked, jumped on the couch, and broke their embrace. She nudged her nose in between Hugo and Alice, trying to join in the group hug. Her tail furiously wagged at the sight of Hugo moving around.

"Were you concerned about me too?" Hugo asked.

Max jumped up and landed on Hugo's stomach.

He winced in pain. "Not there. That hurts. Get down."

He pushed Max back with his arm. She jumped back down.

"Thank you," Alice's reflection yelled down.

Alice pulled back. She slid down to her knees, now positioned between Hugo's legs. She grabbed the outside of Hugo's legs and lost herself in Hugo's eyes.

"I was so scared I was going to lose you," Alice said. "I don't know what I'd do if I did. I couldn't breathe at the thought of being without you. I love you."

"I love you too. I'm . . ." his words trailed off. "I'm sorry. I thought I was doing what was right. What I needed to do. This was all my fault. I needed to fix it."

"Hugo, look at me." Alice placed a hand on his chest. "None of this was your fault."

"Yes, it was," Hugo replied, sitting up. "If I didn't lose my temper that day, they would have never found you. I put you . . . *us* in danger.

The Raskins. This town. It was all my fault. Because I couldn't find a stupid ring."

Alice lowered her head and moved her hand back to his thigh. "It wasn't your fault, Hugo. It was mine." Her eyes lifted to meet his. "I should have taken care of this when it was first a problem. This is my mistake. I should have dealt with it sooner."

"Then would you have met me?"

Alice lowered her head and half smiled to mask her sadness. "I guess not."

Hugo leaned forward. He pulled up her chin, directing her face so he could look her in the eyes. Their faces were inches from each other. She sensed his breath, his aura, his presence. A jolt ran up her spine. Her stomach fluttered.

"Then it's not your fault," he said. Alice's smile grew as his words gushed over her. "I couldn't imagine my life without you. You're the light of my world. I couldn't stand the thought of you hurting. I had to try something. It almost worked too."

Alice chuckled. "Yeah, almost. What was your grand plan?"

He tilted his head to the side, never breaking eye contact with Alice. "I met them at the restaurant. My plan was to stab Sebastian with a stake I made out of a wooden hockey stick. I taped it to my forearm, so they wouldn't see it. After I took him out, I was going to fight her and stake her as well."

"It's not the worst plan. Not the best, but not the worst."

"Your reflection called it 'the dumbest fucking thing she ever heard.'"

"I was being generous. Two vampires at once? By yourself?"

"She said the same thing. It almost worked. I stabbed him, but I hit something. Must have been a rib. I tried to push it in, but the stick broke. He grabbed me. She pushed me over with the table. I was on the floor, pinned between the table and chair. The last thing I remember was her toying with me before biting down. At least they didn't take all of my blood. I do feel lightheaded, though. And my mouth hurts." Hugo rubbed the top of his mouth.

Alice leaned back, her hands dragging to Hugo's knees. Any sense of relief faded as her face turned pale. "Hurts like how?"

"It's like a sharp pain. Stronger than a toothache. Like something is pushing against my teeth."

Alice stood up. She shook her head in disbelief. "Oh, no. Please no."

Hugo let out a howl of pain. He rubbed the front of his mouth. He rocked back and forth on the couch, trying to ease the pain. He covered his mouth with his hands.

Through a muffled voice, he said, "The pain is unbearable. It's like my mouth is ripping apart."

Max tucked her head and backed away in horror. She ran and hid under the black, high-back chair. Guinevere remained unfazed, floating in the air, not moving.

Alice took a step backward. "Hugo, I need you to be still."

A shriek came from upstairs. "Get your ass up here now," Alice's reflection yelled down. "I need you."

Alice sprinted upstairs. Her thick soled boots stomped down onto the hardwood like a thundering herd. She flew through the bedroom and into the bathroom. She nearly slipped on the tile floor, catching herself on the porcelain sink. Horror filled her eyes, widening as she was forced to watch the events unfold on the other side of the mirror.

"Fix him," Alice's reflection pleaded, holding back tears. "He just woke up, and now look at him."

"What's happening to me?" Hugo's reflection asked.

He stumbled toward Alice's reflection before falling forward. She caught him, propping him up. His body dematerialized, first his arms, and then his legs. The dematerialization spread to his torso.

"I don't want to leave you," Hugo's reflection cried.

"I love you," Alice's reflection cried through her tears as she held on to what was left of Hugo's reflection.

"I love y—"

His reflection vanished.

"No!" Alice's reflection yelled as she collapsed to her knees. She buried her head into her hands and sobbed. "No. Please no."

Alice cupped her mouth in horror. Her greatest fear was coming true. They did more than drain Hugo's blood. They did so much worse.

"Alice," Hugo said from the bedroom. "I think I have a problem."

Filled with a sense of urgency, she rushed out of the bathroom and found Hugo standing in the bedroom doorway, his fists clenched.

"I don't think this is supposed to happen," he said as he unfurled his hand.

In the center of his palm were his two, bloody incisors. Blood dripped from his mouth onto the hardwood floor. It pooled into blackish-red splatter—shiny and reflective. "What's happening to me?"

Fear engulfed Alice, causing her hands to tremble as she faced the sheer horror of the situation, leaving her frozen in place. A million thoughts raced through her mind, yet she could act on none of them. She had no answer. She had to see for herself. She had to see their handiwork.

"Hugo, open your mouth," Alice commanded.

Hugo opened wide, pulling back on his lip. Newly formed fangs had pushed out and replaced his incisors, washed red and dripping with blood. Alice bent over, clenching her teeth. She scrunched her eyes closed and tugged at her hair. She let out a barbaric yawp.

"I take it"—Hugo's voice cracked, betraying his attempt to hide his sadness—"it's not good."

Alice let go of her hair. Tears fell down her face. "I'm so, so sorry."

"Does this mean . . .?" Hugo asked. His face was sunken, his eyes red and holding back tears at the revelation of his new future.

Alice somberly nodded.

"Get in here," Alice's reflection yelled as she smacked her side of the mirror.

Alice peered into the bathroom.

"Bring him back. Bring him back now!" Alice's reflection shouted.

Alice entered the bathroom with small steps. Her head went low, and her shoulders drooped. "I can't."

"Why not?" Alice's reflection asked. "Bring him back."

"I can't," Alice answered as her eyes met the mirror image of herself. "I can't because vampires don't produce magical reflections."

CHAPTER 15
THE QUEEN'S KING

Sebastian opened the front door to their house for his queen. Sylvia stormed in without breaking her stride. Sebastian followed, shutting the door. He clutched his chest where he had been stabbed earlier in the evening. He winced with every step. Though the wound had stopped bleeding, it was still fresh and painful. His black shirt was damp as it soaked up blood. He entered the living room. He carefully sat on the black, leather Chesterfield sofa. Every movement sent a sharp pain through his body.

"There's still something in there," Sebastian said. "We need to get it out."

He removed his shirt to reveal a seeping wound on his chest where he was struck earlier in the night.

Sylvia's face twisted in shock; her mouth gaped open in a silent scream and her eyes reflected pure horror. "Get me a first aid kit," she commanded of the ghouls.

They were waiting in the hallway for their masters to return.

"Go. Now!" she commanded.

One scrambled upstairs to do as instructed.

Sylvia knelt in front of Sebastian. “You!” She pointed to another one. “Go get me a towel. A damp one.”

The ghoul rushed into the kitchen and returned with a wet towel. Sylvia snatched it from his hand and pressed it against the wound.

“Are you okay, my love?” She turned her attention back to her king.

“I’ll be fine,” he said. “I think he got close. Thankfully, it hit my rib. We need to get the piece out before it works its way inward.”

“First aid. Now!” she shouted once more. “Unless you want to lose your head!”

“My dear, they’ll bring it. Don’t worry,” Sebastian said.

Sylvia took his hand and kissed it. She fixated on Sebastian’s dark brown eyes. “My love, I couldn’t bear a single day without you. When he stabbed you, I thought you were done for. I would have destroyed him and everyone else in this town if I lost you.”

Sebastian leaned forward. He ran his fingers through her hair, brushing it back behind her ear. “I couldn’t ask for anything less. I wouldn’t demand anything more. That’s my good girl.”

She smiled at him. He leaned back against the couch, draping his left arm across the top of the couch.

The ghoul hurried down the stairs, but was light-footed. He made the minimum amount of noise moving into the living room. He bowed his head and presented Sylvia with the first aid kit. She took it without acknowledging the ghoul.

“Leave us,” Sebastian said. “All of you.”

The ghouls went into the kitchen, opened the basement door, and went downstairs.

Sylvia removed a pair of tweezers from the kit. “This may hurt.”

“Coming from you, it’ll be bliss,” Sebastian said.

Sylvia smiled and plunged the tweezers into his chest. He screamed in agony as the metal pushed deeper. He gripped the fine leather on the top of the couch with one hand and the side with the other. His fingers dug into the leather. He gritted his teeth, wanting to extend his fangs in anger. The pain was intolerable as she probed for the stray wooden shard.

"I haven't found it yet," Sylvia said.

"Keep going," he growled as he arched his neck back. His body tensed.

"Does this make us even, my love?" Sylvia asked.

The memory of their first encounter seized Sebastian's mind, slipping him back to that place so many years ago.

THE DOOR to his French tavern flung open, and a bloodied woman stood at the entrance. Sebastian stood by the bar, holding a broom. Lanterns hung on thick wooden pillars dimly lit the room. A few strands of her strawberry blonde hair draped over her desperation filled face. Blood dripped from her mouth. A bloody wound stood out on her chest. The two creatures of the night locked eyes.

"Please," she begged.

Sebastian motioned with his head to an area behind the bar. She shut the door behind her and ran. She turned the corner and descended a set of stairs to the cellar below. Sebastian rested the broom against a table and went to the lanterns. One by one, he opened the metal and glass door to blow out the candles.

"She went in here," he heard through a window outside.

The door flung open, and the mob consisting of a priest, a farmer, and a man wearing a black coat spilled in. They all held crucifixes. The priest was armed with a wooden stake, and the man in the black coat was armed with a pistol.

"Where is she?" the man in the coat asked.

"Where is *who*?" Sebastian asked.

"The woman who came through here. Where is she?" he asked again.

Sebastian motioned around the empty tavern. The patrons had long since left. The chairs were placed on top of the tables.

"No one else is in this room," he answered. "I've been cleaning up for the night. It's only me."

"She's not here," the priest said as he retreated through the door. "She must have gone down the street."

The farmer followed behind.

The man in the black coat examined the room. He moved to the bar. Sebastian placed a hand on the stool behind him, ready to wield it as a weapon if he got too close. The man in the black coat stopped. Sebastian relinquished the stool.

He turned to Sebastian. "You didn't see anyone come this way?"

"Can't say I did," he replied.

"It's illegal to obstruct the affairs of the Holy Roman Emperor. I'll ask again, where is she?"

Sebastian shook his head. "I don't know who you're talking about."

The man in the black coat gave one last examination and then headed for the door. He stopped as if something caught his eye. He bent down. Sebastian inhaled sharply as he discovered what caught the man's attention. He held his breath. On the hardwood floor was a solitary drop—a drop of her blood. The man in black ran a finger through it, raising his finger closer to his face to further examine it.

Sebastian's heart thumped in his chest. He glanced over to the cellar entrance. His best chance was to grab the broom handle and fend him off to protect her.

The man in the black coat showed Sebastian the blood on his finger. "Rough night?"

Thoughts raced through Sebastian's mind. Thoughts of how to justify a single drop of blood on the floor of his tavern. Anything. Anything plausible.

"Yeah. Some rowdy men came in here. They had a little too much to drink and got into a fight. One of them punched the other in the face. He must have gotten a bloody nose," Sebastian answered. He gulped.

The man in the black coat stood. He wiped his finger across the top of a table. "Well, if you see anything unusual, stay inside for your own safety. There is a vampire on the loose."

"I'll keep an eye out," Sebastian said.

As the man in the black duster opened the door, a cold gust of wind swept through the room. He vanished into the darkness of night; the sound of his fading footsteps filled the air. Sebastian shut the door, the click of the lock echoing in the silence. He breathed a sigh of relief, but the tension still lingered in the air. He knew he had one more nocturnal visitor to confront before the night was over.

Sebastian carefully lowered the only remaining lantern, its soft light guiding him as he moved behind the bar. Sebastian swiftly grabbed a bucket of water, a well-worn rag, and a small, wooden box from a shelf. He then descended the creaky steps to the dimly lit cellar.

A musty scent filled the air. The cold dampness against the dirt flooring. The darkness concealed its secrets, only illuminated by the lantern Sebastian carried. Wine and beer barrels provided excellent hiding spots for the woman now lurking in his cellar. The stairs creaked with every step.

Sebastian stopped at the base of the stairs. His eyes followed the lantern light as he played an unknowing game of hide-and-seek. There was movement off to his left, her strawberry blonde hair shining in the gleaming light. He moved around the barrels.

She cowered in the corner like an animal ready to strike. The full intensity of the lamp light bathed her in an orangish-yellow glow. Her fangs were elongated, and her chin was painted with dried blood. Sebastian wasn't intimidated by her aggressive display.

"Do you not fear me?" she asked.

He moved toward her.

"Stay back," she growled. "I'll tear you to shreds."

He stopped and peered into her eyes. "If you were a real threat to me, you wouldn't have begged so politely to enter my tavern. No. Not you. You look like a woman who doesn't ask, but takes. I would have already been your next victim if not for your wound. Correct?"

Sylvia nodded. She winced, retreating further into the corner. She steadied herself against the wall with one hand and grabbed the left side of her chest with the other. Blood seeped from her chest wound. Her breathing labored.

"I can help you. Will you let me?" he asked as he presented the bucket and rag.

Her fangs retreated. "I'll allow you to help me."

Sebastian moved closer. "I take it you were hit by a bullet. I'm going to guess . . . is it silver?"

Her sapphire eyes focused on Sebastian with a skeptical sense of trust.

"I can't help you if you don't tell me."

"It was a bullet. I don't know what it's made of, but your guess might be correct."

"Please, sit." He motioned to a barrel standing upright.

She climbed on top of it.

"My name is Sebastian. Sebastian Savino. I'm the owner of this tavern."

"Sylvia. Countess Sylvia Dubois."

"Nice to meet you, Sylvia. Or do you prefer Countess?" Sebastian dropped the rag into the bucket, soaking up the water.

"I demand my subjects call me Countess, but I'll make an exception for you."

Sebastian smiled. "Well, Sylvia, I need you to pull back your dress collar for me. Don't worry. I only need to see the wound."

She pulled on the U-shape collar of her crimson-colored dress. Her partially bare chest was covered in blood from her wound. Sebastian sloshed the rag around, wrung it out, and wiped her chest. Delicate swipes as to not press on the wound and hurt her. He helped pull back her collar, but respected her modesty. He wiped under the collar, soaking up as much of the blood as possible.

He dunked the rag once more, picked it up, and wrung out the excess water. He pressed the wet rag against her wound.

"Hold the rag there," he commanded.

She did as instructed, never taking her eyes off him.

"You don't fear me?" Sylvia asked.

"No," he replied as he opened his small box.

He removed a steel instrument almost as long as his forearm. It had a narrow point on one end and two finger loops and a screw on the other. He sloshed the narrow point in the bucket.

"Do you know how to remove it?"

"I run a tavern. Taverns can get rowdy. You're not the first one I've done this for. This is going to hurt. Are you ready?"

She nodded.

"You can squeeze my arm if the pain is too much," Sebastian offered.

"I can tolerate a lot of pain," Sylvia responded as she removed the rag.

"The offer still stands." He brought the instrument up to the wound. He moved to extract the bullet.

"Wait!" Sylvia shouted to stop him from proceeding. "Do I need to ask if it's made of wood?"

Sebastian chuckled. "Do you think I'd go through all of this trouble only to harm you?"

She focused on his brown eyes and didn't answer.

"It's not."

Sylvia licked her lips and wrapped her hands around his muscular forearms. Her fingers dug into the middle of his arm. The pressure of her fingertips intensified as he moved the instrument closer.

"Ready," she said.

He stabbed the instrument into her wound. She grimaced, but never yelled or whimpered. Her fingers dug deeper, finding the soft spot between his two forearm bones. Her grip was excruciating, much stronger than she appeared, but he never relented. He twisted the screw, turning and turning to drive the screw deeper into her chest. She dug her fingers deeper with every turn. He smiled the harder she dug.

Sylvia gritted her teeth, still silent and not yielding to the pain.

"You're doing great," Sebastian said. "Almost there."

He turned and twisted until the screw found the target. He gave it a few more turns to dig into the silver ball. He pulled out the extractor, a silver ball now attached to the end.

Sylvia relaxed her grip and her teeth. She placed the rag on the wound. "Thank you," she said through her labored breaths. She glared into his eyes, hers exhausted and red from the pain. "Why did you do this for me?"

Sebastian put the instrument back in the box. "Years ago, I was strolling through the city at night with my mother. We were followed. She tried not to panic as to not panic me. She hurried our pace, but a man stalked us. He was going to attack my mother when a creature of the night struck first. Its face was cloaked in shadows. I only knew what it was—a vampire. It saved us that night. I never found it again. As soon as I looked upon you and your wound, I knew what you were. It's the least I could do to return the favor."

"It's a good thing that vampire saved you."

"Was it you?"

"No. There are more of us."

"Then consider my debt to the vampires repaid. Let's see your wound."

Sylvia removed the rag. The seeping stopped, and the wound healed over.

"You'll be as good as new in no time," Sebastian said.

"Thank you."

"You're welcome," he replied. "I mean it. You're welcome here anytime. If you get in trouble. If you need a place to hide. If you need a place to feed. You're always welcome here."

Sylvia was silent. Her mouth agape and eyes watered over. "No one has ever shown me this kindness before."

Sebastian matched his eyes to hers. His heart pulsated as he lost himself in her sapphire blue eyes. "You'll always find kindness here. I promise you."

"I think I found it," Sylvia shouted with glee. "I hit something. I have it. Ready?"

Sebastian gritted his teeth and nodded. Sylvia pulled out the tweezers, holding a wooden shard at the end. She placed the splinter on an end table.

Sebastian breathed a sigh of relief as his body relaxed. He covered up the wound with the damp towel. He gazed into her sapphire eyes. "I think this makes us even."

Sylvia smiled. "Let me see your wound."

He removed the towel. The wound healed over. She took the towel from his hand and carefully wiped away any blood with soft, gentle strokes. She fixated on his bare chest.

"Shall we go over and finish the job? I want nothing more than to destroy him for what he did to you."

"No," Sebastian said. He caressed her face, guiding her hair behind her shoulder with his fingers. "Let them wallow for a few days. Have the ghouls watch their movements. They'll panic. Get sloppy. Then we can strike."

Sylvia's soft lips kissed his washboard abs. Gentle, teasing kisses at first, followed by intense presses of desire. He leaned his head back and closed his eyes. His body and soul lit a flame with every tease of her sensual journey. Her lips caressed every contour of his chiseled stomach as she worked her way toward his neck.

"We're so close," Sylvia said.

Her lips brushed against his chest. The warmth of her breath heralded the imminent arrival of her teasing butterfly kisses. Small pecks followed by lingering warmth which sent pleasure coursing through his body. Sebastian savored every moment of her sensual journey.

She stood and placed her knees on both sides of his waist, digging into the leather and straddling him. Her journey continued upward as she followed an invisible path of pleasure from his collarbone to his neck. She mimicked the sensual act of their vampire embrace years ago—kissing, nibbling, caressing his neck. She stopped, pulling away to let her playful tease linger. He wanted nothing more than for her to finish this journey of passion and ecstasy.

"Can you feel it?" she whispered into his ear. Her warm breath intensified his longing and desire.

Sylvia was a tease, and Sebastian loved every minute of it.

"Yes," he whispered back.

"Soon, my love, we'll have our prize."

He worked his hands under her shirt. His fingers traced the contours of her back. She arched her back slightly, closing her eyes and biting her lip. His fingers danced in circles on her back as they wrote in the dark language of love. She opened her eyes. Their eyes locked together in a fiery dance of passion and anticipation. Their breathing synchronized.

Sylvia let the gaze linger, leaving Sebastian in blissful torment.

"And we shall rule together for all of time," he growled. "For our new empire."

Sylvia smiled a devilish grin. "For our new empire," she growled back.

They completed their journey, their two lips joining together in a passionate union. Their souls and bodies unified under a shared desire for each other. An expression of their deep desire. Their deep passion. Their deep love.

Sebastian lost track of all time. It could have been seconds, minutes, or hours. All he knew was bliss.

CHAPTER 16

THE LIFE AND UNDEATH OF HUGO DODDS

Light spilled into the wine cellar as Alice opened the door. The candles of the wall sconces roared to life, illuminating the rest of the darkened room.

"Good evening, sleepyhead," Alice said as she entered.

"Is it morning already?" Hugo asked, rolling over on his side to face Alice. He was laying down, hovering about shoulder height, and covered up to his neck in a blanket draping over him. "Do you know your *Air Walk* wears off after a few hours?"

"It's after sundown, not morning," Alice replied. "And yes. Yes, I did."

Hugo sat up; his legs dangled as if he were sitting on an invisible ledge in the air. He wore a ruffled up, black T-shirt and matching boxer briefs.

"Do you also know what it's like to slam into a stone floor when it wears off?"

Alice stood with her hands on her hips, a smirk on her face, and sadness in her eyes. "Can't say I do."

"Well," Hugo started as he floated down to the ground with his blanket in hand. "Even as a vampire, it hurts. Like a lot. Especially if you're sleeping. I'm leaving a terrible review for this air bed-and-breakfast."

Alice lowered her head and chuckled. "I see you haven't lost your sense of humor."

"Nope. I may be undead, but my humor is very much alive."

Undead. The word sent a chill running through Alice's nerves. She closed her eyes and bit her lip to hide the pain, to stop herself from bawling her eyes out and reducing herself to a blubbering mess on the floor. She kept herself busy—her mind busy—vampire proofing the house so Hugo wouldn't have to lurk in the shadows of her wine cellar away from the sunlight.

Every window was now covered in thick, light blocking curtains. The windows of their bedroom were reinforced with black wood paneling, sealing it off from the outside world, so he could sleep in their bed once again. Alice went through every room to ensure Hugo could move freely throughout the house at any time, day or night. She believed this was her fault, and she would be doing everything she could to make him comfortable.

"I'm kind of starving. It's weird. It's like a different sensation. Like I'm hangry and woozy and irritable all at the same time," Hugo said.

"It's the vampire frenzy," Alice said in a solemn tone. "If you go too long without feeding on blood, you'll frenzy. You'll rampage until the thirst is quelled."

"I take it a candy bar won't fix it?"

Alice chuckled, hiding her tears as she bent over at the comment. She hesitated for a moment before scolding Hugo, but her voice betrayed her true emotions with a playful undertone. "I'll stake you myself if you don't stop with the jokes. This is serious."

"Hey. I know," Hugo replied. "Elizabeth used to joke with me all the time. I never understand how she could joke with everything she was going through . . . until now."

Alice wiped a tear from her cheek.

"I figured I have two options. I can sulk and not change the outcome. Or I can joke and not the change the outcome. If I can't change anything, I might as well laugh. Right?"

Alice laughed, covering her mouth with her hands. "I love you so much right now," she said, her words muffled behind her fingers.

"You only love me because I'm a vampire." He ran his fingers through his hair. Hugo smirked as he lowered his head, his eyes glaring at her from below the top of his eyelids. He winked. "And that makes me more of a scoundrel. I bet you love bad boys."

"I'll stake you right now if you don't calm down," Alice blurted as she crossed her arms.

"The stereotypes of vampires are true. I feel . . . different. Like a teenager again. If you know what I mean?"

"Yes. Yes, I do. You're not the first vampire I've dated, remember? I'm well aware."

Hugo straightened and moved toward Alice, dragging the blanket behind him. "So, how do I stop myself from frenzying? I'm willing to try new things, but I really don't want to cross *that* line." Hugo locked onto Alice's neck.

"Ez is on her way. She's taken care of it," Alice answered, rubbing her neck.

"Good." Hugo breathed a sigh of relief. "How's she doing?"

"Ez? She's okay. Concerned, but okay," Alice replied.

"I meant your reflection."

"Oh. She's . . . she's not well. She's sobbing and wailing and crying." Alice paused, staring at a spot on the stone floor. "She won't talk to me."

"Does she blame me?"

Alice shook her head no.

"Do you blame me?"

Alice locked eyes with Hugo. She wanted to tell him the truth. She wanted to let out every emotion she held back. Anger. Fear. Anxiety. Sadness. Hurt. Despair. All of it. She wanted to lay it all out for Hugo to hear. But she held back. It wouldn't have mattered and would only make things worse. She kept her strong, brave face for him. For her. For *them*.

"I don't blame you."

"Liar," Hugo was quick to answer. "What about Max?"

"I dropped Max off at the Raskins. I didn't tell them about you. I couldn't. I didn't want them to worry. I only told them we thought she'd be safer with them, so the Savinos couldn't attack her and use her against us."

"Good," Hugo replied in a low voice. "I saw her face. I saw the fear. She knew I was different. And now, if I frenzied and did something to her, I couldn't . . . I couldn't forgive myself."

"She doesn't have to stay there forever, just for now."

Hugo nodded in agreement. "Yeah. Just for now."

They locked eyes, not knowing what to say. They stood in silence, frozen. Hugo fiddled with the blanket in his hands before wadding it up into a ball. Alice wanted to shout, to let everything out, but held her mouth frozen.

"Hey, I'm sorry," Hugo broke the silence.

"Don't be," Alice replied. "It's not your fault."

"You can keep telling me it's not my fault, but deep down . . ." His words trailed off.

There was only the silence again.

Alice shrugged her shoulders. "I get it. Like you said, if you can't change the outcome, you might as well laugh."

A smile played on Hugo's lips as he lowered his head and let out a soft chuckle. His eyes roamed the wine cellar, finally settling on the bottle of *Air Walk* resting on her workbench. He stole a quick glance at Alice. "So, what's it like dating a vampire?"

Alice returned a half smile. Her fingers tapped against her arm, rubbing the cotton fabric of her long-sleeve black shirt. Shifting in her stance, she traced one of the stone grooves with her bare foot.

"As I said before, they suck," Alice replied.

"Funny," Hugo said with a hint of sarcasm.

"But those nights—" Alice added.

"What about them?"

Alice twisted in her stance, twitching her eyebrows. She held back all the lurid details she wanted to tell Hugo. The nights became a wild realm, filled with the electric energy of untamed beasts, where lovers reveled in the ecstasy of exploring and indulging in their primal passions. The thrill of dating a vampire was like no other. Alice's heart fluttered as her imagination conjured images of how her and Hugo's nights could play out.

"Let's just say . . . it was fun."

Hugo jumped up to his invisible shelf and leaned back with his hands behind his head. "Care to have some fun?"

Alice dropped her arms to her sides. "Are you going to be like this from now on? Because if you are—"

Hugo jumped down. "I'm joking. But I feel so charged up, I think I'd lose it if you touched me."

"You'll get used to it."

"Hopefully soon or else . . . hopefully soon. By the way, did you see their present?"

"What present?" Alice asked.

"The bag. Did they not leave it?"

"No. What bag? What was in it?"

"Alice, it's—" He paused. "Maybe they put it in my jacket pocket."

"What is it?"

"You have to see it."

He left the wine cellar with Alice closely behind. She steadied herself against the wall as they ascended the creaky wooden steps.

They entered the hallway and moved to the coatrack by the front door. Alice had placed his leather jacket there after cleaning up. Hugo took the jacket and sunk his hand into the pocket. He moved on to the next pocket.

"It's here," Hugo said.

Alice held her breath with anticipation.

He withdrew the gift held within and handed it to Alice.

Alice gasped. Distress clouded her eyes as she concentrated on the sight of the red knit hat. She recognized the hat immediately. It was *her* hat.

She took it from Hugo. Her fingers clutched it tighter the longer she held it.

Alice sniffed it. The fresh notes of strawberries confirmed her signature perfume. Alice's breath shortened. Her heart raced as it thumped against her chest. She gulped.

"Is that what I think it is?"

Alice clutched the hat to her chest with tears in her eyes. Hugo hugged Alice. She laid her head on his chest, finding comfort in his arms. She wanted to speak. She wanted to audibly confirm his suspicion, but couldn't. She was frozen in silence. It was Sam's red knit hat. Her mind slipped back to the night with Sam.

~

"My head is cold. Buy me a hat," Sam commanded Alice. She stopped in the middle of the crowded shopping area on Essex Street.

Alice took a few steps before turning to face her girlfriend. Her hands were on her hips, her head to the side. "I told you to bring a hat. Why didn't you bring your witch's hat?" Alice tugged the brim of her curved pointy hat.

"Unlike you, I prefer not to broadcast what I am, thank you very much," Sam replied.

"Look around you." Alice motioned to the throngs of people overwhelming the street as they continued by in their Halloween costumes. "It's Halloween in Salem. I think you'd fit in."

The sky was dark, and the October air was crisp. Street lamps illuminated Essex Street as it filled with revelers partaking in the Halloween activities. The shops were filled to the brim. Street performers struggled to maintain their space as waves of costumed people moved past. Witch costumes of all varieties. Skeletons.

Classic monsters. Vampires. A couple with carved pumpkins on their heads. It was heaven to Alice.

Sam pouted her lips and drooped her shoulders. "Buy me a hat. Please."

"Why don't you buy it?"

"Because then it wouldn't be special. It would be from you," Sam replied.

Alice blushed and smiled. She rocked back and forth, looking around at the various shops. "Do you really want me to buy you a hat?"

Sam moved closer and held Alice's hands. She leaned in and whispered in a long, drawn-out answer, "Yesssss."

As the melodic word washed over Alice's ear, a symphony of emotions danced inside her soul. The solitary sound warmed Alice's heart in the crisp, cold night. In one word, Alice was transported back to their private evenings, where their expression of love transcended everything. Alice was a sucker, and Sam was playing right into her, toying with her emotions. Alice lowered her head, biting her lip.

There was a pause.

Alice locked eyes with Sam, losing herself in Sam's steel-blue eyes. Alice smiled.

Sam smirked.

"I don't know how you do it, but I can't say no to you."

"Thank you," Sam said with glee. She let go of Alice's hands and headed toward the nearest store. "I want a red one."

~

THREE KNOCKS at the door interrupted Alice's memory. Her head swirled from the rush of emotions. The hallway spun. Alice took a step back to catch herself.

Hugo grabbed her arm. "Are you okay?"

Three more knocks.

"I'm fine." Alice rubbed her forehead. She set the red knit hat on the console table. "I'm fine. The knocks startled me. I'm . . . I'm on edge. That should be Ez at the door."

Hugo let go of Alice. He pulled back the curtain. "It's her," Hugo said as he turned the diamond shape ornate knob to let her in.

"You. Couch. Now," Ez commanded as she entered. She pulled a wheeled cooler behind her.

"Nice to see you too," Hugo said.

Ez snapped her fingers. "Couch. Now."

Hugo shut the door and went into the living room.

Ez stopped the cooler in front of Alice. Her shoulders slumped, and her arms stretched out for a hug. "How are you, kiddo?"

Alice hugged Ez, giving her a tight squeeze. "I'm fine. I'm fine. We're managing."

"You'll be okay, kiddo. You'll be okay," Ez reassured her.

Alice stopped hugging Ez, but kept both hands on her shoulders. Alice motioned with her head to the red knit hat on the console table. "They had Sam's hat. They gave it to Hugo."

"One issue at a time. One issue at a time," Ez said as she searched the hallway. "Where's my little buddy? I have a treat for her."

"I dropped her off at the Raskin's house. We didn't want—" Alice paused. "I didn't want Hugo to hurt her if he frenzied."

"Good thinking. Give this to her the next time you see her," Ez said as she removed a dog treat from her coat pocket. "Please be a dear, and put these into the fridge. Bring me one. I'll go look over our patient."

Ez removed her coat and placed it on the rack.

Alice didn't need to look inside; she already knew what was in there. She took the cooler handle and went into the kitchen.

She opened the refrigerator door. It was packed with food and open wine bottles. She bent down and rearranged the contents. She opened the cooler and pulled out pint bags of blood—donations from a blood drive. Ez had used her connections to secure a month's supply for Hugo. She stacked the blackish-red bags neatly on the bottom shelf. She shut the door and grabbed the last one in the cooler. She went to join the other two in the living room.

"Let me see," Ez said.

Hugo pulled back on his lip to reveal the sharpened fangs protruding from his mouth.

"How do you feel?" Ez asked.

"Nauseous. Woozy. Like my body is on fire and a hand is grabbing and squeezing me," he replied.

"Your body is getting used to the transformation. It'll calm down. Eventually," Ez said. "You're now undead. Your body is at peak physical health. Heart rate low. Cholesterol low. Testosterone and pheromones . . . very high. All at optimal levels. Your body is a perfect specimen of health for someone considered undead. I take it you've had urges of all kinds."

"That's an understatement," Hugo replied.

"It'll calm down, and you'll be fine. From now on, your body will heal fast," Ez added.

"Any chance to fix this?" Hugo asked.

"You'll be fine. Stay out of the sunlight and away from wooden stakes," Ez said. "Now for the fun part . . . feeding."

Alice handed her the pint of blood. A white sticker with an oversize *O* covered most of the blood bag. Ez removed the rubber band and unraveled the PVC tube. She pinched a bloodless portion, withdrew scissors from her pocket, and cut the tube.

"Pinch here," she said as she handed the tube to Hugo. "Now drink."

Hugo placed the tube in his mouth and sucked it like a straw as the blood flowed through the tube. "It's sweet," Hugo said in between drinks.

"Keep drinking," Ez said as she turned to Alice. "Kiddo, let's go talk."

"You can tell me the bad news," Hugo said.

"Drink!" Alice said.

Hugo shrugged his shoulders and continued drinking.

Alice turned to Ez. "Let's go downstairs."

They headed for the basement when the noise of Hugo gagging caught their attention. They turned to see Hugo convulsing and heaving. Alice's face turned pale with fear.

Hugo clutched his abdomen and doubled over. With a mixture of guttural growls and violent belching, it sounded as if his insides were being ripped apart by something unholy.

The sound intensified until a torrent of thick, crimson blood gushed forth from his mouth. The blackish-red, macabre liquid splashed all over the hardwood floor. A splattering hit the red velvet couch and coffee table. A trail of blood dripped from his quivering lips, painting his chin red.

Hugo trembled, his chest rising and falling as he caught his breath. Sweat dribbled down his face. Alice gasped and covered her mouth. Ez observed the events unfold without flinching.

"Ahhh," Hugo wailed in agony. "It burns coming out. It burns."

Ez snapped her fingers. The fluids disappeared. Hugo's chin was clean, and the floor and furniture were free of the pooling liquid.

"Keep drinking," Ez commanded. "You'll get used to it. No matter how hard or disgusting or awful it tastes, you keep drinking. At least one of those a day. Two tonight. Do you hear me?"

Hugo nodded in agreement. He picked up the now almost black tube and resumed with his evening feeding. Ez and Alice continued downstairs.

They made their way into the wine cellar. The heels of Ez's pumps echoed off the stone floor as she entered and shut the door behind her. The lights and shadows danced along the stone wall.

Alice moved over to her workbench, not daring to look Ez in the face for her upcoming scolding. She couldn't. Alice knew this was her fault, and she had to hear it anyway. She twirled a pestle around in one of her mortar bowls.

"How are you doing, kiddo?" Ez asked.

"I'm okay," Alice said.

"I didn't ask if you were okay."

"Don't worry about me. I'm fine."

"Alice," Ez said. Alice snapped over at the mention of her full name. "Don't tell me you're fine. You're not. Just . . . just tell me."

Alice stopped twirling the pestle and turned to face Ez. She crossed her arms and leaned against her workbench. Her eyes watered as she held back tears. Her lips were pursed, holding back the words she wanted to say.

Her fingers danced along her arms to a nervous rhythm only she could hear. A beat created by her anxiety and fears echoing through her soul. Her touch was light, as if she was holding herself back out of fear she'd strike harder in deserving punishment. Each sensation grew her anxiety.

Alice finally said, "I . . . I'm barely holding it together. Holding it together for him. I know what this means. I'm well aware of what could happen, and I'm frightened." Her tapping became more erratic as it matched the unease gnawing at her core.

She continued, "I messed up. I should have brought him with me or stayed behind . . ."

She paused. Alice scanned the room, her eyes darting from corner to corner, searching for an answer. The motionless vats. The empty wine presses. The bottles stacked neatly on the racks. Their special rack in the back. She begged the universe for an answer, pleaded for reprieve, but only found silence.

She stopped tapping and took a deep breath. She gazed at Ez with her red, tear-filled eyes. "I should have dealt with it. If I did, then Hugo would've never met me, and he'd be fine. He'd be great. He'd be normal . . . not what he is now. All because of me." She sobbed as she buried her face in her hands.

The clicking of her heels against the stone drowned out Alice's bawling as Ez moved to hug Alice, the top of her head resting slightly below Alice's shoulders. Ez patted her on the back. Alice breathed deep.

"It's okay, kiddo. It's not your fault," Ez said.

Ez's arm was like the comfort of a warm blanket. Alice closed her eyes and relaxed her hands. She leaned her head into Ez's shoulder. Her anxiety quelled with each breath she took.

"Then why does it feel like it is?"

"He made the choice. He knew what he was doing. It wasn't you. It wasn't your fault."

"Thank you."

Ez gave two taps on Alice's back and let go. Alice stood up and wiped away the tears in her eyes. She sniffled to pull back any further tears.

Ez locked eyes with Alice with an intense, unrelenting gaze. "I need to know. Are you prepared?"

Alice's lower jaw twitched. She attempted to focus on Ez, but her gaze became blurry, which left Ez as nothing more than a colorful blur. Anxiety coursed through Alice's body. Her heart raced. Her neck muscles tensed up. A high-pitched noise drowned out all sounds, leaving her in silence. She tried to gulp, but nothing happened. The gnawing sensation froze her in place.

"Are you?" Ez asked again.

Alice could only nod her head yes.

Ez surveyed the wine cellar, examining all the motionless equipment. Her eyes lingered on the bottles ready for transportation to her club. She turned back to Alice.

"So, what do you want to do? Do you still want to move?"

Alice stood upright and pulled her shoulders back. She took a deep breath. Her anxiety filled veins emptied, replaced with a fiery rage. The rage built in her stomach and spread out to every inch of her body. She furrowed her brow and locked eyes with Ez. Her eyes filled with an intense malice mentally directed at two unseen people.

"I'm not leaving. *We're* not leaving. We take them out or else they take us out. There's no other way. If they want a war, well, they got one."

"Great," Ez said. "That's what I wanted to hear."

CHAPTER 17
PILLOW TALK

Alice leaned against the dark wood entryway casing to the living room. The room was darkened. The lights and candles long since extinguished as the night grew later. The flickering TV light filled in the darkened corners of the living room. Sports highlights played on the TV mounted above the fireplace.

It was a compromise in their home decor. She hadn't much use for a TV, but knew Hugo liked to watch his sports. The house was filled to the brim with her stuff—he hardly contributed anything after he moved in. She gave up the space above her fireplace. They each had their peace of mind. She had her wine cellar. He had his TV.

Her eyes fixated on Hugo sitting on the couch. He lounged comfortably, leaning back with his feet propped up on the coffee table. One leg outstretched, careful not to knock anything over. The other leg had the knee bent and foot pressed against the edge of the table.

He held the remote control in one hand. His other hand was stretched behind his head as if he was using his hand as a pillow. His gaze focused on the moving images of various sports highlights playing from earlier in the day. The day he had sequestered himself in the damp, dark cellar away from the destructive sunlight.

A smile formed in the corner of her lips as Alice traced the outline of Hugo in the flickering shadows. His gray sweatpants formed tight against his legs, leaving nothing to the imagination. His black T-shirt snug against his lean, muscular chest. The sharp jawline of his nearly perfect trimmed beard. His coifed hair. She ended her examination locked on to his icy blue eyes. He seemed at ease, at peace.

A stark contrast to her frazzled nerves which mimicked the wildness of her tussled hair. She ran her fingers through her purple hair, pulling it back behind her ears. She finished and crossed her arms. Her hands buried in the oversized hooded sweatshirt she put on in the chill of the night. *His* hooded sweatshirt.

She leaned her head down and sniffed the cotton fabric. The hoodie smelled of him. His essence. His cedar and vanilla signature cologne. She breathed deep, committing the smell to memory. Harmony and peace filled her aching soul. For a moment, the world was right and normal. A brief time where all was perfect with the world, even if their world was rocked to its core. Something had to be normal, even for a moment.

She let out a soft sigh as their eyes found each other in the darkness. He smiled. Her heart beamed. They didn't need to say a word. The unspoken connection spoke more than any soliloquy, sonnet, or love poem could ever express.

Her heart fluttered, dancing to its own melodic beat, as a gentle reminder of her love for him. The love for moments where they could adore each other and not say a word. The act of being in each other's presence nourished and fulfilled Alice's soul. Being only together.

"You can hide in the shadows and glare at me all you want," Hugo said in a low, gravelly whisper. "But my heart will always smile when my eyes find you."

Alice melted as his words sent shivers of warmth and longing down her spine. The cadence of his voice was like a sweet symphony for her soul. Her heart erupted as it overflowed with passion and desire. Even in times of trouble, a moment like this brought her comfort. Moments where they were lovers without a care in the world.

"Always?" Alice asked with a half smile.

"Always." Hugo smiled with a piercing, narrowed gaze.

Alice buried her head into her shoulder to hide her blushing face.

She took a moment to collect herself, taking a few breaths to calm her fluttering heart, before turning her focus to Hugo. "I'm pretty exhausted. It's been a day. I'm going to bed."

"Goodnight. Thank you for everything today. It means a lot that you would go through so much trouble. I want you to know that I love you."

"Can you join me?" Alice asked. "I missed you last night. I didn't like being alone again. You don't have to go to sleep. I want you to hold me until I do."

Hugo turned off the TV and tossed the remote onto the couch. He stood up, careful not to knock the wineglass and bottle off the coffee table. He approached her with soft steps. His chest puffed out and shoulders drawn back. He placed a hand behind her, pinning her close to the wall. Alice's heart fluttered. She wanted to linger in this moment. He leaned in as if he was going to kiss her, but swept her legs out from under her.

The sudden movement startled Alice, causing her breath to catch in her throat. Instead of falling to the floor, she fell into the safe embrace of Hugo's other arm caressing her torso. She wrapped her arms around his neck to steady herself. They locked eyes, never wavering. He lifted her and carried her up the winding stairs. Their intimate connection strengthened with each step toward the sanctuary of their bed. Their hearts synchronized as if they beat as one.

With Alice cradled safely in his strong arms, Hugo approached the bed with his footsteps echoing softly off the wooden floor. She snapped her fingers, and the covers pulled back. She released her grip around Hugo as he set her on the side of the canopy bed with care. Her feet dangled over the edge. Their eyes never strayed from each other.

Alice began removing the sweatshirt, but Hugo stopped her. His fingers worked their way under the dark gray material. His fingertips glided across the softness of her skin. Alice flinched at the coolness of his touch tracing an invisible line up her body. They grazed her cropped tank top. He picked up each finger and tapped down with tenderness, like a jazz singer playing an instrument to Alice's soul.

He played the soulful notes up Alice's sides. She closed her eyes, wanting to wrap herself fully in the electric sensation of his touch. To let her soul be enveloped in the unheard symphony. She tilted her head and arched her back. With no words spoken, only their rhythmic breathing, she raised her arms to allow him to remove a barrier between each other. Goosebumps formed on her arms as they were bathed in the chill of the nighttime air.

Hugo's hands caressed the small of her back. She arched further, letting out a slight moan. His fingertips caught the elastic band of her leggings. She lowered her arms and lifted herself off the mattress. He pulled the leggings down her hips to expose her matching underwear.

He peeled back the spandex, never rushing. She lingered in anticipation. Her body wanted it to hurry, but her soul wanted it to last forever. He pulled them off and tossed them aside. Another article of clothing removed, shrinking away her protective layer and revealing her raw beauty underneath.

His hands wrapped around her ankles with a gentle touch. He lifted them onto the bed. Alice fell to her side and into the soft embrace of her pillow. Hugo removed his sweatpants and jogged around to the other side. He slid into bed beside her, laying side by side. Working one arm under her neck, he draped the other over her, pulling her closer. Their bodies intertwined.

Alice snapped her fingers, and the lights turned off. She snapped again, and the covers flew over them. They stopped as soon as they covered their shoulders; the unseen force tucked them in safe and sound. His warm breath tickled her neck. She wrapped herself in the embrace of Hugo and their shared bed. Their souls became united in love. Their essence transcended time and space as they melded together into a perfect fit.

"Are you sure you want me this close to your neck?" Hugo asked jokingly.

"Shut up," Alice said. "Don't ruin this for me." Alice wiggled, pushing herself deep into Hugo's embrace, not wanting any space between their entwined bodies.

"Umm . . . If you keep wiggling, I think I'll end up ruining this for both of us. I'm beyond being charged up at the moment."

"Oh yeah?" Alice asked as she pressed deeper against Hugo's groin. His body flinched and tightened.

"Please stop or I'll have no choice other than to roll you over and really show you what this new body can do," Hugo replied.

"Is that a threat or a promise?"

"Both."

Alice smiled. "Fine."

They laid in silence, listening to each other's bodies. Alice lost track of time, unsure if minutes or hours had slipped away. She didn't care. They were together, and Hugo's loving embrace provided her with comfort and safety.

Alice shut her eyes. "Hugo," she said. "Lie to me."

"Lie to you?"

"Yeah. Lie to me. Tell me everything is going to be okay."

"It'll be okay."

"You're a terrible liar."

They chuckled.

"How so?"

"Because we know it's a lie," Alice answered.

Hugo brushed Alice's hair behind her ear. He kissed the back of her head. "Do you want to know what I used to tell Elizabeth?"

"Yes."

"I used to tell her all the time we would beat it. That everything would be fine. But you know what? We both knew it was a lie. We both knew the outcome. And you might think we lost. If you asked me at the time, I would've said yes. But now . . . now I know we didn't lose. We won. We beat it."

"How did you win?"

"Because until the very end, she never changed. Elizabeth was still Elizabeth." There was a crack in Hugo's voice as he teared up. "She went out the way she wanted to go. She held her head high with a smile on her face. She never complained. She never wavered. She was still her optimistic self. It might have killed her, but it never beat her. She won. We won."

Alice sniffled as a tear ran down her face. She clutched Hugo's arm tighter, pressing her face against his forearm.

He continued, "I want you to know, I'm still me. I'll always be me."

"I like that. Never change, Hugo," Alice said. "Thank you for lying to me." Her words trailed off as she drifted to sleep.

"Good night, Alice. I love you."

"I lov—"

Alice fell asleep in the loving embrace of Hugo's arms.

CHAPTER 18

THE NEIGHBORHOOD VAMPIRE

Hugo held Alice as she slept. As he listened to her breath in and out, the rising and falling of the comforter soothed the troubled thoughts of his mind. The minutes and hours blended together, unsure of how much time had passed. It didn't matter. Holding her safe and sound in his arms was what truly mattered. He tried to sleep. He closed his eyes hoping to fall into a restful slumber, but it never came.

The troubled thoughts plagued his mind. He replayed the events from the restaurant over and over. He analyzed every step, every misstep. The lunge into Sebastian's chest repeated constantly, so certain each strike would find the target. Nevertheless, it always failed.

Where did I go wrong? Did I pull his shirt too hard and overshoot it? Why did I have to miss?

With a deep breath, Hugo closed his eyes. He tried to sleep, but a flurry of thoughts filled his mind. Even down in the wine cellar, he couldn't sleep. The same thoughts. The same replays. The same memories. It was a relentless onslaught to his mind. He should be exhausted, like Alice, but his body was coursing with energy, reinvigorated by the two pints of blood he drank.

Maybe I don't need as much sleep. Will I ever sleep again?

His nose twitched. He could smell the blood flowing through Alice's body. The sweet ambrosia of his new life calling to him. Tormenting him. Her neck right there, so close to him.

What harm is there in a taste? Just a sweet, sweet taste.

His fangs elongated.

What are you doing, you monster?

He recoiled, withdrawing his fangs. A shiver ran down his spine. He shut his mouth. Hugo had to get away and do what he had done so many times before when faced with a troubled mind.

Hugo pulled back his arms, careful not to disturb her slumber. Alice shifted. He stopped. She nestled into a new position.

He continued tearing apart their intertwined bodies. He gathered his jeans and socks, piled on the floor from earlier, and continued for the bedroom door.

He paused in front of the bathroom. The thought of checking on Alice's reflection passed. It might wake Alice, and he didn't want to disturb her. He slipped out the door and shut it behind him, turning the knob so it wouldn't make a sound. He pulled on his pants and socks and softly hoofed it down the steps. He put on his leather jacket, slipped into his shoes, grabbed his key hanging next to the front door, and left.

The night air was cold and damp. Dark clouds covered the skies and blocked out the welcoming moon. Ravenhill Drive was quiet. The houses were dark as everyone was in their beds for their nightly slumber—everyone except the neighborhood vampire.

Hugo tucked his hands into his jacket pockets. His shoulders pulled forward. A slight hunch in his posture. He thought of grabbing an umbrella, but the mist was refreshing on his head. He stepped off the porch and began the journey to calm his mind. A journey he had taken countless times . . . only this time, he was alone. There was no Max. There was no Alice. There was only what was left of himself.

Hugo's eyes lingered on his former house, infested and transformed from the welcoming home it was when Elizabeth was alive. Its warmth. Its glow. Its radiance. All gone. Now, it was dark and cold. A tormented shell of its former glory. Hugo gave thought to running up those stairs, kicking down the door, and storming the house. He might not get them all, but he'd take some of them with him.

The house was dark. No lights from any windows. No signs of activity. No movement.

They're not even there. Why don't they camp out and surround the house?

He glanced behind him. The chill in the air sent a shiver down his back, and he briefly considered returning to the cozy embrace of his bed. Back to his embrace with Alice. Yet, a familiar pull urged him to press on.

Guilt, worry, and fear consumed his thoughts, casting a dark shadow over his mind. His once familiar world was a whirlwind of change and confusion. His former life was a distant memory, leaving him adrift and uncertain about how to move forward. Hugo knew exactly what he needed, a long walk to clear his mind.

He took a deep breath, savoring the crispness of the air. The chilly dampness rejuvenated his lungs. Hugo continued his journey.

He approached the town center. The ornate filigree lamp posts radiated like mini stars in the misting nighttime sky. The exterior of the buildings was bathed in an orangish glow. The interiors were dark. The street was quiet. No signs of life.

Hugo passed a street clock. It was well past midnight. He'd been out on these walks this late before. The familiar stillness of the night. He rather enjoyed it. No one asked him how he was doing. No one talked to him. It was only him and his thoughts. His tormenting thoughts. The thought he had of biting Alice a few minutes prior . . . He winced.

He passed Sylvia's, the scene where his old life ended, and this new life began. The dark curtains were drawn, no lights from the door. It was empty. He clenched his fists. The images replayed in his mind over and over.

He had grabbed Sebastian's shirt. It was tight.

Was it tight?

His hand slipped to his vest.

Or did I miss his shirt?

He had a fistful of the vest and pulled.

Did I pull him too far? Did I not pull him far enough?

He stabbed him in the chest. The stake hit something.

Or did I not push hard enough? It all happened so fast.

The memory changed each time it replayed.

He basked in the night sky, choosing not to stand under the awning. Dark clouds rolled past. The mist covered his face. His hair became soaked in small beads like dew on the grass. He closed his eyes.

What do I do now? Please tell me. Please. Help me, Elizabeth.

There was only silence.

He opened his eyes and caught a glimpse of himself in the reflection of the glass door. His solemn face. His rain covered jacket. He pulled back on his upper lip. The sharp fangs were visible in the glass window. He pushed against one fang. Its sharp point pierced his thumb. The drop of blood dripped off his finger as the rain washed his thumb clean. The spot healed quickly. He shoved his hand back into his pocket.

I'm a monster.

He continued, passing a few more buildings. A light turned on behind him. Hugo turned. The distinct warm glow of the interior light illuminated the sidewalk outside. He sniffed. Even in the mist-strewn evening, he could smell it. It pulsed and flowed on the other side of the wall. Someone was in there. He could smell the blood. He turned back.

In the window, a neon sign hung—a hand with an eye in the

center of the palm. A circle filled with stars and moons surrounded the hand. The pink light was like a beacon beckoning him to enter. An older woman struggled as she carried a cardboard box inside.

Her wild, gray hair was tucked under a grayish-white scarf. She wore a multi-colored, tie-dye billowing dress. Hugo recognized her. It was Madame Sophia, the fortune teller from the fall festival. She set the box on the counter, glimpsing Hugo in the window. She motioned for him to join her inside. Hugo grabbed the handle and entered.

Shelves and counter spaces filled the floor of the shop to create a maze-like path through the space. They were half full of various mystical items—crystal balls, candles, incense, statues of Egyptian goddesses. Overwhelmed, Hugo tried to absorb the sheer multitude of items, even with the barren spaces. It reminded him of their living room. She could have raided their living room and still not filled the space.

Our credit cards will be maxed out when Alice learns of this place. He chuckled.

"A creature of the night, I see," Madame Sophia said.

"Excuse me?" Hugo asked.

"Out this late in the misty rain . . . Either you really love the night or something must be on your mind."

"Oh, yeah. Uhh . . . The second, I guess. Needed to clear my head," Hugo replied.

"Do you know what helps me clear my head? Movement. It really helps to calm the nerves," she said.

"Is that why you're here this late?"

"No. No. Heavens, no. I'm running behind schedule. I want to open my shop soon, and I still have to unpack and inventory everything. No rest for the weary."

"Madame Sophia from the festival, right?"

"The one and only."

"Interesting shop. I like it."

"Thank you."

"My girlfriend will love this place. She alone will probably keep you in business."

"Oh, yeah?" Madame Sophia asked. "She must be a very spiritual person."

"You have no idea," Hugo responded.

"Well, tell her to stop by. I'll give her a reading for free."

"Will do."

Madame Sophia tapped the cardboard box she had placed on the counter. "Since you're here, do you mind giving me a hand? There's a heavy box on the ground. I need a second set of hands to lift it."

"Sure," Hugo replied. He moved over to her.

She pointed to a box on the ground. "This one here. I need it on the counter. You grab one side; I'll grab the other."

They bent down. Hugo pulled a corner of the box so he could slide his fingers underneath.

"Lift on three. One . . . two . . . three."

Hugo strained as he lifted. The box was far heavier than he had expected. Madame Sophia lifted the box with ease, as if she had another unseen set of hands assisting her side. Hugo placed his corner onto the counter, grabbed the other end, and slid the box onto the counter. He could smell the blood pumping through her veins. He stepped to the other side of the counter.

"Are you sure the counter is rated for that much weight?" Hugo asked through a small laugh. "What's in it?"

"I hope so," she replied. "Stones and crystals. I overpacked the box, and with my bad back, it makes it easier to pull them out up here. Thank you."

"You're welcome. Well, I better get going and leave you to your work."

"Here, let me give you something," Madame Sophia said.

"That's not necessary. I don't mind it."

She searched the room, not able to find the item she sought. "One moment. Wait here." She disappeared into the back room.

"I don't mind. Honest," Hugo said.

He lifted his foot, ready to make a hasty retreat to the entrance door.

She returned carrying a deck of cards. "Please, let me give you a reading?"

"You don't have to. Honest," Hugo insisted as he backed away.

"A one card reading. It'll be quick."

He slumped his shoulders. "Sure. Okay."

Madame Sophia shuffled the tarot cards, the corners tapping against each other. Each card rushed to take its place in the deck as they fell. She neatly aligned the cards and offered the deck to Hugo.

"Please cut," she said.

He split the deck, setting his top half onto the counter.

She placed the bottom half on top. "Fate has been cast."

She fanned out the cards, waving her hand over the cards, and continued, "Close your eyes and think on your troubles. The answer you seek is here in the cards. When you're ready, tell me when to stop."

Hugo closed his eyes. He thought of Sylvia and Sebastian. The restaurant. Alice. The pain he caused her. The sorrows she hid. Sleeping in the wine cellar. Drinking blood. Their embrace in bed. All of it played like still images in his mind over and over. He focused on Alice . . . on her leaning against the wall frame in his sweatshirt from earlier in the evening. Their time cuddling in bed. How he wished they could spend eternity together wrapped around each other.

"When," Hugo said. He opened his eyes.

Madame Sophia drew out a card and flipped it over. It was an image of a man hanging upside down by a foot on a T-shaped wooden cross, one foot behind him and his arms behind his back.

"The hanged man," Madame Sophia said. "Interesting."

"Is it good or bad?"

"Well . . ." She paused. "It could be either. It's about letting go, perhaps letting go of what troubles you. It could also be a decision you have to make . . . something you're stuck on. Perhaps a sacrifice you need to make. Maybe something in your past. Maybe you have to let it go and accept it."

"Well—" Hugo started. Hugo focused on the card, his eyes tracing every line and word. "There's a lot in my past I need to let go of."

"There you are. If you let go, you can move forward."

Hugo raised the corner of his lip, giving a half smile. He bowed and nodded his head. "Thank you, but I should be going."

"My pleasure. Thank you for your help."

Hugo smiled at her, buried his hands in his pockets, and followed the maze out of the store. He stepped back into the misty rain. As he continued his familiar journey, the light from Madame Sophia's store turned off. Hugo turned and paused. He thought about peeking back in, but continued toward the edge of the town square.

He stopped, listening to the cool breeze rustling through the leaves along the path which led to Wildgrove Park—his usual walking path. The path he took many times before to lose himself, to punish himself.

Her words echoed in his mind. *Maybe you have to let it go and accept it.*

He took a deep breath, filling his lungs with the damp, fresh air.

His eyes followed the cracked sidewalk as it wound its way through a quiet street of Newbury Grove and provided a path home.

Let it go.

Hugo's eyes darted back and forth between the allure of his familiar Wildgrove Park trail and the one leading to Alice. He diverted his path and started for home.

He followed the winding sidewalk through the neighborhood. He passed the silent, folk Victorian homes. Each step bolder, quicker. He pulled his shoulders back. He removed his hands from the jacket pockets. He thought of Alice sleeping in their bed at home, waiting for him. If they were to get through this, they could get through it together. He swung his arms. His pace quickened. He was heading home.

His nose twitched. It stopped him in his tracks. The smell. The intoxicating allure of the sweet, sweet smell. It was close. It was moving. He was drawn to it.

A light spilled forth from a house's front window. A shadow moved inside. His eyes dilated. His nose flared. His fangs drew out. His hands twitched. The shadow continued moving through the home. Even though he had his daily feeding, his new body craved more—something fresh, something warm.

He tried to continue. He tried to move forward. If he could run home, there was a bag waiting for him in the refrigerator. But something stopped him. Something was pulling him. Something wanted him to take a step toward the person inside. His greatest fear was coming true. He couldn't control himself. He lifted his foot and stepped off the sidewalk and onto the grass.

A glow cut through the darkness, bathing Hugo in purple light.

"Hugo . . . Please don't," Alice's voice called to him.

He spun around. She stood on the sidewalk with her hand sticking out of the sleeve of her tailcoat and wielding a purple flame of arcane energy.

"Please don't make me do it," Alice pleaded.

Hugo pulled his foot back. His lips quivered, and his eyebrows drew together. "I- I don't know what came over me. I smelled them and I . . ." his voice trailed off.

"Hugo, please come with me," Alice said as she doused the flame.

"I want to, but I'm scared."

"I know."

"I'm scared I'm going to harm you. I don't know what I'd do if I did."

"Hugo, it'll be okay. We can get through it together."

"There are urges. Uncontrollable urges. It's like my body is on fire. After you fell asleep, I thought about biting your neck. I didn't know what to do, so I left. I thought I was fine," he said, turning toward the house. "And then I smelled them moving around. It was like my body took over from my mind."

Alice moved toward Hugo. "It will be okay."

"Stay back," Hugo said, withdrawing from her. "I'm a monster."

Alice extended her hand, moving closer. "You're not a monster."

"Then what am I?"

"You're Hugo Dodds. The best boyfriend a witch could ever ask for," Alice said. Each step drew her closer to him. She was within arm's length. "Please. Please take my hand. Let's go home."

"I don't want to hurt you."

"You won't."

"We're never going to be the same, will we?"

"No," Alice answered.

Hugo lowered his head.

"That's okay. We'll get through it. We can beat this. Together. You and me. Let it go and take my hand."

Let it go.

Hugo locked onto her emerald green eyes. "Promise me."

"I promise you."

Hugo took her hand. It was warm to the touch.

She pulled him closer, ending in a warm embrace on the damp, cold night. "I love you, Hugo Dodds. I promise you we'll get through this together."

"Thank you," he said as they unlocked their embrace.

"It's late. Let's go home."

They held hands as they journeyed home.

THE THIRD SONATA MOVEMENT

"PRESTO AGITATO"

CHAPTER 19

BLEED THEM DRY

Sylvia held her wineglass of blood and gazed down upon her vampiric subjects cleaning The Heart and Rose from the nightly revelry. They toiled away in silence, mopping the floor and scrubbing the bar after the activities of the various patrons who visited for a night of drinks and dancing.

Those unfortunate souls sought relief from the daily stress of their lives only to be enthralled and bled for the pleasures of the vampires who inhabited the building. They didn't die, but they lost enough blood to be bedridden for a few days. The vampire staff ensured every trace of their sanguine activities was erased.

Sylvia raised the glass to her lips. The intoxicating scent of the blackish-red liquid enticed her senses, filling her nose with a metallic aroma. With a gentle sip, the insatiable hunger which drove her to madness subsided as the sweet warmth coated her taste buds.

Most vampires hated the taste of blood at first, but not Sylvia. She reveled in it. She wanted it. She craved it. She had accepted her fate willingly. Still, there was one thing she didn't have, one thing she sought above all else—immortality. While no longer mortal, her reign as queen of her empire could be usurped and short-lived. She suffered from the same vulnerability as all other vampires.

Her mind was focused on one thing and one thing only—acquiring *The Lovers' Kiss*—the spell she sought for lifetimes. So close, yet still so far. Too much time had passed—a week—since she had turned her new pet in the restaurant. They should have acted by now, attacked in some manner as retribution for her actions on the fateful night their negotiations escalated.

She swirled her glass and took another sip. The nectar of her life tickled her senses. Her fingers danced on the railing, playing an invisible piano as she followed along to the music being played behind her. She finished her glass and turned around, leaning against the rail.

Sebastian sat at the player piano, playing his favorite song "Moonlight Sonata." The keys flourished as he entered the third movement. The song picked up tempo, each key struck with purpose and passion. The song built to its thrilling finish, and with a few dynamic chord strikes, it was over. He turned and smiled at Sylvia.

"I never grow tired of hearing you play, my love," Sylvia said.

"I only play it for you. You're the light of my night and should be serenaded with song," he replied.

Sebastian grabbed the lid and gracefully closed it over the keys. The lid landed without a sound. He locked eyes with Sylvia.

There was a pause. Their game began again.

Sylvia stood and broke eye contact with Sebastian. "I can't play tonight."

"Something troubling you, my queen?"

She set the glass down on an end table and took her seat in the crimson, high-back chair. She nestled into the corner of the chair so she could look at Sebastian. She crossed her leg and continued to play her invisible keyboard on her knee. "Do you think it's odd nothing has happened?"

"I'm sure they're waiting for us to make the next move."

"It's been a week. They haven't done anything. Surely, they would have slipped up by now."

"Maybe their move is to not make a move. Maybe they're waiting for us to mess up."

"Still . . . I don't like it."

Sebastian stood and sauntered toward Sylvia. He straightened his vest and tugged a few times on his necktie. He towered over her, glaring down. She loved him looming over her. For all her drive and ambition—her dominance and control—she loved to surrender herself to him. It was her release. Her ecstasy. Her pleasure.

Her heart fluttered at the sharp inhale of breath in the still moments of silence.

Loud crashing noises broke the silence below. Sylvia snarled, ready to spring up to yell at those toiling away below. Sylvia hated noise. She couldn't stand it. After her vampiric transformation, loud noises bombarded her senses, crushing her head by a cacophony of sound.

Sebastian placed a hand on her shoulder, inviting her to sit back down. "I've got this," he said before moving to the railing. He placed both hands on it and leaned over. "If there is one more sound—one more noise—I'll come down there and rip off your heads. Is that understood?"

Sylvia shifted in her chair, never taking her eyes off Sebastian. She wanted him. She craved him. She needed him. She loved silence, but she loved Sebastian more.

He returned. "I'm sorry, my love. It won't happen again."

She smiled and gazed up into his dark brown eyes. Even on the dimly lit balcony, she could always lose herself deep in his eyes. Sylvia bit a portion of her lip, leaving a fang exposed. She wanted him to see her fang—the same fang that transformed him into a vampire many years ago.

His chiseled, stoic face glared back. A small corner of his lips betrayed him and arched up into a smile. Maybe she did want to play their game after all.

"What's our next move?" Sebastian said.

"I should use his blood to enthrall him to bring the spell to us," Sylvia suggested.

"Do you think it's wise? We have enough for what—one, maybe two attempts at best. What if she stops him? Then we lose our leverage."

"We should force them out," Sylvia responded. "But how?"

Sebastian paused. He drew his hand to his chin and lips.

After a moment, he asked, "What if we only have to force her out? We could draw her to the Raskins' home, leaving him inside."

Sylvia glanced away, lost in thought as the idea sparked new ones in her mind. "Yes. It could work. You could draw her out. Then I only need to use a small amount of his blood to enthrall him."

"He can let you in, and you won't have to worry about a thing."

"I'd have free rein to look through the house. I could compel him to tell me where the spell is hidden. No one would stop me." The mere thought brought a glimmer to her eyes and a sly smile to her face.

"We'll send the ghouls to the Raskins' house right before sunset. It will force him to stay in the house. She'll have to respond, and it will leave him all alone."

"With only a small amount, I'll need to look him in the eyes to enthrall him. He won't answer the door for me," Sylvia said.

"Of course not. Wait until a few minutes after sundown. Then frantically pound on the door like you're one of the Raskins seeking help."

"Yes. That will work. When he looks outside to see who's there, I can enthrall him to let me in."

"And everything we ever wanted will be ours."

She stood. "Everything we ever wanted," she said with a smile. She breathed in, every inhale deeper than the last. Her heart raced at the thought of being this close to the end of their goals. "Tomorrow."

He took a step closer to Sylvia. "Tomorrow night," he said in a whisper.

They stood in silence. His musky scent tantalized her senses. She bathed in his aura. Jolts of emotions coursed through her body. Every essence in her being was alive. She wanted him more than ever. She gulped.

Sebastian placed his hand beneath her chin and tilted her head up. His thumb traced an invisible line from the end of her nose, over her lips, and down her chin. Her knees buckled. Her shoulders tightened, and a shiver went down her back. She smiled.

"We're so close my love. Can you feel it?" his gravelly voice whispered.

"I can feel it," she replied in a hushed tone.

"Do you want it?"

"Yes," she whispered.

"I can't hear you," he said through a mischievous smile.

"Yes," she said louder.

He leaned in to kiss her. Before they became reacquainted, he paused. The distance between them was an ocean of anticipation. She waited with bated breath for him to close the final distance. She was held in sweet torture as his breath mixed with hers.

"Are you sure?"

"Yes!" she shouted.

"That's my good girl."

Their bodies pressed together as their lips reunited once more. The smoldering fire of their longing fused their hearts and souls together. They closed their eyes, slipping into the eternal bliss of their personal paradise. An eternity of immortal love where time lost all meaning, and there was only a single thought remaining: Sylvia would burn the world down for Sebastian.

CHAPTER 20
DANCING UNDER THE PALE MOONLIGHT

"What is it?" Hugo shouted.

Alice ran to the stairs to investigate the commotion.

"You have to slow down," Hugo said into his phone as he ran down the stairs into the living room. He was still in his black T-shirt and boxer briefs from the day's slumber.

"What is it?" Alice asked as she followed behind.

He covered the phone with his hand. "I don't know. Carol called me in a panic." He placed the phone on speaker. "Carol, Alice is here. What's happening?"

Her voice came through the speaker, "They're outside the house. They're trying to get in."

"Who's trying to get in?" Alice asked.

"These four men. They're outside trying to break down the door and smash the windows," Carol said with a hint of panic in her voice.

"They followed us home from the store," Oliver yelled into the phone.

"What do we do?" Carol asked.

"I'm going to shoot them," Oliver said.

"Don't shoot them," Hugo said.

"Whatever you do, don't open your door," Alice yelled. "As long as it's closed, you'll be safe."

"What if they get through the windows?" Carol asked.

"They can't get through," Alice reassured her.

Hugo put the phone on mute. "The windows will hold, right?"

Doubt coursed through Alice's mind as she recast the spell in her mind. She took a sharp breath and held it.

Did I forget a step or mispronounce a word? Were the defenses weakening? No . . . No, I pronounced each word correctly. It will hold. It should hold.

She exhaled. "They should hold . . . I think."

"We have to help them."

Alice checked the clock. "I can go."

"I'm coming with you."

"The sun's still up for another fifteen minutes."

"Damn it," Hugo said with an expression of anger. "You go. I'll join you as soon as I can."

"Stay here."

"But I want to help."

"I think they cracked the window!" Carol shouted.

Max barked at the would-be intruders.

Hugo unmuted the phone. "Carol, listen to me. Take Max and Oliver and go to the basement. Wait there. Alice is on the way."

"Please hurry," Carol said.

The call ended.

"I didn't hang up," Hugo said. He tried calling her back, but it went to voicemail.

Alice and Hugo exchanged glances of anxiety and fear, their eyebrows arched and mouths gaped open.

Alice snapped her fingers, and her coat and hat flew into the living room. She slipped her arms through the sleeves of the coat as if someone was helping her put it on. The hat came to a rest on her head. She buttoned up and pulled her hat snug.

"I've got them," Alice said.

"Do you want me to follow you?"

"Don't. Stay here in case I send them this way. You'll need to let them in."

Hugo shook his head. "Fifteen minutes to sunset?"

"Fifteen minutes," Alice confirmed. "I'll have to drive."

"Be careful."

"I'm always careful. Besides, I'll have backup." She winked to Hugo and then whistled. "Gwennie, let's go."

The floating broomstick followed Alice to the door. Alice grabbed the broomstick handle. She paused and they nodded at each other.

"I'll be back," she said.

The sunlight poured into the darkened hallway as she opened the door. She trotted to her awaiting SUV. Alice placed Gwennie in the backseat before climbing in. The engine roared to life. Alice and Gwennie took off on their mission.

Alice tapped the steering wheel with every passing moment. She controlled her breathing, inhaling and exhaling with every twist and turn of the vehicle. Flashes appeared in her mind. Flashes of death and destruction. She had traveled this path so many times. It should have only taken her minutes, but time passed like thick molasses. The visions and the endless possibilities weighed heavily on her mind.

Would her defenses hold? Were the Raskins okay?

Her heart pounded. Her mind raced. She held her breath.

The tires of Alice's black SUV screeched as she brought the SUV to a stop in front of the Raskin's home. Alice drew in a sharp breath as the four ghouls, armed with rocks and other heavy landscaping stones, smashed their improvised instruments into the windows of the single floor folk Victorian home.

Even after the ghouls' bombardment of the windows, the defenses Alice had conjured held firm.

After unsuccessful attempts to break through, they moved onto the next window. Two ascended the stairs to the covered porch spanning the full length of the front. The ghouls alternated turns striking the front doorknob with their stones. Through all of their efforts, all of their might, it all proved fruitless. The door held.

She rolled down the back window.

Guinevere popped halfway out of the window.

"Wait here," Alice commanded. "Wait for my signal."

The broomstick retreated inside. Alice opened the door and leapt out, charging into battle as she ran up the walkway, stopping halfway between the street and porch steps.

Alice Primrose snapped her fingers and conjured a purple, arcane flame of energy in each hand. She raised her head, peering out from under the brim of her curved witch's hat. The hem of her black and purple tailcoat flowed in the breeze of the late autumn evening. Her shoulders pulled back and the balls of arcane energy were at her hips.

Like a gunfighter ready for a shootout, Alice was prepped for the quick draw of battle. She inhaled a deep breath, determined to defend her friends . . . *No. Not friends. Her family's home.*

"Four against one," Alice said. "Not good odds for you. I'm feeling merciful, so I'll offer you a choice. Leave or perish."

The ghouls held onto their stone implements. They trudged down the steps, raising them above their heads, ready to strike. They picked up speed, racing toward her.

"You want to dance? Let's dance," Alice said.

She flung her arm forward, sending the arcane flame hurtling toward the lead ghoul like a bowling ball careening toward a rack of pins. It struck him on the chest and exploded in a dazzling display of arcane sparks. He dropped his stone implement and fell backward onto the cement walkway. The ghoul writhed in pain and evaporated into a cloud of dust.

They continued their march, now closing in halfway to Alice. She threw the other flame, striking one more on the side. He fell to his knees, writhed in pain, and turned to dust as well. This didn't stop the other two. They continued their relentless march, rushing faster. They were within striking distance.

Alice took a step back. She snapped her fingers to produce more arcane flames. They closed in too fast. She couldn't concentrate enough to produce the purple flames. The ghouls leaned into their blow, bringing their stones down to strike at Alice.

With a quick jump to her right, she tucked and rolled on the ground to avoid the stones crashing down on her. The ghouls smashed the stones into the sidewalk where Alice once stood. She rolled on the ground and sprung to her feet, ready for the next round.

The ghouls turned to continue their pursuit of Alice. They stepped onto the grass, but stopped. They were frozen, unable to move forward. Alice blinked a few times, unsure of what was transpiring. Her heart and mind raced, but she never let them distract her from the two ghouls standing before her.

They dropped their stones and pivoted, sprinting in the opposite direction. The ghouls disappeared into the darkness as they rounded the corner of a home.

Alice exhaled as she kept an eye out for other would be intruders. Night had fallen and shadows lurked around every corner. The street was quiet and dark. Porch lights weren't yet illuminated to fight back against the darkness. A car or two drove past; their drivers curious enough to glance Alice's way before continuing.

The hair stood up on Alice's arms. Something was off. They wouldn't run away. She continued her search. Her eyes were ever vigilant against the moving shadows. She held her breath, listening for anything.

There was nothing, only silence and the rapid beats of her pounding heart. A shiver ran down her spine.

Guinevere popped out of the back window, ready for her signal to join in the fight. Alice held up her hand and motioned the broomstick to go back. It retreated once more into the vehicle.

Alice snapped her head at the sound of grass rustling behind her. She couldn't see anything in the shadows between the houses. She produced another purple flame. This time, her mind was full concentrating on her conjuring abilities. She held her hand aloft, the purple flame now a lantern to guide her way.

The purple light fought back against the darkness. She moved forward, each step deliberate and with purpose. Alice entered the space between the two houses. The Raskins had a simple picket fence with ample viewing into their backyard. Alice dispersed the flame and placed her back against the side of the house. She peered around the corner to avoid being seen by whatever made the rustling noise.

The backyard was covered in darkness and the pale light of a waning crescent moon. She breathed deeply, trying to soothe her racing heart. Her fingers twitched with anxiety. Her shoulders tensed. She stood still as she listened intently for any movement or sound lurking within the shadows.

There was nothing.

You're imagining things.

Alice exhaled deeply and relaxed her shoulders. She crept to the front of the house. She continued to scan the area with her eyes. Ever alert. Ever vigilant. Satisfied the area was clear, she jogged up the porch steps to the front door.

"Carol. Oliver. It's Alice. Can you hear me?" Alice shouted.

There was no response.

Alice's breathing labored. She tried to open the door, but it was still locked. Half-smiling, she pulled out a key from her pocket.

"You can't win," a voice growled.

Alice dropped the key back into her pocket. She spun around and ignited an arcane flame in her hand.

"We are too many. We are everywhere," the voice continued to taunt her.

She recognized the voice. *His voice.* Sebastian was here, hiding in the shadows. Alice frantically shifted her head, checking for any signs of him.

"Did you really think you could stop us?" His voice came from the end of the porch.

Alice moved to investigate, raising the purple ball of energy to her shoulder.

"Blood will flow through the town streets. We will destroy everything you care for," he taunted.

His voice sounded like it came from back at the door. Alice doused the purple flame, allowing the darkness to cover the porch. Her breathing increased, nearly drowning out her thoughts. She had to concentrate, be smart in her actions. She tiptoed along the side of the house, trying not to make a sound. The creaky old wood of the porch betrayed her position. She stopped and crouched down, ready to spring into action.

"I see you, little witch. We've always seen you. Watching you. Hunting you. Stalking you. You never knew it," his voice echoed.

It sounded as if it was right in front of her, yet there was nothing there. Only the darkness.

"You still have a choice. You can join us. Join us and we'll spare your precious town. Your precious friends. You'll have everything you ever wanted. Everything you ever needed. All we want is for you to turn over the spell, and devote your life to us."

He tempted her with his rich and velvety words, like an intoxicating elixir plucking at the heart strings of her deepest desires. His words teased and manipulated her into surrendering. She gulped, trying to clear her head of his false promises. Alice knew it would never be as they promised. They would control her, dominate her. She would never be allowed to live the life she wanted. She would be made into a servant of the Savinos, bending to their whims. It would never be enough. They would extract all they could from her, and when they finished, they would dispose of her.

"Join us," he tempted once more.

Alice closed her eyes, trying to focus on where the voice was coming.

He continued, "It's the only way."

Alice snapped her eyes open. His voice was coming from above her. He was on the roof. Alice leapt forward over the railing. She tucked into a somersault and rolled along the ground. She sprang to her feet, conjuring a new arcane flame. He lurked on the roof above the porch, illuminated by the pale moonlight. She threw the flame at her tempter.

He dodged out of the way. She threw another, barely missing him as he rolled to safety. He retreated up the roof, sliding over the point. He popped his head above the point of the roof. Alice couldn't hit him from this angle, not without destroying part of the roof. He snarled toward Alice.

"Consider this my official rejection notice!" Alice yelled.

"You'll never get another chance," he growled back.

"I don't need it."

"Then so be it. This night, the streets of Newbury Grove will run red with blood."

"You're not a very good bluff," Alice said. "I took out two of your ghouls. I've driven you into cowering behind the roof. I appear to have the king cornered. I believe in chess I'm supposed to yell out 'check' or is it 'checkmate?'"

He laughed. "What makes you think you have me cornered?"

"I don't have you cornered," Alice said. "But my white knight does." She whistled.

Guinevere sped from the open window of Alice's SUV like an arrow toward Sebastian. He slid down the back of the back of the roof as the grayish-white broomstick shot above his head. Guinevere circled around and followed him.

Alice took off in a sprint around the side of the house. She braced her hand on the picket fence and leapt over. The backyard was empty. Patio furniture was knocked over where Sebastian had possibly landed. A small shed occupied the corner of the backyard. There was nothing else in the backyard.

"Do you see him?" Alice asked the broomstick.

Guinevere circled in the sky, unable to find its query. Alice ran over to the shed, a new arcane flame in hand. She ran around it, unable to find any signs of Sebastian. She gave the shed door a firm yank, but it refused to budge as it was locked. The backyard stretched out before her, devoid of any signs of another person.

A black SUV, parked in front of the houses which lined the street behind the Raskins' house, roared to life. With a squeal of its wheels, it sped off down the road.

Guinevere chased after it.

Alice whistled to stop the broomstick. "Let him go. Get back to the car. I'll check on the Raskins."

The broomstick gave a final look at the SUV speeding away and then retreated to Alice's vehicle.

Alice ran to the front of the house. She pulled the key from her pocket and unlocked the door.

"Carol, Oliver!" Alice shouted. "It's Alice."

She entered and shut the door behind her.

The house was dark. She entered the living room, which branched off into the kitchen and bedrooms. The living room was decorated with well-kept furniture, personal pictures, and a TV. Beige curtains, framing the front window, were more decorative than functional. Inch thick blinds were drawn shut to seal off the outside world from looking into the house.

"Carol, Oliver!" Alice shouted again.

A sound came from the kitchen. The basement door squeaked open, and she heard footsteps ascending creaky wood stairs.

"Stay back!" Oliver yelled. "I'm armed. We have a dog too."

Max went running up the stairs and into the living room, greeting Alice with the wag of her tail. She whined, wanting to jump up on her. Alice bent down to scratch her behind the ears.

"Are you two okay?" Alice asked. "They're gone."

"Put that thing down before you hurt yourself," Carol said.

"It's better to be safe," Oliver said.

Carol and Oliver Raskin entered the living room. He carried a wooden baseball bat.

"I had this in case they made it inside. They don't like wood, right?"

"Yeah, but—" Alice said as she stood.

"See, I told you." Oliver lowered the wooden bat.

"You'd have to stab them with it, though," Alice finished. She gave Carol a hug and then Oliver. "Are you two okay?"

"A little on edge," Carol said. "But we're fine."

"They're gone. I don't think they'll be coming back," Alice said.

"Where's Hugo?" Carol asked.

"He's at home," Alice answered. "He stayed behind in case you needed to make a hasty retreat."

"No one is going to run us out of our home. Not even some vampires," Oliver said.

Alice paused. A passing thought pressed on her mind.

This was too easy.

"Something doesn't seem right," she said. "It was only one of them. They're always together. Why would one attack here? Unless—"

As the horror of the situation played out in her mind, Alice's stomach sank and twisted. Yet again, the Savinos were a step ahead on the chessboard.

"What is it?" Carol asked.

"I need to go. Keep the door shut. Don't leave until dawn." Alice left, slamming the door behind her.

CHAPTER 21
SEEING HERSELF IN

Hugo focused his attention on his phone as he finished putting on his clothes. There had been no response. No call. Nothing. It was silent, and he didn't like it. Helplessness washed over him as the unknown surrounded him. He had no idea if the Raskins or Max or Alice were safe. There was only silence and waiting.

He paced around the bedroom, trying to ease his mind. He stopped outside the bathroom door. It was dark and quiet inside. The sounds of Alice's reflection's wailing had long since stopped. He flipped on the light switch.

"Go away," Alice's reflection yelled. "I want to be left alone."

Hugo ignored the request and entered the bathroom. He turned to face the mirror. Alice's reflection was huddled on the floor in the corner of her bathroom, fixated on the wall. A purple bathrobe was wrapped around her like a child being swaddled. Her head was bent over.

Hugo placed his hands on the ornate gold frame of the mirror and leaned in. He tried to speak, but the words failed him. He knew no matter what he said, no matter how sincere, he couldn't undo the damage.

He could only say, "I'm sorry."

"Is that supposed to make me feel better?" Alice's reflection said.

"No, but I wanted to let you know I'm sorry."

"Do you want a cookie?"

Hugo lowered his head. "She's putting on a brave face for me, but I need to know. How is she doing?"

"I thought we had this discussion about knowing her innermost thoughts?"

"Yeah, well, I guess I'm failing the test now."

Alice's reflection didn't move.

"I need to know. I need to know how she feels. How you feel."

Alice's reflection glanced over her shoulder, a scowl on her face. Mascara ran down her face, and then tears followed.

"You want to know how I feel?" Her eyelids narrowed.

"Yes."

She got up from her corner and stormed to the mirror. Her bathrobe unfurled to expose Alice's comfort clothing of choice—black long sleeves with matching leggings and bare feet—as it flowed behind her. She arrived at the mirror and gave it a good smack with her hand.

"I'm fucking furious," she answered. "And she is too. She might be talking a good game right now, but she's furious."

Hugo let go of the frame and dropped his head. He couldn't look her in the eyes.

"She's furious because she blames herself. Not you," Alice's reflection continued.

Hugo arched his eyebrows, shocked by the answer.

"She was too scared to deal with this on her own and wanted to run. That's all she's ever done. Boy troubles? Run away. Girl troubles? Run away. Career troubles? Run away."

He thought Alice would certainly blame him, not herself.

"And I blame her too. The one thing in this world she actually ran toward was you, and now look!"

Hugo rubbed his neck where he had been bitten. He paused and then touched his retracted fangs with the tips of his thumb and index finger.

"You're the only thing she cares about, and she let you down. We let you down." Alice's reflection fought back tears as she focused on where Hugo's reflection last stood. "Now I've lost the only love I've ever had. You were the only one she did this for. There were no other reflections. Just you . . . And he vanished in my arms. There was nothing I could do. I could only watch, never to get him back. Do you know how that feels?"

Hugo pinched the spot on his left ring finger where his wedding ring had been. He held it only for a split second before recoiling his hand. He had slipped back into old habits from a previous life. She was hurting as much as he was hurting when his black onyx wedding ring had occupied his finger. He knew exactly what she needed to hear.

"I do," Hugo said.

Her eyes were red and bloodshot. Black, mascara filled tears streamed down her face.

Hugo continued, "I know that feeling all too well. The exact feeling I had with Elizabeth. I know what it's like being forced to watch someone suffer and perish. The feeling of helplessness. I went through it again when Alice was hurt, and I didn't know what to do. But do you know what I learned?"

"What?" Alice's reflection asked in hushed words.

"It took me a while. It took Alice helping me through it. Even though I might not have changed the outcome, at least I was there. They weren't alone, and that's all they could have asked for. I was there for Elizabeth. You were there for my reflection. That must count for something."

Alice's reflection wiped the tears from her eyes. She examined her blackened fingers from the running mascara. She drew water from her sink, washed her hands clean, and wiped them on her purple bathrobe.

"I guess you're right," Alice's reflection said.

"It hurts. It doesn't get easier, but you have to keep going. We'll find a way to fix this. Even if *The Lovers' Kiss* didn't work, there has to be something. We'll bring him back. I promise you."

She sniffled to hold back the tears welling up. She smiled. "Thank you."

"I promise when this is all done, we'll keep trying."

Thunderous knocks rattled the front door, varied in their tempo—the sound of panic. It drew the attention of Hugo and Alice's reflection.

"Sounds like she's in trouble," Hugo said. "Is she?"

"I feel fear, panic. I think so."

"On or off?" Hugo asked as he started out of the bathroom.

"On, but shut the door," Alice's reflection answered.

Hugo shut the door behind him and darted out of the bedroom. He flew down the stairs and pulled back the black sheer curtain covering the inset window.

"Alice?" Hugo asked.

Sylvia, face to face with only the glass between them, locked eyes with Hugo. Her pupils dilated and her irises flashed red. "Look at me," she commanded. "Lose yourself in me."

Hugo's eyes dilated and flashed red.

Sylvia smiled. "Now, be a good pet and let me in."

Hugo tried to resist. Every fiber in his being screamed for him to not let her in, but something compelled him. Something took control. Sylvia was taking control over him, forcing him to act against his will. But how?

He turned the ornate diamond knob and opened the door. Sylvia entered. Her hands were concealed within the pockets of her crimson velvet jacket. The swallowtail hem extended down to the back of her knees and sashayed with every step as her high heels clacked against the hardwood.

"Thank you. Now shut the door. Stand there until I tell you to move, and don't speak unless I tell you to do so. I want your eyes to follow me around," she ordered.

Hugo shut the door as commanded and remained motionless. He tried to scream. He tried to yell, but was frozen, held in place by an unseen force. His arms tightened. Fear overwhelmed him.

They had breached the door. They were inside.

Sylvia tapped him twice on his left cheek and traced her fingers down under his chin. "Good boy."

Sylvia examined her surroundings, settling on the console tables lining the hallway. She picked up one of the amethyst crystals scattered across the tabletop. She turned the crystal around, examining every cut edge. "Your girl really loves purple, doesn't she?"

She tossed the crystal. A piece broke off as it hit the hardwood floor.

Hugo couldn't move, frozen in silence. His arm shimmied as he clenched his fists.

Sylvia tapped on his shoulders as she passed by into the living room. "Whoa," Sylvia said as she discovered the various objects decorating the room. "I don't know if I should be impressed or worried the two of you are becoming hoarders. There's so much."

She took in her surroundings. The red velvet couch. The black high-back leather chair. The gnarled fingers of purple, black, red, and white candle wax frozen in place as they dripped over the edge of the fireplace mantle. The bookshelves filled with various oddities and cherished memories.

She turned her attention back to Hugo. "Why don't you join me in here? Come." Sylvia smacked her thigh as one would to get the attention of a dog. "Sit in the middle of the couch."

Hugo did as instructed, never taking his eyes off Sylvia. He traversed in silence as he maneuvered around her and took his place on the couch.

"Good pet."

I'm going to stab her myself. So, help me. I'll stab her.

Sylvia tapped her hands together as she surveyed the room. She stopped and brought them to the side of her face, leaning her chin on the back of her hand. "So many places to look. I don't know where to begin. Don't tell me yet. I love a good hunt."

She stood in front of the fireplace mantle. Her eyes traced the gnarled finger like wax dripping over the edge of the mantle. The light of the candles burned bright as they awaited the oncoming darkness of night.

"Don't answer, but I hope you know this is a fire hazard," Sylvia said. Her fingers traced around bubbled wax drippings. "I mean, one little bump and this whole house could go up in flames."

She flicked the candles off the mantle. Their flames extinguished in mid-air as they tumbled to the floor. They bounced off the ground a few times before rolling around to their final spots.

Sylvia smirked at Hugo. "A fire safety spell. Smart." Sylvia stalked to her next target.

Sylvia stood in front of one of Alice's many shelves, packed to the brim with books, macabre items, and covered in the winding vines of plants nestled on top. Sylvia pulled out a book and flipped through the pages. "A history of witches during the Middle Ages," Sylvia read aloud. "Fascinating, but all a lie. They always leave out the parts of history they don't want you to know. Like how witches nearly wiped out us vampires. All because they wanted to protect their precious humans. You may see it as protection. I see it as defiling the natural order of things." She tossed the book over her shoulder.

Hugo clutched the seat cushion, his fist full of the red velvet material. Fire and malice in his eyes. He made the most of what little bodily control he had.

She turned to Hugo. She smiled a devilish, knowing grin. "You know, she could have easily hidden the scroll in one of these books, but I don't think that's her style. No, she's far too intelligent to hide it there. But what if she hid it behind this bookcase?"

Sylvia grabbed the edge of the case and pulled it forward. The contents spilled all over the hardwood floors. The potted plant shattered, sending dirt scattering with the pieces of dark green ceramic. There were no secret compartments in the bookcase or wall.

Sylvia raised her hands in the air and chuckled. "Oops. Guess I was wrong."

Hugo's fingers dug deeper into the cushion. He clenched his teeth. His arms shook.

Sylvia pouted her lips. "I hope my game of hide-and-seek isn't making you upset. I don't like it when my pets are upset."

She dug her hands into her pocket and moved closer to Alice's memory shrine. "What do we have here?"

She surveyed the old family pictures and heirlooms—the various crystals, flowers frozen in time, sets of keys, a quill, and the box containing Hugo's wedding ring. Her hand hovered over each item, unsure of which item to pick up first. They lingered over the masterfully crafted wooden box, the picture of Elizabeth's smiling face resting behind it.

Hugo watched in silent horror. He let out a barbaric yawp only his mind could hear. He was powerless to stop her. His arms and legs were bound to the couch by unseen shackles. He wanted to jump up and fight her, but couldn't.

Sylvia picked up one of Alice's family photos—an older photograph from the late nineteenth century. Her eyes lingered on the photo, narrowing the longer they fixated on the image. Her sharpened fingernail screeched across the glass as she traced Xs over both images.

The picture of Alice's great-great grandparents always caught Hugo's attention when he glanced at the memory shelf. The black and white photo was worn and starting to fade. In the picture, there was a rugged, scruffy man wearing a black cowboy hat, armed with two six-shooters by his side. He stood with an arm draped around the shoulders of a beautiful woman. She wore a dark blouse over a long-sleeve lace shirt, a black walking skirt which dragged along the ground, and a witch's hat. Both appeared to be in their late thirties.

Sylvia dropped the picture frame, cracking it in splintering spiderwebs of broken glass.

"Oops," Sylvia said.

She snared a set of keys with her finger. She twirled them around as she surveyed the rest of the area. She examined Galahad's remains atop the shelves. She paused, twirling the keys faster and faster.

Don't you dare touch him or so help me!

After she was done playing, she flung the keys across the room. "Nope. I don't think she'd keep it up here. Maybe you can tell me where the spell is located."

She strutted over and stood in front of Hugo. Sylvia dropped to her knees, placing her hands on his. She leaned in, working her hands up his legs as she spread them apart. Hugo's knuckles turned white as he gripped the cushion as hard as he could.

"You know, I could give you anything you want. All you have to do is ask."

I want you dead, bitch.

She worked her hands further up his legs, stopping on his upper thighs. "Do you want me? They don't have to know. It could be our little secret." She tapped his legs.

Hugo fought back every tantalizing urge of excitement. His thoughts focused on Alice.

She touched his chest with her right index and middle fingers, playfully marching them down his torso. She indulged herself with every prolonged press of her fingers.

"Look at me," she said. He did as told. "Are you enjoying my gifts? I want you to answer me with yes or no."

"No," Hugo replied.

She leaned back on her heels and pouted her lips. "No? Do you not appreciate what I've done for you? Answer me."

"No," Hugo replied again.

She tilted her head, pressing her lips together. She leaned in deeper. She laid on top of him, raising her head until it was next to his. He could smell the mixture of perfume on her body and blood on her breath.

She traced his jaw with her finger. "Maybe you need to be shown how to use your gifts—all of your gifts. I could show you. I could show you how fun being a vampire could be. Answer me yes or no. Would you like me to show you?"

Hugo wanted to throw her off and grab the wooden stake. He wanted nothing more than to drive it right into her chest. Yet, he couldn't. He couldn't take his eyes off of her. He had no choice but to respond.

He narrowed his eyes. "No."

She pulled back. "You really are no fun, aren't you?" She tapped her knees. "I guess I'll be on my way. So, why don't you tell me where your little girlfriend keeps The Lovers' Kiss spell?"

Don't tell her. Don't do it. He screamed, a scream only he could hear. He hesitated. He resisted.

"Tell me!" she commanded once more.

With all of his willpower and might, he resisted once more.

"I won't ask again," she commanded as she moved her finger over his neck. Her sharpened fingernail dug into his neck.

"Downstairs," he responded.

"See, it wasn't so bad. Where?"

He tried to keep his mouth shut, but the compulsion overwhelmed him. "In her cellar."

"Where in her cellar?"

"Behind a stone above her workbench."

"Thank you," she said as she stood up. "Wait right here. I'll be back." She winked at him and left the living room.

Hugo could hear her opening the basement door and descending the creaky steps.

What have I done? Forgive me, Alice.

His heart raced. Sweat ran down the back of his head. He wanted to move, to stop her, but the unseen force kept him frozen in place.

He still had control over his eyes, even though his body and head couldn't move. His worst fear was confirmed—the front door was closed. With the door shut and Alice's key in the house, there would be no rescue coming. He was alone, at her mercy, and she knew it.

The ticking of the grandfather clock was excruciating. His heart sunk with each passing movement.

Tick. Tock. Tick. Tock.

She had been gone for what felt like an eternity. Thoughts raced through his mind as to what she was doing down there. What she could do. What she would do.

Tick. Tock. Tick. Tock.

His eyes shifted to his right. He could only see the shelves out of the corner of his eyes. He wanted nothing more than for Galahad to spring to life, fly down the stairs, and stab her in the heart. He poured his entire essence and soul into his wish.

Come on, buddy. I need you. Please. Do something.

The broomstick didn't move.

Tick. Tock. Tick. Tock.

The clacking of her high heels grew louder as Sylvia ascended the basement stairs. She entered the living room holding a bottle of wine with a disappointed expression on her face. She stood in the entryway and leaned against the door frame, tilting her head. She tapped the bottle with her fingers as she held it in her hand.

"I found her little hiding spot," Sylvia said. "But it seems the little witch moved it. Apparently, she doesn't even trust you with its secret hiding spot."

Hugo tried to smile, but couldn't.

"I did find this, though." She held the bottle so Hugo could see the label: *The Lovers' Kiss Hugo & Alice*. "Looks like you two actually made a batch. Did it work?"

Hugo resisted and remained silent.

"Answer me!" Sylvia shouted.

"Yes," Hugo replied.

"Good." She smiled and moved toward Hugo, placing the bottle on the coffee table.

Sylvia positioned her knees on the couch between Hugo's legs and hands. She straddled him, sitting on his lap and wrapping her arms around his neck. Her strawberry blonde hair tickled Hugo's face as she moved her hips around to get a better position.

"You're a lucky man, Hugo Dodds," Sylvia said in a flirtatious voice. "Every time I think about taking your head off, I always come up with a reason to keep you alive . . . or undead, as it would be." She laughed with villainous glee.

His head trembled with anger.

She leaned in closer, her breath washing over his lips. In a low, seductive voice, she said, "Does this excite you?"

"No," he responded.

"It excites me. I do have to warn you, though. Sebastian can be a very jealous lover. If he should find you, I can't imagine what he'd do to you. Maybe I'll tell him. Maybe I won't. How would Alice react? Would she be furious? Or . . . would she want to join in on the fun? You know, Sam spilled every little detail about their relationship to me. She was so helpful."

Hugo's whole body shook.

Sylvia laughed. "I think I touched a nerve. Okay, I'll leave. I know when playtime is over. But before I go, I want you to do something for me. I want you to let her know it was me. Can you do that for me?"

He didn't answer.

"Answer me," she commanded.

"Yes," he replied.

She laughed, flicking her head so her hair flipped over her shoulder. She leaned in and whispered into his ear. Her breath was torturous with every word.

~

Hugo's ears perked up as he heard the distinct sound of Alice's footsteps echoing on the gray wooden steps of the porch. The partially open front door gave a glimpse of Alice, frozen in place before she could even knock.

"Hugo!" Alice shouted, freed from her momentary hesitation.

She rushed through the door with Guinevere following.

"Hugo, are you okay?"

She slammed the door shut before darting into the living room.

Hugo remained in the same position as before, his body tense and unmoving. His hands still clutched the seat cushion. He wanted to move, he wanted to talk, but the unseen force still held him in place. His eyes focused on Alice.

Alice moved through the living room with a stunned expression on her face as she examined her surroundings. The candles on the floor, the knocked over bookshelf, and the shattered potted plant. She removed her curved witch's hat and bent down to pick up the set of keys from her memory shrine. Alice locked eyes with Hugo.

"Hugo, what happened here?" Alice asked.

"Say her name," Hugo commanded.

"Say whose name?"

"Say her name," Hugo commanded again.

Alice dropped her hat to the ground, her expression of concern morphing into anger. "Sylvia."

"Say *her* name," Hugo commanded once more.

Alice paused. The grandfather clock ticked and tocked a few times, cutting through the silence of the room. Alice glared at Hugo, her tongue holding back the words she needed to say.

After a pause, she said in a low growl, "Sylvia Savino."

Hugo sprang up from the couch, the unseen hold relinquishing its compulsion over him.

"I'm going to stab her. I swear, with every fiber in my being, I'll stab her." He sprinted out of the room toward the basement door.

"What happened?" Alice asked as she followed him.

"She was in the cellar looking for the spell," he answered as he bounded down the steps.

The light was still on from when Sylvia had been there.

"How did she get through the door?"

"There was a panicked knock at the door. I thought it was you. She mind-controlled me through the window on the door."

He rushed across the basement to the open wine cellar door. Hugo stopped, his face sunken as the flickering lights from within illuminated the damage inside.

"Vampires can't enthrall other vampires. She must have some of your blood from before the transformation . . ." Alice's words trailed off as she stepped into the entryway.

The cauldron and other items from Alice's workbench were strewn across the stone floor. The hourglass shattered as its sands spewed into the crevasses of the stone floor. The wine presses smashed. The vats run through with the grape stompers. The bottles awaiting a trip to Ez's place all broken. The once pristine cellar was now the latest victim of the Savinos' wrath.

Alice entered with a horrified expression on her face.

"Alice, I'm—" Hugo started. "I'm so sorry. I thought it was you. There were panicked knocks, and your reflection said you were in a panicked state."

Alice surveyed the damage. Pages torn out of her grimoire and tossed all over. Her apothecary cabinet emptied and contents spilled out. She bent down and picked up one of the cracked mortars Hugo had given her as a Christmas gift.

Hugo lingered over the barren opening in the stone wall, once the hiding spot of The Lovers' Kiss. "She said she couldn't find the spell."

"I moved it," Alice responded as she turned her attention to the back corner and her special wine rack. The rack containing over a dozen bottles of *The Lovers' Kiss* brewed potion lay on the stone floor, each bottle smashed.

"She took one. She showed it to me and took it," Hugo said. "What about the Raskins? Are they okay?"

"They're fine. I held off Sebastian. I took out two of their ghouls."

“They wanted us separated,” Hugo said. “I’m sorry. I’m so, so sorry.”

“It’s not your fault. Grab your stake.” Alice said, turning to Hugo. Revenge spewed forth from her eyes. “This ends tonight.”

“Time to storm the castle?” Hugo asked.

“It’s time to storm the fucking castle!”

CHAPTER 22

STORMING THE CASTLE

Alice bolted out of the front door onto the darkened porch. She tugged and jostled the brim of her hat to make sure it was snug on her head. Hugo followed, slamming the door shut. He held the wooden stake from the vampire hunter's kit upside down in his right hand, ready to strike at any given moment.

"They have to know we're coming," Hugo said as he pulled on his black leather jacket.

"Good," Alice responded. "They better be ready for a fight."

"Two ghouls down, right?"

"Yep. Two left."

"Two of us against the four of them. I like those odds," Hugo said. "What about the mind control?"

"Don't make eye contact, and you'll be fine."

"Oh, I'm going to," Hugo said with a smirk as he turned his head toward Alice. "I want to see the horror in her eyes as I drive this stake through her heart."

Alice smiled back at Hugo.

They left a trail of ghostly clouds of vapor from their breath as they charged down the gray steps and across the yard. The sky was dark, only illuminated by the waning moon. Ravenhill Drive was silent, except for the two pairs of feet trudging through the frosting grass in the cold autumn air.

Alice snapped her fingers, and the Savinos' porch light went out. They stomped up the white steps and into the darkness. They cared not for stealth or a tactful approach. They wanted to announce their presence. Alice wanted to let them know their reckoning was coming. She raised her hand to fling the door wide open.

"Wait," Hugo said as he blocked her hand. "Let me go first."

"I can handle it," Alice said.

"I know, but this could be an ambush. What if they're waiting for you to enter and then try to bite you? What at they going to do to me . . . turn me into a double vampire?"

"Good point."

Hugo approached the door, readying himself in a fighting stance. He held the stake shoulder high, primed and ready to strike. "I can smell them in there."

He took two quick breaths and gave a nod. Alice snapped her fingers to unlock the door. Hugo lifted his hind leg, lurched forward, and kicked the door wide open.

The house was dark. Alice could only see the faint outlines of the inhabitants inside. Multiple pairs of eyes, more than the expected four, leered back at them through the darkness. The sounds of growling and snarling emanated from within. The house was full of vampires.

"There's more than four," Alice said with a high-pitched panic in her voice.

"Good. I love a line brawl," Hugo said.

He charged inside with a barbaric yell, the wooden stake held high. He made it two steps before he was confronted by a frenzied vampire trying to claw at his neck. Hugo tugged at the vampire's clothing to pull him off balance. He flung the attacking vampire against the wall, knocking down a few decorations. With a seamless motion, he drove the wooden stake into the vampire's chest. The vampire screeched as he turned to ash and dust.

"One," said Hugo.

The next vampire closed in behind Hugo. He grasped around Hugo's torso and flung him over his shoulder. Hugo groaned as he slammed face first onto the ground. The vampire climbed on top, biting toward his neck. Alice snapped her fingers, conjuring a flaming purple ball of arcane energy. She entered the house and flung it at the vampire.

It exploded in an array of arcane magick. The vampire wailed in pain, falling off Hugo. Hugo rolled over and stabbed the vampire in the chest, reducing him to dust.

"Two," Alice said.

The next vampire charged down the hallway, her fangs elongated and screeching. Alice threw another ball of arcane energy, hitting her square in the chest. She fell backward, writhing in pain on the ground. Hugo jumped up, moving to finish the job.

Two vampires ran in from the living room, tackling Hugo. Alice's stomach twisted in knots at the sound of Hugo screaming in agony as his ribs crashed into the wall. Her heart thumped against her chest.

Without hesitation, she attacked with two more purple spheres of arcane energy. One struck a vampire in the head, knocking him to the ground. The purple sphere hit the vampire in the shoulder, momentarily pulling him off Hugo.

Hugo clutched his ribs and stabbed the dazed vampire in the chest, turning him to dust. Hugo twirled around, jabbing the vampire on the ground.

"This is why I wanted to go first," Hugo said.

He twisted and struck the other vampire writhing on the ground behind him, reducing her to only a trail of dust. The hallway was clear.

"Two minutes for boarding," Alice said with a smirk. "Five for fighting."

"Why, Ms. Primrose, are you flirting with me?" Hugo asked with a half-smile. He stood up, wiping the sweat off his brow.

"Just a bit of foreplay, dear." She blew him a kiss before biting her lips.

Seeing Hugo charge into the house, fighting, sweating, his hair a mess, breathing heavily . . . She was seeing Hugo in a new light. No longer the compassionate lover, but a force of power and aggression. Her stomach fluttered. Her body tingled. Her muscles tightened. It unlocked something deep within. Something . . . primal.

The stairs thundered as three more vampires tumbled down.

Focus!

"Get behind me." Hugo wrapped an arm around her, pulling Alice behind him.

Hugo's hand placed on her waist ignited a flame throughout her whole body, causing a yearning for him as he rushed past. He stood between Alice and the vampire onslaught.

Touching my hip isn't helping.

Alice launched a few more flames toward the descending vampires. The wood railing exploded as the arcane spheres struck against it, sending the vampires recoiling in fear at the flying splinters.

"Watch it with the splinters!" Hugo yelled as he braced himself.

"Sorry," Alice said.

The advancing vampire was met with a swift and powerful motion as Hugo slammed the vampire against the wall. Continuing his counter attack, Hugo drove the stake into her chest. Another vampire turned to dust.

The next vampire slashed Hugo across the neck, leaving a streak of blood as one fingernail dug into him. Hugo recoiled in pain, gripping his wound with his open hand.

Hugo slugged the vampire in the face, knocking him back into the other descending one. It was only a moment as the now lead vampire rose and lunged for Hugo's neck. The vampire crashed Hugo into the wall. The shock knocked the wooden stake free from his hand. Hugo gasped for air as the vampire crushed his neck.

The last vampire on the steps leapt over the railing, knocking Alice to the ground. Her hat flew off and rolled down the hallway. He straddled her, his knees pinning her arms to the ground.

"They said we could do whatever we wanted to you," the vampire growled as he leaned in.

The heat from his breath washed over her. Horror filled Alice's eyes as his elongated fangs drew closer. Alice kicked and shimmied, struggling to free herself. His weight was too much.

"Hugo, get him off of me!" Alice shouted.

He didn't reply. She couldn't see him, only the sounds of him gasping and gurgling for air. The sound of knocking against the wall, like feet kicking, was the only response. Hugo never answered.

"You should see what they're doing to your boyfriend. Won't be long now," the vampire taunted.

Alice screamed once more, "Hugo!"

There was no response, only the sound of a body slamming into the wall.

"Do you know what I want to do to you?" the vampire asked Alice as he leaned in closer. "I bet you taste sweet."

He lurched forward, driving his fangs at her neck. Alice narrowed her eyes and snapped her fingers. The splinters shot up into the vampire's back. He reeled backward, letting out a howl. Alice snapped her fingers again, driving the splinters into his heart.

His face contorted as his body turned to ash and disappeared. The pile collapsed onto Alice, covering her in the dusty remains of her vampire attacker.

"Disgusting!" Alice yelled.

She snapped her fingers, and the ash particles scattered away from her. She rose to her feet.

She snapped her fingers again. The wooden stake flew into her awaiting hand.

"Hey, you," Alice said to the vampire.

Her words drew his attention, but he still held onto Hugo's neck.

She continued, "Catch."

Alice snapped once more to produce a new arcane flame and hurled it toward the vampire. It struck him in the face. Hugo fell to the ground as the vampire relinquished his grip. The momentum forced the vampire backward, slamming it into the wall at the base of the steps.

Alice charged, let out a primal scream, and stabbed the vampire in the chest. He was reduced to dust. Alice collapsed onto the bottom step, away from the pile of ashes, and propped herself against the wall to catch her breath.

Hugo coughed and struggled to breathe. He rolled around on the steps as he soothed his throat and gasped for air.

"Are you okay?" Alice asked.

"Ten-minute game misconduct," Hugo struggled through his coughs. "You're out of the game, buddy."

"I see you haven't lost your sense of humor." Alice chuckled.

"It's undead . . ." Hugo said through his gasps. "Just like me."

"What a night. Any more of them?" She handed Hugo the wooden stake.

Hugo sniffed. "Yeah, I can still smell some."

"Fantastic," Alice said as she stood up. "Let's check upstairs." She extended her hand and helped him to his feet.

Alice snapped her fingers. Her hat flew onto her head. She adjusted the brim, so it was in its proper position.

Hugo arched his eyebrow and gave her a discerning look.

"What?" Alice asked as she gave it a final tug. "I need my hat."

"Do you know how much I love you?" Hugo said with a smile.

Hugo fell forward, catching himself against the wall with his right hand. He was inches from Alice's face, his arm cutting off her escape route.

A shiver ran down to the base of her spine as the internal flame reignited. Alice squirmed in the tight place between the corner and

Hugo's outstretched arm. Her eyes flared. She relished him pinning her against the wall.

Not now!

This was definitely a different side of Hugo—a side she hadn't seen before, but had only heard about in his stories. His aggressive hockey style played out in a hallway battle with vampires. She would have to explore this later when they got home.

She scrunched her eyes as she glared at him. Her smiled faded into pouty disapproval. "How could you think of such a thing at a time like this?"

"I thought you were—"

"Exactly," she cut him off. "I know what you were thinking. Shame on you. Get your hormones and pheromones in check. We have a job to do."

She smiled and winked at him as she ducked under his arm to move past him. She pulled up the hem of her tail coat, so he had to stare at the curves of her hips in the tight leather pants as she ascended the steps.

Hugo chuckled and followed. "Foreplay, indeed."

Alice glanced back at him with a smirk.

They approached an open spare bedroom door. Hugo hurried past Alice as they stepped into the room. It was barren. No furniture, boxes, decor, or knickknacks. Only a rug covered the center of the room.

"What were they doing in here?" he asked.

"We probably don't want to know."

"Let's check the other bedroom."

They closed in on the master bedroom. Alice checked with Hugo. His eyes focused on the antique brass knob.

"Are you ready for this?" Alice asked.

"Not my room. Not my house," Hugo said. "Open it."

Alice snapped her fingers, and the door flew open. Hugo rushed in with Alice following behind.

"They're not here," Hugo said. He kicked over a foot stool. "They're not here."

Alice's heart sank. They were alone in the bedroom. The bed untouched. The furniture in its proper place. Crimson curtains were drawn over the windows, heavy and thick enough to block out the sunlight. Hugo approached and pulled them back. The windows were boarded up so no light could enter.

The bed was meticulously made and flawless. Each fold of the sheets and covers was immaculate. The black and red pillows sat in their proper place. Alice approached the side of the bed. She jerked back the bedcover and sheets, spilling the pillows on to the floor.

"I thought we didn't have time for that?" Hugo joked.

Alice glared at him and didn't respond. He gulped and backed away.

"I thought about returning the favor and trashing her place," Alice said as she pulled the covers completely off the bed. "But I thought of something better. I want to send her a message." She removed two playing cards from her pocket.

"The Queen and King of Spades," Alice said as she placed them on the bed. "I want her to know we were here. In her room. Touching her bed. I want her to question what we did in here."

Hugo strode across the room. Alice recognized the look in Hugo's eyes. It moved beyond flirtatious. He wrapped his arms around her waist and pulled her close to him.

She gasped. He gazed into her emerald green eyes. She melted in his icy blues as his hands traveled down the small of her back. Alice was enthralled by his heightened pheromones, drawing and pulling her closer to him.

"Why let them guess?" he whispered into her ear. "My heart is burning . . . yearning for you right now. Let's remove all doubt."

His words dripped over her like sweet ambrosia, tickling her senses. She wanted him too, but not here. Not in this defiled place he once called home. No. It would have to wait.

"What has gotten into you?" Alice said.

Hugo shook his head, his mouth agape. "I don't know. It's like the anger and rage is fueling everything inside. It's as if all my senses are exploding at once. I'm having a hard time controlling it. My body is calling for you. Is this what it's like to frenzy? Am I frenzying?"

"You're not frenzying. Vampirism heightens everything. It's like pouring gasoline on a candle. It's also what makes nights . . . fun," Alice responded. "Hold it for later. Trust me."

"You're such a tease."

"I know." She grinned at Hugo.

"Come on. Let's check the basement," Hugo said. "I can still smell them. They must be there."

They charged down the steps and back into the hallway. They traveled through the dining room and into the kitchen. No signs of anyone.

Hugo approached the white door leading into the basement. He gripped the brass knob.

Alice nodded.

He flung open the door. The warm, incandescent glow of the basement light greeted them. They used their eyes to communicate with each other to go down, both nodding in agreement. He gave a three count with his fingers, and together they rushed down the stairs.

Hugo descended the steps with Alice following behind him. One of the ghouls stood at attention against the cinderblock wall. It was unmoving, smiling back at them. Hugo charged the ghoul and pinned him against the wall. He brought the wooden stake up to the ghoul's throat.

"Where are they?" Hugo shouted.

The ghoul was silent, smiling back at Hugo.

"Where are they?" Hugo shouted once more at the ghoul, who smiled an unnerving, unwavering grin.

"They won't tell you," Alice said. "She entranced them to not speak."

"If he's no use to us, then what's the point of keeping him alive?" Hugo asked as he readied the stake to strike.

Alice seized Hugo's hand, preventing him from striking. "Because we're not like them. He's not a vampire. He's not attacking us. Let him go."

Hugo grunted, releasing the ghoul who remained still—smiling and smiling. Hugo stormed off around the corner.

Alice bent over and rubbed her hands over her face. She closed her eyes and shook her head. *Why? Why put us through this and not be here?*

"Alice!" Hugo shouted. "Come look at this."

Alice opened her eyes. The basement was barren. Nothing scattered across the gray floors. Nothing stacked up against the cracked cinderblocks. Yet, something was around the corner. Alice kept an eye on the ghoul as she rounded the corner. He didn't move. The ghoul only smiled.

As Alice turned to find Hugo, the sight of a wood door, blackened with iron ornate fixtures, inlaid into the cinderblock wall, greeted her. The last remaining ghoul stood guard with an unnerving, overstretched smile.

"How?" Alice asked.

She didn't recognize the door, but she knew what it held within and where it could lead. She wasn't the only witch who could conjure a door to a secret location.

"I thought you said vampires can't cast magick," Hugo said.

"They can't," Alice said.

She touched the door and tried to pull on the handle. It wouldn't budge. She examined the edge of the cinderblocks around the door. Shock filled her eyes. She recognized the arcane symbols. They were protection symbols, similar to the ones protecting her house.

"How did they do this?" Hugo asked.

"Someone cast it for them," Alice said. She slugged the door with the palm of her hand. "Someone is working for the Savinos."

She hit the door over and over. The blows of her hand echoed in the barren basement, each blow harder than the last. She clenched her teeth.

"Someone betrayed us," Alice continued.

Tears welled in her eyes as she pounded on the door. Her hand numbed and turned red with each blow. The skin scraped and blistered. She didn't care. She was going to either break through this door or break her hand.

Alice flinched and held her breath as Hugo's hand closed around her wrist.

"Hitting it won't open the door," Hugo said.

"No, but it damn well will make me feel better."

Hugo hugged her. She buried her head into his shoulder and sobbed.

"You know who did this, don't you?" Hugo said.

"It can't be true. It can't," Alice cried.

"They didn't give us the hat to let us know they hurt her. They gave it to us so we knew Sam was working for them," Hugo said.

CHAPTER 23

DANCE NIGHT MACABRE

Alice sat in her bay window, the curtains drawn back, observing the Savinos' house. She leaned against the wood frame with her legs outstretched, waiting for any signs of movement. The room was dim, only lit by the flickering of the candelabras resting on the console tables in the hallway, so she could see the outside world clearly. A black shoulder bag rested on the dining table. She was still, except for the rising and falling of her chest as she breathed in and out to calm her nerves.

She was dressed for combat—boots, her leather pants, Victorian style tailcoat hugging around her like a protective suit of armor, and her witch's hat secured on top of her head. She was primed and ready for action. Scouting. Waiting. Eyes focused.

She could see to the street and around the back. If anyone left the house, she would know. The street was quiet. Dark. No movement. The rain drenched night sky cast a dark shadow on Ravenhill Drive. Only the orangish glow of the porch lights pushed back the night sky from engulfing the street with an inky darkness.

Hugo entered from the kitchen carrying two tea cups. He handed Alice the black cup. It was warm to the touch. Steam rose from the dark liquid inside, forming ghostly apparitions against the coolness of the air.

"Thank you," Alice said before taking a sip. The liquid warmed her soul.

"Any changes tonight?" Hugo asked.

"No," Alice said. "It's been three days and nothing. I would expect them to respond by now. Not even during the day. I haven't seen them come or go. No ghouls outside checking on us. They must be using the door in their basement to move in and out. I bet it's connected to their nightclub."

"They can do that?" Hugo asked.

"Yeah. You can create connections between magical spaces. I used to have a connection to Ez's place until . . ." Alice paused, peering deep into the dark liquid of her tea cup. "Until I came here. It's why Ez has to pick up the stuff."

"Maybe you can reconnect them when this is all over."

Alice took a sip. "Maybe."

"What if they up and left?" Hugo asked with a slight hint of hopeful sarcasm. "After all, she didn't find the spell."

"If only." Alice took another sip. She curled and stretched her toes inside the boots. "No, they're waiting for us to make a mistake. We have to be patient."

"Are you sure about this? Is the rain too much? Are you sure you don't want me to go with you?"

"I'll be okay by myself. The rain should provide cover," Alice assured him. "We've run through the scenario. It should work."

"Need I remind you about the last time I ran through a scenario?"

She tilted her head, raising an eyebrow with a sly smile. "The last time you didn't have me," Alice said with a wink. "Besides, I'll have Gwennie to protect me."

Hugo leaned in to kiss her on the cheek. "Be careful."

"I'm always careful—well, most of the time." Alice smirked.

Something in the window caught her attention. A black luxury

SUV pulled in front of the house. Alice straightened. An unknown figure dressed in a black suit got out.

"Must be their driver," Hugo said. "I don't recognize him."

Alice remained silent. Her eyes focused on his every move. The driver opened an umbrella and strolled up the sidewalk to the Savinos' house.

"This is it," Alice said.

Alice handed the cup to Hugo before standing. She seized the strap and flung the bag over her head and shoulder.

"Everything just like we talked about. Nothing more."

"Deal." Alice headed for the back door.

In one swift motion, Hugo clasped her hand, instantly halting their progress. Alice turned back to face him, her eyebrows shooting upward in surprise at his unexpected grasp. He rushed in and wrapped his arms around her waist, drawing her to him. He leaned in and kissed her on the lips. The passionate embrace was like two lovers familiarizing themselves as if it was the first time. She wrapped her arms around his back, pulling herself even closer. She wanted it to last forever, but she needed to hurry. They pulled back.

Hugo's eyes glistened as his icy blues gazed once more at hers. "I love you. Now go get them."

She winked at him, tracing her fingers along his back and across his chest as she pulled away.

"Gwennie!" Alice shouted and then whistled. "Time to go."

The grayish-white broomstick floated into the dining area from the living room. Alice turned and left through the kitchen and out the back door with the broomstick following behind.

Alice snapped her fingers and darkened the area in the backyard. The air was cold and damp. The rain was pouring harder than she'd like. The drips of water splattered on her hat and coat. She swung her legs over the broomstick and settled into the worn, leather brown seat.

Her fingers wrapped around the gnarled grooves of the handle. With a push off from her feet and a gentle pull of the handle, they rose to the top of the house. Alice peered over the gabled points of her folk Victorian home, as she waited in the shadows for the emergence of the Savinos.

Sylvia proceeded down the walkway side by side with Sebastian as he held an umbrella over both of them. The driver followed behind. Sebastian held the car door open and closed it once Sylvia entered. He proceeded to the other side, while the driver climbed into the driver's seat. After a moment, the SUV drove off.

Alice's eyes traced every step and every move. Her breath quickened. Her heart raced. Her mind was ready. She pulled back on the handle, giving a slight jump, and the broomstick took off into the rainy night sky.

Alice followed the vehicle as it made its way through the town center, out past Wildgrove Park and onto US-42. It picked up speed. Alice matched it.

A vast number of barren farmer fields, once dense with corn, streaked by as Alice continued her pursuit. The combination of wind and rain splashed against her face. Water dripped into her eyes. It burned as it forced the sweat into her eyes.

She wiped her face against her arm sleeve, but only briefly. She didn't want to lose sight of the black SUV below her. She tilted her head forward, using the brim of her hat to help shield herself. She dug the heels of her boots into the foot pedal for support. She rose higher into the night sky. The low-hanging clouds shrouded her movement.

The SUV turned onto the highway and headed for Columbus. Alice knew exactly where the SUV was going, where she had hoped it was going. She leaned in lower to the broomstick.

"You're doing great, Gwennie," Alice said. "Keep it up."

Darkness faded, replaced with an eerie orange glow as if a great fire rose up to combat the rain. The lights of the city came into view. Houses gradually replaced the farmers' fields and then office buildings. The SUV picked up speed. Alice and Guinevere fell behind.

"Come on, girl. A little more." Alice leaned in closer, her chin nearly touching the rain-soaked handle. "Give me just a little more."

The broomstick shook. It pushed itself as hard as it could. The broomstick fish-tailed back and forth as it struggled to match the speed.

Alice pulled up on the broom handle, slowing their speed. The SUV sped away. Alice leaned back, giving Guinevere a reprieve.

She patted the handle. "You did good. Don't worry; you did good," Alice said. "We know where they're going. We'll have to meet them there. Ready?"

The broomstick bobbed up and down as if to answer *yes*.

"Let's go," Alice said as she leaned forward.

They took off.

Alice journeyed across the city, hiding in the clouds and away from prying eyes. Cars and other vehicles populated the freeways below. The streets were quieter, but still had far more activity than she was used to in Newbury Grove. She rose as high as she could, without getting completely enveloped. She had a maximum height she liked to fly, and this was pushing her limits.

Alice recognized landmarks as she worked her way to her destination. Familiar streets led to freeways. The buildings of The Ohio State campus appeared. She knew she was close. She cut across campus to High Street. Even the rain drenched night couldn't stop the bustle of High Street as college students and other adults worked their way from bar to bar.

The black building of The Heart and Rose came into view. Alice maneuvered to approach the building from behind to begin her descent. She snapped her fingers to darken the area as much as possible, so she could land undetected on the roof. She stuck out her feet and met the roof below.

She flung her leg over the broomstick and stepped onto the roof. "You did good, Gwennie. You did really good," Alice said in a low voice as she rubbed the top of the handle.

She swung the bag around and flipped the satchel open. She removed a homemade device.

She swung the bag around and flipped the satchel open. She removed a homemade device—a newly carved wooden stake, very similar to the one from her vampire hunting kit, with two metal rings around it. She slid the rings over the front of Guinevere and snapped her fingers. The bolts tightened, but not tight enough to crush the broomstick.

"Bayonet secured," Alice whispered. "Follow me."

Alice jogged over to the fireplace chimney jetting out of the roof with Guinevere trailing behind. With a snap of her fingers, the metal safety guard slid off the chimney, allowing her to peek in.

The chimney was far too small for her to jump through, but large enough for her broomstick. The chimney was mostly for show, and as expected, no fire raged down below. The thundering, dark synthwave beats echoed up through the brick chimney, as well as the sounds of people partying inside.

"Head inside and wait for my signal. Then exit the chimney and get into position. Come get me if we need to abort the plan. Ready?" Alice asked.

The broomstick bobbed up and down.

"All right. I'll see on you the inside." She tapped the brown leather seat.

The broomstick rose and descended into the fireplace chimney.

Alice flung open her black bag. It contained another homemade stake, a few vials of her blue potion, a small pouch of spell components, and a metal flask—all instruments used to fight vampires. She said a few words of the arcane language and snapped her fingers. A dark cloud appeared inside the bag, obscuring the contents. To the uninitiated eye, the bag appeared empty.

Alice pulled out the metal flask. She twisted off the top and drank the entire contents. Alice moved to the side of the roof and placed her hands on the ledge. She searched her surroundings. No one was paying attention to her. Various inebriated people yelled to each other as they hopped from bar to bar along the busy street out front. Others ran as the rain drenched the street.

The building on the other side was dark and unoccupied. The side street below was empty, perfect to make an unseen entrance. She closed her eyes, took a deep breath, and leapt over the side. She stepped down, as if descending invisible stairs, to the ground below. Alice scanned up and down the side street, making sure no one was coming for her. Satisfied, she made her way around the corner.

She pulled her hat low, hiding her face and eyes from any onlookers. A few people left The Heart and Rose bar, stumbling as they ventured down the sidewalk. Alice grabbed the closing door. She pulled the door back and was met with the overwhelming beats of the rhythmic music from within. It was dark inside; flashing lasers and pulsating lights cast minimal light onto the dance floor. Alice took a deep breath and entered.

"Five dollars," the doorman yelled over the sounds.

Alice raised her head to look him in the eyes. "I believe your boss is expecting me."

The doorman pinched the microphone clipped to his shirt. "She's here," he said into it.

There was a pause. The music blared, pulsed, and echoed through the building.

"Let me see inside the bag," he continued.

Alice opened and presented it to him, hoping he found an empty bag. Alice took in a sharp breath as her heart beat faster. His hands hovered over the opening for a moment. Her heart skipped a beat.

The doorman lowered his hands to his sides and nodded his head as if he was satisfied with the contents. "Please enter. Mrs. Savino has been expecting you."

Alice exhaled. She closed the bag and entered deeper into the nightclub. She maneuvered around the dancing bodies—obstacles put on the black and white checkerboard dance floor to keep her from her intended target. Alice scanned the room, constantly checking for any signs of trouble. The thick crimson curtains covered the windows. Lights from the bar provided little relief from the darkness. The mixed crowd of various ages and genders focused their eyes on her as she weaved her way through.

They didn't stop. Each one smiled as they spotted Alice, taking great glee in seeing her. A few showed their fangs as they moved their hips and bodies back and forth to the rhythm of the pulsating music.

Some made eye contact with Alice and then bit down on the neck of their human dancing partners, indulging themselves. The vampires released themselves from their sanguine kisses, their mouths dripping with blood. Two streaks of crimson red flowed down their dancing partners' necks like tears. Their enthralled eyes glazed over as they swayed with the beats of the music.

Alice stayed on her toes, putting all her weight forward to keep herself ready for action. Her body tightened, and her breath shortened the deeper she entered the nightclub. Alice constantly swiveled her head around to keep an eye out for any vampire brave enough to be the first to attack. She thrust her hand into her bag, wrapping her fingers around the makeshift wooden stake.

Alice was surrounded by vampires and humans under the vampires' mind control.

The crowd formed a circle around her, entrapping her. Alice stopped and twirled around. Her path to the front door was blocked off. The vampires kept their distance as if ordered to hold back.

The back of Alice's right heel twitched, sending small reverberations up her leg. She exhaled to steady herself, but the leg continued to twitch. The hair on her arms stood up. A chill ran down her spine. A small bead of sweat rolled down the back of her neck. She was losing her cool.

Focus. Alice went to her one source of peace, the one thought to calm her nerves and give her the strength to continue—Hugo. She exhaled slowly.

Two figures stood at the balcony railing, lording over the dance floor below. Their silhouettes were unmistakable. The Savinos stood high in their court, glaring at her, controlling what happened next. Sylvia tapped her fingers on the railing and then raised her hand. The music grew louder. The beats more oppressive. The sounds of synthetic drums pounded Alice's senses. It drowned out her thoughts. The crowd blurred. She was losing track of her surroundings.

Focus.

Alice raised her arms. "You wanted my attention. Well, you got it," she shouted. "Here I am."

The Savinos didn't move. The circle closed in. Her throat tightened as if the bodies were suffocating her. She shifted her feet, ready to make a retreat. She moved her head back and forth, keeping sight of all angles around her. The darkness shrouded their bodies in shadows; only faint outlines against the flashing light showed.

The vampires and enthralled humans closed in. Their bodies continued to sway with hypnotic motions to the beats of the music. Some smiled. Some opened their mouths to display their fangs.

"I thought you wanted to talk!" Alice shouted.

Sylvia tapped the railing. The circle closed in on Alice, now within an arm's length. She spun around, keeping track of everyone close to her.

She gave a thought to pulling out the stake, but something much more explosive might be called for to clear them away from her. Her heart pounded as if it was going to burst through her chest. She couldn't breathe. Any moment, one could lash out, and then it would be a feeding frenzy to tear her apart.

Run. Get out. Now!

Alice raised a foot, ready to ascend to the sky and make a hasty retreat. The vampires wiggled closer, almost on top of her. Their breath whispered against her, a chilling warning of how quickly things could escalate. Alice released the stake and pulled her hand out of the bag. She snapped her fingers and conjured two flames of arcane energy. They bathed the area in a purple glow.

"Enough!" Sylvia shouted.

The crowd backed away, but still maintained their circle around Alice. The music stopped, a relief to Alice's ears.

"Have you come to surrender?" Sylvia asked.

"I've come to negotiate," Alice said.

Everyone else laughed, their laughter echoing throughout the bar.

"What do you have to negotiate with?" Sylvia asked.

"I know you didn't find it," Alice answered. "You'll never find it without me."

The clacking of Sylvia's nails tapping on the railing filled the silence as it permeated through the room. "I'll tear your house apart until I do. My little pet will let me in again. He's a rather good kisser."

Alice's nose flared. *She's trying to get to you. Don't give in.*

Alice asked, "Who said it was in my house?"

Sylvia stopped her tapping. She furled her eyebrows, her eyes opening wide. "You're bluffing."

"Are you willing to risk everything on your belief that I'm bluffing? It's so close. Right there in your grasp for the taking . . . yet so far away. I have friends. Well-connected friends. It could be anywhere. Once again, you were close, and it slipped through your fingers."

Sylvia stood in silence, unmoving. She gripped the railing, squeezing it. Sebastian leaned over to whisper in her ear.

Sylvia raised her hand and slammed it down. "Fine. Name your price."

"Come down here, and let's talk like two adults, but first, tell your goons to back away," Alice commanded.

Sylvia snapped her fingers, and the crowd pulled back.

Alice dissipated her arcane flames. She breathed a sigh of relief. "Come on down. Let's make a deal."

Sylvia and Sebastian retreated away from the railing, disappeared momentarily, and reappeared descending the steps. The crowd parted, filling in behind them, as they approached. Alice could see them with more clarity. They donned matching outfits—crimson Victorian swallow-tail coats which hugged their well-defined torsos.

The black lapels and cuffs matched their pants. Sylvia wore a white shirt while Sebastian wore a black one.

"You have my attention, witch," Sylvia said. "Name your price."

"I want you gone. All of you. Your whole colony of vampires. Gone," Alice said.

"I rather like it here. Newbury Grove could be a wonderful home for us vampires. A perfect seat for my new empire," Sylvia said.

"What do you say to those demands, witch?" Sebastian asked.

"Then you get nothing," Alice answered.

Sebastian rubbed the left side of his chest. "I haven't forgotten what your boyfriend did to me. Maybe, as part of negotiations, we ask to return the favor. What do you say, my love?"

Sylvia smiled wide enough to expose her vampire fangs. "I think it would only be fair. A stab for a stab. And I assure you my dear Sebastian won't miss . . . unlike my little pet. Of course, there's always the other option. Off with his head."

They chuckled.

Alice narrowed her eyes. She pulled back her shoulders and puffed out her chest. "Leave him out of this. You've already done enough to him. This is between you and me."

Sylvia and Sebastian laughed.

"You think it's only between us? Oh, you poor, poor child. This war has raged for centuries. There was an uneasy peace. I'm the one fanning the flames. I'm the one seizing control. This is my opportunity to be queen of a new empire—a vampire empire—with my king by my side," Sylvia said. "We will rule together."

Sylvia and Sebastian locked eyes and smiled as they held hands.

"We offered you a position in our new empire once," Sebastian said. "You should have accepted it. I take it you found our lovely gift in the basement." He smiled a devilish grin.

Alice checked her surroundings. The circle of vampires held back. She turned back to the Savinos. Her eyes narrowed.

"This is my home. Those people are my friends. What makes you think I'll give them up to you?" Alice asked. "This is my life."

"*Life?*" Sylvia asked. "Life is death's playground, and I'm merely one of death's instruments. I've seen what you call life. Torment. Torture. Destruction. Grief. Loss. Acts all done in the name of what you call life. Under my empire, life will take a new meaning. Life shall be everlasting."

Sylvia motioned to the vampires around her and continued, "We need humans to exist. We'll be their rulers. Sympathetic rulers. But those humans will have a new life. A life free from want. Free from desire. A good life."

Alice clutched her fists. She turned a shoulder toward Sylvia. She dragged her foot back and shifted her weight forward.

Sylvia continued, "Just think. We're here, right here, right now because of one witch so many years ago. All she had to do was grant immortality to a king. But because she was so shortsighted, we're standing here. Many have fought. Many have died. Sebastian and I have killed quite a few . . . You aren't immune from this war yourself. It's bigger than us, but we have an opportunity. With that spell of yours, we could end years of suffering and bloodshed. Well, hopefully not all bloodshed."

The vampires laughed.

"What makes you think this one spell will end it all?" Alice asked.

"Because I know the spell transcends death itself. I may be undead, but we aren't immortal. With the spell, we—my king and myself—we can truly become immortal," Sylvia answered. "Now give it to me, or the streets of Newbury Grove will run red with blood."

"I'll stop you," Alice said. She removed the wooden stake, ready to strike at any vampire brave enough to test her resolve.

A few vampires rushed in front of Sylvia and Sebastian, blocking Alice's path of attack.

"Do you think you're going to stake all of us with one little toothpick?" Sylvia asked.

Alice yelled out, hoping Gwennie would hear her cue, "I'm *ready* to stake each and every last one of you. Especially you, your highness."

Everyone laughed—Sylvia and Sebastian, the vampires—everyone except Alice.

"Look around you. You're surrounded. No one is coming. You're alone, you little witch." Sylvia took a step closer to Alice. Her eyes full of rage. Her fangs elongated.

Alice bent her knees, ready to jump. "Who said I'm alone? I'd look up if I were you."

Sylvia stepped back and frantically scoured the ceiling. She gasped as an object cloaked in shadows appeared at the railing where she once stood. Waiting high above was Alice's broomstick. Guinevere lurched forward at lightning speed.

"Sebastian!" Sylvia cried out.

Armed with its wooden bayonet, it shot straight for Sylvia's heart. Sylvia tried to move, but she was trapped by the crowd of other vampires.

"No!" Sebastian shouted as he jumped in front of Sylvia. He shielded her as Guinevere pierced the wooden bayonet into Sebastian's back and retreated backward.

Sylvia held Sebastian as they collapsed to the ground. They locked eyes one final time as he slowly turned to white ash. Fear and horror dominated her face, causing it to contort in shock. Her mouth gasped as if to let out a scream, but she was silent.

Sebastian's legs and arms disappeared as his body was erased from the world. His eyes rolled and head tilted back. One final expression of agony appeared on his face before he was gone.

Sylvia held out her hands. The empty fingers, once cradling Sebastian, trembled and curled into half-closed fists. She let out a barbaric yawp and then shrieked, "Kill her!"

The vampires rushed in. Alice leapt into the air and climbed higher as if she were ascending an unseen staircase. Streaks of purple bombarded the vampires below. They were knocked unconscious from the explosions of arcane energy.

Some of the vampires grabbed Sylvia, lifted her up, and whisked her away. Sylvia tugged and pulled in protest as she screamed and yelled.

"Sebastian!" Sylvia yelled. "My love . . ."

Alice used her magick to fling the stake at Syliva. A vampire jumped in front of Sylvia, shielding her from the attack.

The stake didn't kill the vampire; it merely lodged into his arm. Alice followed with a ball of arcane flames. Explosions erupted around Sylvia as the flames struck vampires, knocking them to the ground. They weren't dead, but seriously wounded. Surrounded by chaos, Sylvia's bodyguards grabbed her by the arms and dragged her away.

She screamed out, "No! Take me back to him."

They ignored her pleas, and they disappeared into the hallway.

The remaining vampires tried to get at Alice. They clawed at the space above them, but she was well out of their grasp. They threw bottles, glasses, and other objects at her. Alice dodged them, continuing to climb higher, running circles around the space above the nightclub dance floor.

Alice pelted them with the arcane flames. Some burst into ash as they struck the vampires in the head with enough force to blow it off. It was a mad scramble for salvation, and Alice was playing the role of the destructor.

Guinevere circled toward Alice, ready to pick up its new rider. Alice took a few steps and leap frogged over the broomstick and onto the seat. Guinevere buckled as she caught Alice. She flung a few more flames at the vampires below.

With Sylvia gone and most of the vampires scrambling, there wasn't much more she could do. They spun around, searching for an exit. The doors were too close to the ground for their retreat; they needed to be higher. Alice threw a purple flame at one of the crimson curtains. The window shattered in an explosion of glass and fabric.

Alice leaned forward and flew out the window. She made a hasty retreat for home.

CHAPTER 24

THE COUNTESS AND THE TAVERN KEEPER

"Let me see!" Sylvia shouted as she pushed her way through the small assortment of vampire bodyguards. Streaks of black ran down her face as her tears mixed with her mascara. Fury and anger blazed from her furrowed brow. "Let me see! That's an order from your queen."

Her wall of defense parted, and she was free to return to the scene where her life shattered. The spot where Sebastian, her lover—her former lover—her King was slain. She rushed down the hallway back onto the dance floor.

She stopped. All eyes fell on her as their Queen was rendered silent. The vampires and their ghouls took steps away from the now empty spot where Sebastian once stood.

Sylvia covered her mouth with her left hand and stretched out her right. Extending it into the void, hoping to pull him back to life as she moved closer to the scene of the crime. She stopped and knelt to the ground on both knees. She sat back on the heels of her feet.

Her hand trembled and twitched. She needed to caress the spot he once stood, but her body held her back. If she didn't confirm his absence by touching the emptiness, then he'd still be there. Somewhere. At least she hoped.

A tear left a black, viscous trail down her pale face. Her sapphire blue eyes rendered a bloodred to match her crimson jacket. Her hand hovered over the spot. She dared not touch the emptiness. The once raucous nightclub was silent.

Sylvia pressed down on two of the cold checkerboard tiles where Sebastian previously stood. She dragged her fingers across the floor, hoping, praying, she would find some remnant of Sebastian. There was only emptiness.

Sebastian Savino was gone.

Sylvia closed her eyes, seeking solace in her memories. She wanted to see Sebastian once more time. She needed to see him again.

~

SYLVIA STOOD in the dark hallway leading to her grand, illustrious ballroom below. She hid in the shadows, listening as the sounds of a string quartet and other revelry found their way up the staircase and into her ears. She detested music and sound. She demanded silence from her servants and caretakers of her French countryside manor. However, tonight was different.

She adjusted her masquerade mask. Its crimson color matched her flowing gown. Her heart raced. She had turned many humans to vampires, but this was different. Tonight was the night she would lose her lover and gain a partner.

The clock struck midnight. The string quartet silenced their bows. Twelve gongs echoed throughout the hallway. Sylvia straightened herself, ready to proceed for her grand entrance.

A voice shouted from down the staircase, "Ladies and gentlemen of the Court of the Crimson Rose, the Countess welcomes you to her Midnight Rose Ball. I now present to you, our leader. The illustrious grand lady of the manor. Our Countess. Sylvia Dubois."

She was summoned on cue. The darkness gave way to a brilliant light. It took Sylvia a moment to focus as her eyes strained, but it soon became very clear. She stood at the edge of the staircase to examine her small empire below.

The ballroom was rectangular with an ornately decorated, cavernous ceiling inscribed with red and gold filigree. The ballroom stretched up to the second floor where Sylvia stood overlooking her court below.

The grand staircase split into two as it descended to the black and white checkerboard ballroom floor. Red carpet decorated the center of the stairs. Red drapery slung over the marble handrails. Large windows lined the long back wall. Their red curtains were pulled back to provide an excellent view of the darkness outside.

Chandeliers provided most of the light, filling every space of the room. They were made of dark cast-iron, twisted and molded into sharp angular points like fangs. The largest chandelier held the privilege of being placed in the center of the room. Red wax dripped from the candles like gnarled fingers reaching down for the guests below.

Candelabras and other candlesticks were strategically placed around the room to illuminate all the dark corners, so no deed would go unnoticed to the Countess's watchful eyes. Vases of red and black roses filled in every available spot along the walls. Waiters carried trays of black goblets and waited for the guests to partake in the drink.

The women were dressed in the most exquisite gowns—a menagerie of various shades of blacks, deep reds, purples, and dark greens. Spider-web like lace crawled over their arms and chests, exposing the right amount of skin to be seductive, but concealing enough to tantalize the mind. Their ballgown skirts floated in the air as they moved with grace and elegance. Their hair meticulous and pulled back to show the curves of their faces and jawlines.

A test for her lover—her tavern keeper. She scanned the faces. She didn't see the masque of her tavern keeper near the beautiful women. He passed. Now test two.

The men wore more subdued clothing to not stand out in the crowd. They wore black waistcoats with matching vests and pants. They lacked any identifying marks. Face to toes, they wore all black. Outside of hair and physical height, it was difficult to tell them apart.

Everyone wore black masques, except for one. The target she sought below. Her prize. Her lover. Her future partner.

A tall, muscular man weaved his way through the crowd. He never took his eyes off her at the top of the grand staircase. He wore a white masque and black clothing, except for a red vest. He moved closer to her. She smiled.

Sylvia took a deep breath and started down the grand staircase. She was a sight of wonder, beauty, grace, and elegance. Her strawberry blonde hair was parted to the side to expose the right side of her face. Her sleeveless, red, flowing gown hugged the curves of her body before billowing out like melted candle wax. She commanded the attention of all eyes in the room.

Her long legs appeared from behind the billowy gown with each step before being enveloped by the skirt once again. Each step was made with the grace and poise of a dancer. She made no noise as she descended to her subjects. Her fingers lightly touched the drapery on the railing, not for support, but to trace an invisible line with her fingertips.

The men plucked the red and black roses from the vases and surrounded her as she descended the staircase. She scoffed at their offerings and turned them away. Dejected, they faded back into the crowd. She worked through the congregation of people offering her a rose for a dance. They held the roses in their hands, but she turned everyone away without giving them a second thought.

Her eyes, alert to every detail, scanned the crowd for her tavern keeper. Standing at a distance, the man in the white masque carefully inspected the suitors' attempt to vie for her attention. *Perhaps he's unsure if he wants to partake in his test?*

On and on, Sylvia rejected the offerings of would-be suitors. The tavern keeper plucked a red rose and plunged himself into the crowd.

He worked his way toward her, pushing aside his competition. A passing grade so far.

The masked tavern keeper broke through to the inner circle and stood there, waiting for her to acknowledge his rose. He didn't offer the rose like the others. He held the stem between his teeth. Sylvia stopped in front of the tavern keeper.

Her eyes assessed every part of him, from the white masque to his toes, before they connected with his brown eyes. The tavern keeper didn't hold out his right hand. Instead, he raised his left and waited. She closed her hand around his and leaned in close. She bit the rose stem. He relinquished. Sylvia pulled back with the rose firmly in her mouth.

The string quartet played a waltz. The crowd parted and retreated toward the wall. The floor was theirs and theirs alone. Her tavern keeper took the lead. They moved as one. Their eyes met, aflame with passion, mirroring the intensity of their movements. They spun to the music. He stopped, yet Sylvia continued to spin away.

The tavern keeper held her hand firm and stopped her from spinning off into oblivion. Sylvia's eyes focused and locked onto his. A word didn't need to be uttered. They spoke only in the dark language of desire.

The tavern keeper held the pose, his arm extended firmly into the air. Time stretched endlessly, as if it could have been an eternity or a fleeting moment. Either way, it was torture. Pure torment of her body being separated from her lover. Yet, despite their separation, their eyes locked and their souls intertwined once again.

With a flick of his wrist, she spun back. He caught her against his chest, collapsing his right arm around her waist. Her left arm gracefully wrapped around his shoulders. They continued their waltz. Their bodies intertwined.

The guests disappeared into a blur as if only Sylvia and her tavern keeper were left on the dance floor. Their faces touched. He bit the rose stem. They held it together. They continued their waltz until the string quartet finished in a flurry.

The room broke into applause. Sylvia let go of the rose. She leaned in closer and gave a small kiss to his neck. The tavern keeper shivered, then he pulled back and held the rose in front of her. The Countess gracefully accepted the rose the rose and smelled it, committing the wonderful aroma to memory. She clutched it close to her chest. They locked eyes once again before the Countess turned away.

"Thank you all for attending my ball. Please, enjoy the refreshments and partake in the merriment," she addressed the crowd. "Now if you'll excuse us."

The Countess took the tavern keeper's hand and led him to the grand staircase. She hiked up the stairs, never letting go. They flaunted down the hallway like royalty, their backs straight and chests puffed out. The light faded and darkness enveloped them. There were no candles to light the way. Though it was dark, the Countess knew the way.

She opened a door at the end of the hallway and motioned for him to go inside. Her heart raced with anticipation and delight. Her breaths were short with excitement. She could smell the blood coursing through his veins. She could hear his elevated heart rate, the thumps against his chest. She didn't give a comforting word, only an impish smile. He entered the room, and she followed.

The light of a few candles fought against the darkness, but they could only do so much. The room was grandiose, yet intimate despite its high ceilings. There were no windows. The room was filled with a canopy bed against the back wall and a velvet couch placed near the center of the room. A desk and towering bookshelves filled the side wall. An armoire stood alone against another wall. There was only one door. There was no other escape.

She closed the door behind her and turned the lock. She moved with the grace of a stalking predator. Each step light and with purpose.

She closed in on her evening prey. The light danced and flickered off him. The desire in his eyes from moments ago had faded into something much more fearful, like a frightened animal. The tavern keeper backed away and stumbled onto the couch. She stood over him.

"You passed your test," she said. "You dance well for a tavern keeper."

"You'd be surprised what you can learn from travelers passing through a town," he replied. "Especially from a Countess."

"Oh?" She sat next to him and leaned in closer. "And what exactly have you learned from me?"

"You really love the color red."

The Countess chuckled and whispered into his ear, "I love it more than you know."

She ran her fingers through his dark hair before making her way to the strap around the back of his head. Her fingers followed the path to the velvet mask. She could hear his heart beating faster. The blood coursed through his veins.

"Shhh. It'll be okay," she said to calm his nerves.

It didn't work, as she sensed his heart rate increase.

She pulled back to lift the mask above his head. Her heart fluttered in anticipation as the tavern keeper's rugged face was fully revealed. The Countess held the mask up to the dim light to examine each curve. She studied it for a moment before tossing it behind the couch.

"I don't think you'll be needing this any longer," she said.

Sebastian Savino's breathing labored. She traced his jawline with the back of her hand down to his chin. She gently placed a finger on Sebastian's lips.

"Shush," she said. "It will be over quickly. Enjoy it while you can. Take it all in. Everyone should be as lucky as you."

The Countess removed her masque and gazed into his brown eyes. Her sapphire blues reestablished their connection to his soul, the same connection they had on the dance floor. Sylvia's fingertip traced an invisible path from his lips, down his throat, and over to the place on his neck she had kissed earlier.

She circled the spot continually, like she was committing it to memory. Sebastian gulped. He shifted on the couch. His breathing increased. Each breath was shorter than the last. She paused.

"This is what you want, right?" she asked. "All of this tonight was for you."

"I do," he answered. "Countess, I do want it."

"Excellent," she said as she leaned in closer. "After tonight, we'll no longer be a Countess and a tavern keeper. We shall be a King and Queen. The start of a new empire. Do you want that?

"Yes," he whispered back.

He tilted his head. She kissed his neck again before licking it. Her eyes met Sebastian's one last time, and she smiled. Two sharp fangs elongated from her mouth.

"After tonight, you'll never want or need again," she whispered into his ear. "You'll awaken into a new world where we'll be together. Forever. But first . . ."

She leaned in and placed her lips onto his neck. Each fang pierced deep into his neck. His body twisted and contorted in anguish. Her hand moved across his chest in a feeble attempt to soothe him. She repositioned herself, attempting to ease the transition. She moaned with ecstasy as she drank the blood. His blood. Her lover's blood. Her King's blood.

He crushed the arm of the couch with his grip. His fingernails jabbed into the wood. She yanked his hand away, wrapping her fingers into his. Their hands clasped tight. Sylvia released her bite, satisfied the transformation would commence. Blood dripped down her chin, bringing back memories of the night they first met.

The last thing Sylvia said before Sebastian blacked out and gave up his former life were the words, "I love you."

Sylvia opened her eyes, hoping, begging, praying this would only be a nightmare. Hoping she would wake up and find Sebastian waiting for her. For Sebastian to swoop in and help pick her up off this dance floor, where they would continue with their empire. But there was no Sebastian. Only the scattered ashes of his body.

She snarled, elongating her vampire fangs in anger. She stood and marched down the hall toward a doorway. She descended the steps into the basement of the building, followed by a small assortment of vampiric guards. Streaks of black ran down her face as her tears mixed with her mascara. Fury and anger overtook her eyes. The musty odor of the well-aged basement filled her senses as she breathed deeply with an inner rage.

Embedded into the wall was a wooden door with ornate iron fixtures, similar to the one in their basement. She circled a few times in front of the door. She clenched her fists and breathed deeply. She could only think of Sebastian. His ashes scattered to the wind. She would never see her husband, her lover, her confidant, her King again. Her memories were haunted by the horrified expression on his face as they locked eyes one last time. Her heart raced. Adrenaline pulsated through her body.

"Bring me the bottles. Both of them!" she shouted. "Do it now!" Her voice reverberated off the stone walls.

Her accompanying guards entered the wooden door. They hurried back, carrying two bottles and a glass. Sylvia snatched the glass from one of their hands.

"Pour!" she commanded.

They each poured the contents into the glass. Red wine came out of the bottle labeled *The Lovers' Kiss Hugo & Alice*. Blackish red contents poured out of the second bottle labeled *Blood From My New Pet*. The two liquids sloshed and intermixed until the goblet was nearly full.

Sylvia recited an old, forbidden language, not conjuring the powers of the arcane, but something much darker. She chugged the unholy concoction in one gulp, never stopping for air. Trickles of red liquid dripped down the sides of her mouth. Her eyes dilated. The irises turned red.

"Hear me. Lose yourself in me. Heed my words, my command," Sylvia growled. "I command you, Hugo Dodds. I command you to *kill the witch*."

CHAPTER 25

A GOTHIC PROPOSAL

Clouds swirled like a thick ichor in the night sky, obscuring any light from the moon. The oppressive rain spattered against Alice's face and body. Not a pouring rain, but a steady drip slowly eating away at a soul. Her drenched hat seeped onto her hair. Her tailcoat provided protection from completely soaking her. A late November chill was in the air, biting away at her face and hands as she held onto the flying broomstick.

"Come on, girl, give me a little more," Alice said.

The broomstick fishtailed in the night sky.

"I know. I know. We have to hurry."

For all of Alice's and Hugo's planning, it only half worked. Only one of the Savinos perished on this night. Sylvia most likely had an easy path back to Newbury Grove through her magical room. If only Alice was so lucky. She had to get back before Sylvia could retaliate.

Alice relied on the lights of the cars below to find her way home, not wanting to cast a light in the sky and draw attention to herself. She followed the serpentine like roads as she retreated from the city and into the country. Soon, the treetops of Wildgrove Park appeared and then the orange glow of the town center. A few more turns and the awaiting comfort of her purple house came into view.

She snapped her fingers and dampened the light on the front porch as she landed. She jumped off. Her heart raced, powered by the adrenaline still coursing through her body. Alice twirled around, vigilant and ready for an ambush. There was no movement. No signs of vampires rushing up her porch. An eerie stillness descended on Ravenhill Drive. The only audible sound was rain spattering off the roof and against the wood siding.

Alice gulped and breathed in deeply to calm her nerves. When satisfied she was alone, she produced a brass key from her coat pocket. She inserted the key into the black door and turned the diamond shape knob. Alice gave a whistle to Guinevere and entered the purple house. The broomstick followed behind.

Alice kicked the door shut with her foot as she removed her tailcoat and bag, placing them on the coat rack. She tossed her hat onto the railing newel post and then snapped her fingers. The water disappeared, leaving her hat, coat, and purple hair now dry. Alice glanced down the hallway. Hugo wasn't there to greet her.

"Hugo!" Alice yelled. "Sebastian is dead. Gwennie stabbed him in the heart. They whisked Sylvia away before we could take her out. I'm sure they'll retaliate soon. We need to be ready."

There was no response.

"Hugo?" Alice called once more.

The house was dark. The light from the candles above the fireplace spilled into the hallway, casting a dancing glow on Alice. There was no sound. Alice's heart raced once more. Her eyes acclimated to the darkness, revealing the hidden details of the objects on the console tables lining the hallway. There were still no signs of Hugo. She gulped.

"Hugo, this isn't funny."

She peered into the living room. No signs of Hugo. Alice could hear the beats of her heart in her eyes. She moved down the hallway, taking small steps. She entered the dining area. No one was sitting at the table. She continued into the kitchen. She found only darkness in the empty kitchen.

"Hugo, I'm not in the mood for games!" Alice shouted.

Guinevere bumped against the basement door, catching Alice's attention.

"What is it, girl?"

The broomstick continued bumping against the door.

"Is he down there?"

Guinevere rammed the door twice more before turning to face her witch. Alice approached the door with soft steps, trying not to signal her approach. The flooring creaked and moaned with each step, betraying her position. She was a few feet from the door, reaching out with her hand for the knob.

The door flung open, blocking her view of who exited. A figure grabbed Guinevere, pulling it back behind the door. The crack of wood breaking over a knee filled the hallway.

"No!" Alice said and went for the door.

Someone pulled it back and then forcibly slammed the door into Alice's face, momentarily stunning her.

Alice covered her face with her hands to assess the damage. Nothing was broken, and she wasn't bleeding. The numbness hid the pain. She lifted her face in time to see the figure throw the broomstick down the stairs and slam the door.

"Alice!" Hugo shouted.

As Alice laid her eyes on the outline of Hugo standing before her, her heart skipped a beat and she stood frozen in shock.

"Run!"

Hugo charged her. In the heat of the moment, her mind went blank. Her heart pounded in her chest as her boyfriend charged toward her, leaving her frozen in terror. He wrapped his arms around her, lifting her off the ground. He squeezed her tightly, constricting his arms around her torso. This was no endearing hug. Hugo was trying to crush her ribs.

She struggled to breathe, each gasp for air more odious than the last. She couldn't move. Her hands were caught between her body and Hugo. She couldn't use them to call forth the magick to save herself. The muscles in his forearms tightened to constrict her further. She let out a gasp. He slammed her body into the hallway wall, knocking over the console table. Its contents spilled onto the floor.

"Why?" Alice mustered through tears and the pain.

"I can't stop it. I'm being forced to watch while she's controlling me. You have to stop me."

He reared back and slammed Alice once more into the wall. She winced in pain. Alice gasped for air as his arms constricted her further. Hugo lifted her up and reared back.

Alice wiggled a hand free and snapped her fingers. The amethyst rock flew from one of the console tables and struck Hugo. He grimaced in pain as the rock shot at him with great force, causing him to lower Alice, but not to let go.

"Do it again," Hugo said. "Harder."

"I can't," Alice struggled to say. "I won't."

"Harder!"

"If I can get to my bag—" Alice started.

"Hit me again!"

With a swift motion, he effortlessly hoisted her over his shoulders. Alice's heart raced as she plummeted toward the floor behind Hugo. Alice tensed up, expecting to hit the floor, but hovered in midair. Hugo reared back and tightened his grip, preparing to slam Alice to the ground. She snapped her fingers once more. Two more rocks flew at great speed, striking Hugo in the back. He yelled in pain as he released her. Alice fell to the ground, catching herself with her hands. As she struggled to catch her breath, Hugo's towering figure loomed over her.

"Run. Get away!" Hugo yelled.

Alice rolled away from Hugo and sprang to her feet. She dashed into the living room through the second entryway. Hugo was right behind her.

Alice snapped her fingers. Her black shoulder bag flew into the living room. Hugo snared Alice's arm. She twisted to the side, freeing herself from his grasp.

The momentary deflection allowed Hugo to close in on Alice. He bent down, landed his shoulder into her stomach, and tackled her to the ground. The hardwood floor knocked what wind she had regained out of her. She gasped and winced in pain. It was all a blur. She couldn't think or act or do anything.

The black bag landed next to them on the floor. Hugo grabbed the bag and smashed the contents on the floor. He jumped on top of her, straddling her legs.

He held down her arms and placed his hands over hers. Each finger interlocked with hers so she couldn't call forth any magical abilities. She tried to move. She tried to wiggle free, but she couldn't. Hugo's red eyes bore down onto her own with an intensity that sent a chill down her spine, filling her with abject terror as her boyfriend—her lover—pinned her to the floor.

Alice couldn't breathe. She couldn't think. Her eyes were filled with terror and fear, but she never looked away from Hugo. She didn't know if Gwennie was okay, hurt, or even alive. Alice was helpless.

Time froze. The ticking of the grandfather clock disappeared. She could only hear her heart beating against her chest. No one was coming to rescue her. It was only Hugo and herself.

Hugo opened his mouth and, in a display of intimidation, showed his elongated fangs. Alice tried to kick, but couldn't under his weight. Hugo bent down, going for her throat. As his body lifted, Alice seized the opportunity to rotate her hips and free one of her legs. Using her knee as a shield, she jabbed it into his stomach to keep Hugo from getting closer.

Hugo pressed down, but Alice held him firm. He wouldn't release his hands, so she dug her knee further into the center of his torso. They were locked in a stalemate, each trying to position for leverage in the ensuing battle.

"Hugo, please. Please stop," Alice pleaded.

"I can't. She has control."

"I don't want to hurt you." Tears streamed down her cheeks as his pair of once icy blue eyes bore down on her, now in a haunting shade of crimson red.

"It's okay. You have to."

Alice shook her head. "No."

"You have to. She won't stop. I can't stop until you're dead. You have to do it." He put pressure on her as he leaned forward.

A pain shot through her as her hip and leg twisted.

"No. No. NO. There must be another way."

"There isn't. It's okay. Trust me. It's okay."

Alice sobbed, struggling to find the words. "I can't. Don't make me."

"This is how I win. It's my choice." A tear fell from Hugo's eyes onto Alice. "I was told by the fortune teller I needed to make a choice . . . and I'm making it. This is how I beat it. This is how I win."

Alice was silent. She struggled to find the words, but they failed her. She knew what Hugo was going to ask of her, but she didn't have the strength to do it. She couldn't do it. She refused, yet she didn't know what else to do.

"It's on the coffee table," Hugo said.

Alice searched for the dreaded object, but only found the underside of the table.

"I think I can try to let go of your hand if I concentrate hard enough."

She focused back up to Hugo. The vampire fangs tried to inch closer to her neck. The pain shot up her leg and hip and through her spine. She didn't know how much longer she could hold him. Tears flowed down her check.

"Before . . . before you do it," Hugo said through his tears. "I need to ask you a question. A question I've been trying to ask you since the night in the Raskins' store."

"Anything," Alice replied.

"You've brought me so much joy over the last year. I was in a dark place. I never thought I was going to get out of it. I was thinking bad thoughts. But then one night, I met the most beautiful, most loving, most caring person in my entire life . . ."

Hugo paused before continuing, "You bewitched me from the first time we met. I'm so glad you followed me into the woods, or else I might have never had the courage to ask you out. You rescued me. I don't want to spend the rest of my life with anyone else except you. I love you. You're the moonlight that guided me out of the darkness. You're my everything. Alice Primrose, will you do me the honor of being my wife and marrying me?"

"Yes," Alice cried. "Yes. Of course. Of course, I'll marry you."

Hugo fought and managed a smile as he loomed over her. "Look up behind Galahad. There's a black box. I've been holding on to it for a few weeks."

Alice nodded.

"Tell the Raskins I love them, and I'm sorry for putting them in this situation. Take care of Max for me," Hugo said.

"Of course," Alice said.

"She likes her treats and whatever you're eating. She barks a lot, but she's a good girl."

"I know."

"And I'm sorry."

"It's not your fault. Don't blame yourself."

Hugo gritted his teeth and snarled. His left hand shook as he struggled to free it from being entwined with Alice's. He dragged his fingers a few inches to the palm of her hand, freeing her fingers to call forth her arcane powers.

"I want you to know that you're not a good witch. You're a great witch. Thank you for everything."

Alice snapped her fingers. The wooden stake rose from the coffee table. She positioned it directly behind Hugo.

"I don't want to do it," Alice pleaded once more.

"It's okay. It's okay," Hugo reassured her, managing a half smile.

"Lie to me. Tell me it'll be okay."

"You'll be okay," Alice sobbed.

"You're a terrible liar."

"I learned from the best."

"I love you."

Alice's heart sank. A surge of emotions coursed through her soul —a chaotic mix of fear, agony, anger, love. Her body tensed. The room blurred until there was only Hugo. She wanted desperately to see his icy blue eyes one more time, not the red monstrosities peering down at her.

She pressed her thumb and middle fingers together. She paused, wanting to stretch every last possible moment they had together before she had to perform her dark deed. The moment was an eternity and an instant all at once.

Hugo nodded at her. She knew it was time. He inched closer to her neck, once again opening his mouth to display his vampiric fangs. She didn't know how much longer she could hold him back. Her knee slipped. She couldn't wait any longer.

Alice said her final words to Hugo, "I love you too."

She snapped her fingers, and the wooden stake impaled Hugo in the back, piercing his heart. He arched backward as his legs and arms turned to ash. The line rapidly worked its way up his torso. His face contorted in pain and suffering before it disappeared.

Hugo Dodds was no more.

The wooden stake fell to the floor, though Alice never heard it drop. Hugo's ashes scattered to the wind and disappeared. She closed her eyes and cried, but nothing came out. With her hands, arms, and legs now free, she writhed in agony on the floor. Alice curled into a ball, rocking herself back and forth. She tried to cry, but produced no sound.

She was lost in the pain of losing Hugo—the only one who truly cared about her. Her lover. Her betrothed. She took in a breath. Finally, Alice let out a barbaric yawp, filling the once happy home with pain, suffering, and torment.

CHAPTER 26
A CROSSED LOVER

The grandfather clock chimed three times. Dong. Dong. Dong. 3 a.m. The witching hour. The house was silent. The wails of agony had long since stopped. There was no movement. It was silent, except for the constant ticking of the grandfather clock.

Alice laid on the hardwood floor using her arm as a pillow. She had lost track of how long she laid there. She couldn't remember if she fell asleep. Her arm, however, fell asleep ages ago. She didn't care. The numbing pain relieved the pain in her heart—her soul. She focused on the instrument of her torment—the wooden spike. Her face remained devoid of any expression.

Her eyes never wavered from the point of the wooden stake, the instrument of death. Hugo's contorted, agonized face was still fresh in her mind. She wanted to remember the good times—his smiling face, a passionate kiss, anything. She could only remember his final moments.

She breathed in and out, each breath slow and shallow as if she questioned why she took her next breath. Every inhale a moment of solace. Yet, every exhale carried a lingering sense of melancholy as she questioned if she could go on with the burden of the world.

Her life was gone. Everything she knew had crumbled before her. All at the hands of Sylvia Savino in her pursuit of becoming queen of a new empire. Her wine cellar was smashed to pieces. Her friends, the Raskins, lived in fear for their lives. Her lover, her best friend, and soulmate was dead. There was nothing left for her. Sylvia won.

All because of a stupid spell. A spell her family had given her as a burden. There was one who begged her, pleaded with her to make the spell. They wanted to use it to their advantage. Alice's mind slipped back to the event that set all of this into motion.

"What are you looking at?" Sam's voice jolted Alice.

A shiver ran down her back.

"Did I scare you, the great Alice Primrose?"

Alice laughed. "You didn't scare me. I was just concentrating. Startled, more like it."

Sam draped her arm around Alice's shoulder, hugging her close as if she was preventing her from running away.

Alice wanted to run away.

"So, what are you concentrating on?"

Alice rolled up the scroll and stuffed it back into its wooden box. "It's nothing," she responded. She picked it up, stuffed it back into its hidden hole, and pushed the stone shut. "It's just a spell. Don't worry about it."

"Well, it must be something if you're doing your best to keep it hidden. What is it?" Sam asked.

"It's nothing."

Sam leaned in and whispered into Alice's ear. "What is it?"

Sam's breath over her ears tantalized Alice's soul. Sam knew every button Alice loved to have pushed. Every tease excited her mind, body, and spirit. A longing within craved a deeper connection with her girlfriend.

"I can't tell you. You shouldn't have seen it," Alice said.

"Ms. Primrose, are you keeping secrets from me?"

"Nooooooo. It's something special, and I don't like people knowing about it."

Sam freed Alice from the binding of her arm. She leaned back against Alice's workstation and crossed her arms to push up on her chest. She pouted her lips and batted her eyes. This was Sam's seductively, manipulative way to get what she wanted, and it worked every time. Alice's heart fluttered.

"If you tell me, I'll let you do that thing you like." Sam batted her eyes again.

Alice bit her lip and smiled. She hid her face, lost in thought about their nightly exploits. She loved Sam and their little playful back-and-forth teases. It was fun, exciting. It was ambrosia for her soul.

"It's a love spell," Alice relented.

"A love spell?" Sam asked, standing up. She placed a hand on Alice's shoulder and tilted her head. "Ms. Primrose, have you been putting a love spell on me?"

Her touch sent a wildfire through her body. Each passing moment was glorious torture as her body craved Sam.

"It's not like that," Alice responded.

Sam placed her other hand on Alice's other shoulder. She turned her slightly, so they were face to face. Sam tilted her head forward. The smoldering expression on her face caused Alice's heart to melt.

"So, what's it like?" Sam asked.

She leaned in. Their bodies pressed against each other. The magnetic pull between their two souls drew them closer.

She continued in a low whisper, "Tell me."

Alice wanted to tell her. She wanted to tell her everything, but she couldn't. For all of Sam's teasing and flirting, Alice's intuition beckoned her to not reveal the truth. The less Sam knew, the better, so its true secret remained hidden.

"It's a spell to strengthen the bonds between two lovers. That's all."

Sam pulled back, still holding onto Alice's shoulders. "Then let's make it."

"We can't," Alice said.

The pouty, flirty expression on Sam's face was replaced with a discerning look "Why not?"

"Because I promised my grandmother I wouldn't make it."

"Forget your grandmother. Let's make it and see what it does."

"I'm not going to do it."

Sam let go of Alice. She slumped her shoulders and smacked her hips out of frustration. She turned away from Alice. "Why not?"

"Because it's a stupid spell," Alice said. She thought of an excuse, a lie to tell Sam to get her to stop asking. "I think it only works once, and both people have to be in love."

Sam asked, "Are you not in love with me?"

The question sent Alice into a tailspin of emotions. What was holding her back from telling her the truth? Why not make it? Did she love Sam? The question repeated over and over in her mind. She didn't know the answer.

"I am," Alice said.

Sam crossed her arms and glared at Alice. "You are what?"

"I'm in love with you," Alice said.

"Are you sure?"

Alice hesitated, her gaze sweeping around the room, stalling, trying to find the right words. Any words to defuse and end this conversation. All she could muster was the word, "Yeah."

"Yeah?" Sam said. "Just yeah?"

"What about you? Do you love me?" Alice turned the tables on Sam.

Sam shrugged her shoulders. "Of course."

"Just 'of course'?" Alice asked.

"I mean, of course I love you."

"What do you love about me?"

Sam paused; her eyes wandered around the wine cellar. "I love that you make wine. I love that it allows us to do things we couldn't do on a simple bartending salary."

Alice narrowed her eyes. "Is that all you love me for? Making wine?"

"No," Sam replied. "But I like that you love it."

Alice stood in silence, staring at Sam.

Sam shifted in her stance, turning away from Alice. "Don't look at me like that."

"Like what?"

"Like I did something wrong."

"Do you only love me because I make wine?"

"Well, I mean, it's great. You do it well. And we can use it to get out of here, to some place better."

Alice crossed her arms. Her whole body shook with a raging fury. She could barely contain herself from lashing out. Was Sam only interested in her as a means to an end, using her as a manipulative pawn? Was this entire relationship a front? Was her suspicion correct? Did her infatuation blind her from seeing the truth?

"What about me do you love?" Alice asked. "Me. Not the wine."

Sam ran her hands through her golden blonde hair. Her eyes searched around the wine cellar as well. She was stalling, searching for an answer because she didn't have one. And Alice knew it.

"I love your purple hair."

"My hair?" Alice shouted. "I asked you what you loved about me, and you said my hair?"

"Yeah. I think it's hot. It's sexy. You're sexy," Sam responded. "What do you want me to say?"

"I want you to tell me what you love about me."

"I did!" Sam shouted. Their voices had escalated to a shouting match. "What about me? What do you love about me?"

Alice dropped her arms to her sides. "I love your personality. I love how you make me feel excited to see you. I love how my stomach is filled with butterflies, and my heart flutters when you're near me. I hate how much it hurts when we're apart."

Sam took a step back. She placed a hand on her hip, bowed her head, and tussled with her hair. "Wow. I don't know what to say."

"Do you only love me because of the wine?"

"I love that you can help us get out of here where we could have a better life. Don't you want that?"

"I would do this if I wasn't paid. Would you still be with me if I stopped making wine?" Alice said.

Sam threw her hands up into the air. "This conversation is ridiculous. I don't have to answer. You know how I feel. I'm leaving." She stormed off toward the cellar door.

"Where are you going?"

"I'm going to give you time to cool off from this mind-numbingly, ridiculous conversation."

Alice stood there, alone, in the cold, damp wine cellar.

~

KNOCKS on the basement door brought Alice back to the present. Alice didn't know if those knocks were new or if she had blocked them out the entire time she laid on the floor. The room and all her prized objects came back into view. She sat up, rotating her arm to restore feeling. She snapped her fingers, and the basement door flung open.

Guinevere flew into the living room. The end of its broom handle was cracked and hung limp by a small bit of still connected wood from where Hugo had snapped it over his knee.

"What did he do to you?" Alice asked.

Not Hugo. It was Sylvia. She did it. Not Hugo.

Guinevere hung in the air. It focused on Alice and then on the wooden stake on the ground. It lingered there as if it was examining the instrument and piecing together what happened. It focused back on Alice. Guinevere moved toward her and nestled against her chest and side of her head, leaning in as if to give her a hug.

Alice wrapped her arms around the wounded broomstick. A tear fell down her face. "Thank you. It'll be okay. It's okay."

They held their embrace for a moment.

Alice continued, "Let me heal you."

The broomstick pulled back so Alice had a clear view of the damage. She moved the cracked piece back into position. She cupped her hands around the broom handle, squeezing tightly. She leaned in, breathing into her hands. She called forth the power of her magick with the language of the arcane.

She let go.

Guinevere pulled back, with the handle now straight. A scar remained where the cracks had once carved through the ash handle.

"Sorry, I can't do anything about the scars. But in full honesty, it makes you look like a badass. A badass, vampire killing broomstick."

Guinevere leaned into Alice once more before pulling back.

Alice stood. Her eyes caught the black broomcorn with streaks of purple and red sitting on top of her memory shelf. She moved over to the book case, blindly searching around behind the broomcorn until it made contact with the object. A black, velvet box. She pulled it down.

Her eyes lingered on the diminutive box she held in her hands. She flipped it over and over, examining every inch. She knew what was inside, yet she hesitated, knowing it would be the last gift Hugo gave her.

Her hands trembled as she moved her thumbs to the seams. She took a deep breath and gently slid her thumb up. The soft creaking of the hinge added to the suspense in the air. As the lid lifted, Alice's eyes twinkled at the illustrious item held within the box. A slight smile, once thought to be lost forever, returned to her face.

Nestled in the black, velvety cushion was a ring of absolute perfection. It was a thin, onyx band with a purple amethyst crystal in the shape of a heart. It glimmered and glistened with an ethereal elegance as if it was carved by the powers of the arcane. With a gentle tug, she freed the delicate ring from the soft bed inside the box, then placed the black box onto the memory shelf.

Alice held the ring in her hand, twisting and turning to examine every bit of the surface. She raised her left hand and hovered it over her ring finger. She paused. Her heart beat against her chest. She breathed deeply to soothe her nerves.

"I'll marry you, Hugo Dodds," Alice whispered as if to a ghost standing in front of her.

She placed the ring on her finger with tender care. She twisted the ring around a few times—mimicking the gesture Hugo had done following his loss—before placing it in an upright position. She tapped the amethyst crystal with the tip of her finger.

Alice focused on the memory shelf. The black box of her engagement ring rested next to the wooden box holding Hugo's wedding ring. Her eyes drifted to the various other mementos from her family's past. The pictures of long-gone family members.

The cracked picture of her great-great grandparents—the cowboy and the witch. No doubt the spell was in the picture, hidden and safe within her witch's hat. Her relatives, acting out of a sense of duty, did what was necessary to safeguard the spell.

She recalled the vivid details passed down from her grandmother about how her great-great grandparents valiantly protected a small western town from an ominous shadow wizard in search of the spell. They were successful in their duties, fulfilling their charge with unwavering determination.

Alice's eyes landed on the photo of herself in a loving embrace with her grandmother, Bee. She was the next to shoulder the burden. Her grandmother fulfilled her duty, ensuring the spell remained hidden without a trace. And now, the burden was placed on Alice.

There was no escape from her destiny. The days of hiding were over. In order to fulfil her duty and honor her family legacy, she must rid the world of the vampire menace known as Sylvia Savino.

She breathed in, releasing the tension held deep within her soul.

Alice lifted her head with a renewed sense of purpose. She squinted; her eyes narrowed in concentration on the hickory broomstick resting on top of the bookcase.

Her smile vanished, replaced by a resolute expression conveying her unwavering determination. A brilliant idea flickered into existence in her mind, like a flame dancing in the darkness. Galahad, her horse-dog, left her with one last parting gift.

"I know what I must do. Please. Please be with me. Protect me," she whispered. "Especially you, Hugo."

She turned and marched across the living room, past the fireplace, and through the entryway. Alice charged up the stairs. Her boots slammed into the wood with every step. She arrived at the top and went to open the spare bedroom door.

She paused, giving thought to the other occupant of the house. Alice needed to have a discussion with herself first.

Alice passed through the bedroom and into the bathroom. She flicked on the switch. "We need to talk," Alice said.

"I already know," Alice's reflection said. Her head hung low. "I'm sorry."

Alice nodded. "Thank you, and I'm sorry for you too."

Alice's reflection lifted her head and nodded with a slight smile. "So, what are you going to do?"

"What I must," Alice replied. She hung her head low, not wanting to look her reflection in the face. "You do know what that could mean, right?"

"Yeah, I know," her reflection said. "Promise me one thing. Promise me no matter what happens, you'll stab that bitch in the heart."

Alice locked eyes with her reflection. "I promise you this ends before sunrise, one way or another." Alice turned to leave.

"Wait, let me see it," Alice's reflection said.

Alice lifted her ring in front of the mirror.

Her reflection smiled. "I love it. He showed it to us a few weeks ago. I gave him my approval." She lifted her hand to reveal her ring.

Alice smiled. "You've been keeping this from me the whole time?"

"There's a lot you don't know. Somehow, I inherited him as a client for his own personal therapy sessions too. He wanted to make sure it was perfect. I told him anything he did would have been perfect, but this . . . this is special." She glanced at her ring. "Now, go get her."

"Thanks," Alice said. She pointed to the light switch. "On or off?"

"Leave it on," her reflection said. "In case you don't come back."

"Thanks for the vote of confidence."

"Telling it like it is."

Alice left the bathroom and went back into the hallway. She entered the spare bedroom with its various boxes of hers and Hugo's stuff. She made her way to the closet and opened the door. She removed a few boxes and took out the hat box her grandmother gave her years ago.

She opened the lid and removed the black witch's hat. She plunged her hand inside, finding the hidden pocket. She removed *The Lovers' Kiss* scroll and laid it next to her. She packed up the hat and returned it to its rightful place in the closet. She picked up the scroll and left the bedroom, closing the door behind her.

Alice jogged down the stairs and back into the living room. Guinevere floated in the same place. Alice picked up the wooden stake off the floor and added it to her budding collection of items in her hand. She strode over to the memory shelf and grasped Galahad resting on top. She removed it from the display stand.

"Gally, I need one final favor from you. For Hugo. I need more stakes. I hope you'll forgive me," Alice said to the inert broomstick.

She pulled on the string holding the broomcorn together. The red, purple, and mostly black bristles rained down to the floor, leaving only the brown hickory handle. Alice took all her gathered items and left the living room, heading for the basement.

CHAPTER 27

THE SECOND VAMPIRE-WITCH WAR

Alice parked her black SUV on a side street, about a block from The Heart and Rose. She turned off the ignition and waited, surveying the street. It was silent. Calm. Blissfully unaware of the battle to unfold.

She gathered herself. No more fear. No more hiding. No more running. It was almost sunrise. By the time the sun rose, she would either free herself from the tyranny of Sylvia or else she would see Hugo once again. There was no other way. This would end here.

Alice turned in her seat to face Guinevere floating behind her across the back seat. "If I don't come back, I need you to fly to Ez. Find her. Take it to her, do you understand?"

The broomstick bobbed up and down in agreement.

"I'm counting on you. If I don't come back or someone tries to get you, deliver it to Ez. You're a good broomstick." Alice patted the broom handle.

She turned and pushed the button to roll down the back window, so Guinevere could make a rapid escape. Alice grabbed her black bag and witch's hat resting in the passenger seat. She was about to open the door when a gentle tap on her shoulder caught her attention.

Twice more the broom handle tapped her. Alice gave two taps back, opened the door, and exited the SUV.

The rain had long since stopped, leaving the earthly sent of petrichor lingering in the air. She flung the bag over her shoulder and put on her hat. She tugged on the brim a few times to ensure the slightly curved, wool hat was in its proper place. Alice removed two wooden stakes, fashioned from the remains of Galahad's broom handle from her black bag. She clutched both in her hands and strode toward the nightclub. She picked up speed with every step, nearly breaking into a sprint to reach the building.

Alice ducked behind parked cars, keeping them between her and the building. The curtains were drawn. A new one was draped over the window she had shattered earlier in the night. There was no movement, at least none she observed. She moved from car to car, hunched down to not be seen. Once she ran out of cars, she sprinted to the corner of the building and stopped.

The street in front of her was silent, quiet. An occasional car would drive past, but there were no unusual movements on the street. Alice peered around the corner. Two vampires, both sizable brutes dressed in black, stood guard outside the entrance.

Alice pulled back and placed her back to the wall. She clutched both wooden stakes in her hand, raising them up to her chest. She took deep breaths, trying to soothe her beating heart. Adrenaline coursed through her veins, and malice shone in her eyes. She took one more deep breath, held it, and exhaled, allowing her body to relax.

For Hugo.

She lunged around the corner and whistled. The guards spun around to face her. One closed in on Alice, while the other pinched a microphone clipped to his black shirt.

Alice didn't think, she didn't question, she didn't hesitate. She hurled one stake at the charging vampire, swiftly reloaded her right hand, and flung the second stake at the other. The stakes soared through the air, hurtling toward their targets. The vampires side-stepped the path of the stakes, as they continued their assault. Alice snapped her fingers. The wooden stakes course corrected and hit their intended targets with precision.

Both pierced the vampires' chests, turning them to dust. The wooden stakes bounced off the cement sidewalk. Alice snapped her fingers on both hands, and the stakes returned to her. She strode with confidence, eyes on the door handle. She snapped a finger, while holding the wooden stake. The door flew open. More vampires spilled into the night air.

Alice was ready for them. She struck the first one in the chest, sending him to an ash strewn grave. A hand snared the sleeve of Alice's black tailcoat, attempting to pull her inside. Alice lurched in, surprising the vampire, and struck him in the chest. Alice spun, pirouetting on one foot, stabbing another would be assailant. With her fluid movements, she unleashed her dance-inspired techniques to swiftly dispatch the first wave of vampires.

More rushed in from the back. Alice flung the stakes into her coat pockets and delved her left hand back into her black bag, searching for something hidden within its depths. She produced a handful of sharp splinters and hurled them at the attackers. As she focused on the oncoming vampires' chests, she could see the glint of their fangs and snapped both of her fingers. The sharp splinters effortlessly tore through them, causing them to collapse like a fragile house of cards as they turned to dust.

"Sylvia!" Alice shouted, still near the entrance. "Let's finish this."

Clapping emanated from the balcony. Not in congratulations, but to mock Alice. In the dim light, Alice found her query. The clapping built into a thunderous applause before stopping on one magnanimous clap. Standing at the balcony railing, wearing her crimson coat and pointing her clapped hands at Alice, was Sylvia Savino.

"You survived. A pity. I had such great plans for my new pet," Sylvia said.

"You took everything from me!" Alice yelled.

"Consider us even," Sylvia replied.

Alice let out a barbaric yawp and threw the wooden stake at Sylvia like a diminutive javelin. She spun around, transferring the stake to her other hand, and threw the second. She snapped her fingers. Both stakes raced toward Sylvia's chest.

Sylvia stood her ground. The stakes floated in the air, inches from Sylvia's chest, as if some unseen force held them. An *arcane* unseen force.

She glared at Alice. "Do you think I wouldn't be prepared for you this time?" Sylvia asked. "You'll have to do more than stab me in the heart if you want to kill me."

The wooden stakes floated past Sylvia and fell to the ground.

"How?" Alice asked.

"You might have taken my new pet from me, but I'd like to introduce you to my original pet. I believe you know her," Sylvia said. She turned to someone standing behind her. "Sam, please don't be shy and come say hello."

Alice's mouth dropped. The blonde hair. The rolled-up sleeves showing off her forearm tattoos. She was unmistakable. The sight of her former lover standing next to Sylvia overwhelmed Alice in a state of shock and horror, left at a loss for words. All thoughts escaped her. Her shoulders drooped. She took a step back toward the entrance.

"I have to say, she's been most helpful in my little operation here," Sylvia toyed with Alice. She turned to Sam. "Go say hello."

Sam turned, heading for the stairs.

"Over the railing," Sylvia commanded. "I like the more dramatic entrance."

Sam turned back, placed her hands on the railing, and leapt over. She landed on her feet on the floor below, crouching down to catch herself. She held there for a moment and rose to meet Alice.

"Hello, Alice," Sam said in a monotone voice. Her eyes were red like Hugo's. "I'm so glad you could join us."

"Join is a . . . subjective term," Sylvia said from above. "Joining me is off the table, but I'll give you two options."

Alice shifted her weight forward, turning her back foot. She focused on Sam, then Sylvia, and finally back to Sam.

Sylvia continued, "Option one, you hand it over now, and I'll let Sam dispatch of you. It'll be quick, painless. Option two, I'll rip you apart myself. It'll be slow and painful. You'll beg for mercy. I'll give you none before finally taking off your head."

"Sam, please don't do this," Alice said. "Snap out of it."

A red flaming sphere of arcane energy appeared in Sam's hand, and she threw it. Alice dodged out of the way. The sphere smashed against the DJ booth, sending parts of the wood platform flying into the air. Sam produced another flame and continued her barrage.

Alice kept running, zigzagging across the black and white checkerboard dance floor toward the bar. She placed her hands on the railing and leapt over, rolling down to the floor below. More and more red flames slammed into the shelves above. Bottles shattered. Alice turned her back and covered her head to shield herself from the shattered glass and liquid raining down on her. Alice was covered in a cocktail mixture of wine and an assortment of liquor.

"Come on," Sam taunted. "Let's play like the old times. You remember the old times, don't you?"

Alice could hear Sam's shoes clacking against the dance floor as she approached. "I won't fight you."

A reddish glow bathed the area above Alice. Its light emanated in all directions along the shelves behind the bar.

"We could have been something," Sam said.

One side of the bar led back to the dance floor. She'd be an easy target for Sam. The other end led to a secured room used to store the liquor. There were no windows behind the bar, leaving Alice without a means of escape. Sam was closing in from above. Alice's heart beat faster, slamming into her chest as her mind went blank.

"An arcane power couple. Me and you. Together," Sam said.

"How about you stop and we talk it over?" Alice lied.

There was no escape. The light grew brighter, now spilling over the bar top. The clacking on the dance floor had stopped. Sam was above her. Alice was trapped.

"Goodbye, Alice," Sam said.

Alice brushed against an aluminum tube dangling behind the bar —the tube of the soda gun. Sam leaned over the bar to throw the flame of arcane energy, but Alice was quicker on the draw. She withdrew the soda gun from the holster and sprayed Sam in the face. She recoiled at the attack. The sticky soda soaking her face broke Sam's concentration, and the red flame dissipated.

Alice rose to her feet. She dug into her bag and leapt over the bar. Alice retrieved a small, glass vial of bluish liquid. She ran up behind Sam, wrapping her arms around her. Sam whipped Alice back first into the bar railing.

Alice cried out in pain as the wood railing plunged into the middle of her back. She steeled her resolve and didn't let go. Sam tried again, but Alice was prepared. She kicked her leg back into the bar, preventing Sam from punishing her again.

Alice snapped her fingers, and the cork stopper flew out. "Open wide and drink this." Alice jammed the vial into Sam's mouth.

The liquid poured out. Sam choked, but Alice didn't stop. Not until she drank a good portion of the liquid. Once satisfied, Alice removed the vial.

Sam bent over, her blonde hair covering her face. She coughed and grasped her throat before falling to her knees. Sam let out a guttural gurgle and collapsed to the ground.

Alice's eyes watered. She wiped away a tear with her sleeve. Her betrayer, her former lover, now lay motionless on the floor.

Alice removed another wooden stake from her bag—the same wooden stake she pierced Hugo with through his back. She returned her attention to the balcony. Sylvia was gone.

Alice's ribs burst like fire as she was slammed into the bar railing. Alice dropped the wooden stake. Maddening screams echoed throughout the venue. A mixture of Alice's wails and Sylvia's bloodthirsty howls. Sylvia reared back and slammed her again.

Alice struggled to breathe as it knocked the wind out of her. She tried to clutch her abdomen, but Sylvia maintained a tight hold this time. Sylvia lifted Alice and plunged her facedown into the ground. What little wind remained in her lungs was now gone. She could only mouth the pain of agony.

Sylvia threw the wooden stake into the storage room. Sylvia kicked Alice in her side, forcing her to roll over on her back. Sylvia stood over Alice.

"Funny, this was the same position he was in," Sylvia said. Her hair was messy. An expression of subdued rage was on her face.

A purple arcane flame manifested in the palm of Alice's hand, but Sylvia stepped on it, driving her heel into Alice's palm. Alice screamed in pain. She rolled over, clutching her wrist, trying to free her hand.

"I think I've had enough of you, little witch," Sylvia said, showing her teeth. Her vampiric fangs elongated. Sylvia lunged for Alice's throat.

A ball of red arcane energy slammed into Sylvia, sending her backward onto the middle of the dance floor.

"No one messes with my Alice!" Sam shouted. She threw another red arcane flame at the vampire.

Sylvia writhed in pain.

Alice smiled. She stood up and snapped her fingers. The wooden stake flew into her awaiting hand. Alice and Sam locked eyes.

"Are you okay?" Sam asked.

"I will be in a moment," Alice replied.

Sylvia crawled toward the basement. Every time she tried to stand, she collapsed back to the floor and screamed in pain. Alice and Sam closed in on Sylvia. Alice took her time as she enjoyed seeing her suffer.

"How?" Sylvia asked. "I controlled you."

"I sell a lot of wine. Do you know what else I sell?" Alice asked. "I call it *Drink Me* juice. Anytime you're drunk, hung over, poisoned, or in this case, enthralled, you drink the potion, and it sobers you right up. I sell more of it than I do wine."

Alice and Sam stood over Sylvia, shoulder to shoulder. A red flame was in Sam's hand and the wooden stake in Alice's.

"You didn't think I was going to come into battle with you and not prepare myself against your hypnotic gaze, did you?" Alice asked.

Sylvia rolled to her back, raising a hand to keep them at bay, while trying to crawl away. "I beg you," Sylvia said. Alice raised the stake above her head. "Please."

Alice's arm twitched as she held it there. Her heart pounded against her chest. Her mind raced.

Which witch are you?

Every fiber in her being wanted her to lunge it directly into Sylvia's chest. For everything she did—to the Raskins, to the town of Newbury Grove, to Sam, to her, to Hugo. Alice wanted to pierce Sylvia's heart with all her might.

You're not a good witch. You're a great witch. Hugo's words ran through her mind. She lowered the wooden stake.

"What are you waiting for?" Sam asked. "Do it."

A sense of relief fell over Sylvia. She struggled to catch her breath.

"No," Alice said. "I determine how I win, how I beat you. Stabbing you is too easy. No, I want you to pay."

"Alice, stab her," Sam pleaded.

"Sylvia Savino, for your heinous crimes and disturbing the peace between witches and vampires, I hereby place you under arrest of the Coven of the Moon. You'll be tried and imprisoned until it's been deemed your punishment has been completed," Alice said. "And I'll recommend a life sentence."

"Don't let her live," Sam yelled. "Do it!"

Sylvia narrowed her eyes. She smiled and laughed. "What makes you think you can hold me? I've escaped more places and more situations than I can count. I've seen people come and go. I'll take great joy in standing over your grave."

"You can't let her go," Sam pleaded.

"You don't have the guts, you little witch. I'll track you down. You can't hold me forever," Sylvia said.

"Stab her!" Sam yelled.

Alice turned to Sam. "No! She goes to prison."

"You're weak, little witch. You've always been weak," Sylvia taunted.

"Then I'll do it," Sam screamed as she snapped her fingers.

The wooden stake flew out of Alice's hand and into Sam's.

"No!" Alice screamed as Sam plunged the stake into the vampire's chest.

Sylvia let out a chuckle as the stake pierced her heart. Her legs and arms turned to dust. The erasure line worked up her torso until finally her contorted face disappeared forever.

"What did you do?" Alice asked. "Why?"

"She deserved it. She deserved it for what she did to me," Sam said.

"That's not who we are," Alice said.

"That's not who you are. But it's who I am."

Alice slumped her shoulders. She covered her face with her hands and sobbed. Every emotion overwhelmed Alice, and she could no longer hold back. It was over. It was finally over. The Savinos were no more.

Sam wrapped her arms around Alice to console her. Alice pushed her away.

Sam tapped the thick end of the wooden stake in the palm of her hand. "I guess I deserved that."

Alice snapped her fingers. The wooden stake flew out of Sam's hand and into Alice's awaiting hand. She tossed it into her bag.

"Why?" Alice asked. "I want to know why you told them."

Sam scanned around as if to find the right answer. "I thought if people knew, then we could sell it and make some real money. Money that allowed us to get out of our stupid lives and do whatever we wanted, instead of working behind a bar."

"Did you ever love me?" Alice asked.

"Of course, I did. That's a dumb question."

"Did you love me for me or because of what I could do?"

Sam paused. She crossed her arms, bit her lips, and lowered her eyes.

"Did you love me for me?" Alice asked again.

Sam lifted her head to meet Alice's eyes. "I did love you. I loved the idea of what you could do for us even more. Look. I'm sorry. I only had the best intentions in mind. I was going to get you an offer, and then we could escape to a beach some place. The two of us. I never meant for any of this to happen."

A tear ran down Alice's face. It rolled down her cheek and onto the floor.

Sam threw her hands into the air and slapped them to her sides. "I'm sorry. I'm sorry for everything."

"Hugo loved me for me. He's the only one who ever loved me for me, and he's gone," Alice said.

Sam rubbed her forehead. "I don't know what else to say. I don't know how many times I can apologize. I'm sorry."

"I didn't know if you were still alive or what after I found the door in their basement." Alice retrieved Sam's red hat from her black bag and handed it to her. "I brought it in case I found you."

Sam examined the red knit hat before locking eyes with Alice.

"At least we had Salem," Alice said.

"At least we had Salem," Sam replied, giving a half smile to the red knit hat.

Alice gave Sam a kiss on the cheek. "Goodbye, Sam," Alice said and left the nightclub, leaving Sam alone.

Alice made her way back to the black SUV. She opened the door and removed her hat and bag. She tossed them into the passenger seat before entering. Guinevere poked at Alice's shoulder as she sat down.

Alice placed a hand on the ash broomstick. "It's over, Gwennie. It's all over."

She pulled out her phone and sent a text message to Ez before tossing the phone to the seat next to her. Alice sat in the car, unmoving. The morning sky came alive with a kaleidoscope of colors; rays of red, orange, and purple peered over the tops of buildings as the sunlight pushed back against the darkness.

Alice sobbed.

After a moment, she wiped away her tears. Alice started the SUV, rolled up the back window, and took off.

CHAPTER 28

THE DARK NIGHT OF ALICE'S SOUL

"He's gone," Alice said into her phone through her tears. "Hugo's gone."

"I'm sorry, kiddo," Ez's voice said through Alice's phone. "Hugo was a good man."

Was?

The word stabbed into Alice's heart, Alice's soul. *Was*. As in Hugo was no more, a thing of her past. Alice sniffled and wiped away the tears from her eyes. She had sobbed on the car ride all the way home. The cathartic end to the Savinos broke down the flood barriers, and her tears had flowed all morning.

Alice was frozen, unable to speak back to Ez. She didn't know what to say. All she could think about was Hugo, her fiancé, and his contorted face as the wooden stake pierced his heart. The image was burned into her soul for all of time.

"How are you doing?" Ez asked.

Alice gulped. She wiped away the tears flowing down her face. "I'm fine. Just fine."

I'm fine, by the way.

Hugo's words to her from the night they met tore through her mind. She wasn't fine. She never would be again. Her body, her mind, and her soul craved Hugo. She wanted nothing more than to celebrate this victory with him by her side. She was finally free from her past. There was no longer a need to hide. She was free from those who tried to use her, hurt her. But she couldn't. The wooden stake pierced more than Hugo's heart—it also shattered a portion of her soul.

"I spoke with the Vampiric Conclave. They agreed it was a business dispute. Nothing more," Ez said.

A business dispute?

"They thanked us for taking care of the Savinos. Apparently, they were a thorn in their side as well," Ez continued. "If it makes you feel any better, I told them to shove it, and if another vampire shows their face around any of us, the next time it won't be a *business dispute*."

Alice sniffled again. "Thanks."

"I also told them there's a new owner of Red Heart Distribution, and they can call her Ms. Primrose," Ez said. "I'll make sure the Raskins get everything back."

"Thank you," Alice said.

"I'll send a crew to clean everything up. What about Sam?"

"I left her in the nightclub. I don't know where she went," Alice replied.

"Don't worry about her. I'll keep an eye out for her. Do you need anything?"

Alice needed Hugo back. "I'm good. I'm at the Raskins' house. I'll break the news about Hugo to them, then I'm going home. I need to sleep. I don't know what I'm going to do next."

"Take your time. Take all the time you need. If you need anything, *anything*, I'm only a phone call away," Ez said.

"Thank you."

"Alice, I want you to know I'm very sorry you had to go through this. I'm proud of you. I'm proud you stood your ground and took care of them. I know it wasn't easy, and it hurts now. It'll never be okay. I want you to know I'm always there for you. You're like a daughter to me."

There was a pause. Alice wiped away a tear from her eye. "Thank you. You're the best friend anyone could ask for. I'm so sorry you had to get involved in this too."

"Go home. Get some rest, then we'll figure out what to do next together. I love you." Ez hung up the phone.

Alice sat in her SUV, parked in front of the Raskins' home. She focused on the light blue colored house. Its white trim shone brightly in the early morning sun. She sat there frozen, waiting to tell them what had transpired. She didn't know what to tell them. How could she? They were unaware of the fact that Hugo was a vampire, and now she had to tell them he was dead.

Her lips quivered. Her body hurt. She wanted to yell and scream and break everything. It wasn't fair. It wasn't fair she had to go through all of this. It wasn't fair she had to be the one to tell them. She didn't ask for any of it. There was still one more thing to do, one last torture the Savinos had to put her through. She got out of her SUV.

She trudged up the entryway, each step heavier than the last. She stood in front of their white door. If she didn't knock, then he'd still be alive. Alive in their hearts and minds. If she knocked, then he would die yet again. She hesitated, not wanting to do it. She couldn't. Not to them. Yet, she had no choice. It had to be done.

Alice knocked on the door.

Carol opened it and peered around the corner. "Sweetie, what's wrong? Come in."

Alice entered their home. She batted her eyes, trying to hold back the tears, but failed. They flowed down her cheeks. She wiped them away, but they continued. The deluge of tears flowed. She started bawling.

"Hugo . . ." She stopped. She couldn't finish the sentence.

"What about Hugo?" Oliver asked as he came into their living room from the kitchen.

Max barked and ran to greet Alice.

Alice dropped to her knees and hugged Max. Alice buried her face into Max's fur to hide her tears. She scratched behind the dog's ear. Max sat down, wagging her tail across the carpet, excited to see Alice yet again.

"I'm so sorry," Alice sobbed.

"What's wrong?" Carol asked.

Alice faced the Raskins with her bloodshot eyes. "Hugo . . ." she tried to speak again.

Carol covered her mouth in shock, taking a step back. Oliver wrapped his arms around her, embracing his wife.

"They turned him into a vampire a few weeks ago," Alice continued.

Carol stumbled as she placed her hand on the arm of the couch, and Oliver helped her sit down. Both of them were at a loss for words.

"He didn't want you to know."

"You should have told us," Carol said, fighting back tears. "I thought we didn't keep secrets."

Alice shook her head. "I'm so sorry."

"Is he okay now?" Oliver asked.

Alice shook her head. She wanted to tell them, but something held her back. Her eyes were red, and tears fell down her face.

"Sweetie, please tell us. Is Hugo okay?" Carol asked.

"They were able to control him, and he attacked me," Alice started. Alice's words failed her once more. It was as if an invisible force closed around her throat and squeezed. She couldn't continue, yet she had to. "He told me to stake him. It was the only way to stop him."

"Oh, no," Oliver said.

Carol let out a gasp and covered her mouth.

"I didn't have a choice. He wanted me to do it. He told me to do it. I *had* to do it. He died in my arms. He turned to dust in my arms." Alice buried her face into Max.

Carol bent over crying. "My Hugo," she wailed. "Not my Hugo."

Oliver placed his hand on her shoulder.

"I'm sorry," Alice said through her tears as she rose from her bent over position. She couldn't look at the Raskins. "I'm so sorry."

"What do you need us to do?" Oliver asked in a stoic voice.

Alice raised her head and wiped away her tears. She breathed deeply, trying to calm her nerves. "I don't know. I don't know yet."

"What about the vampires?" Oliver said.

"They're dead too," Alice replied. "I took care of them earlier this morning. It's over. It's all over. Ez is working to get everything back to you shortly."

"What do we do, Oliver?" Carol asked. Tears streaked down her face. "What do we do?"

"I don't—" Oliver began before a crack in his voice stopped him. He paused, still stoic, yet unusually silent. "I guess we'll have to figure it out."

Carol turned to Alice. She couldn't tell if Carol was still in shock or furious at her for what happened to Hugo. The moment could have been a second or a century. Time stopped.

"He was going to ask you a question," Carol said through her tears. "Did he?"

Alice held up her left hand to show them the thin onyx band with a purple amethyst crystal in the shape of a heart. "It was the last thing he asked me."

Carol stood up. "Excuse me," she said. She went down a hall and shut the bathroom door behind her.

Oliver's eyes followed his wife, but he turned his attention back to Alice. He hugged her. "It'll be okay."

"It won't. This is all my fault," Alice said.

"It's not your fault," Oliver said.

"How is it not?"

"I'll tell you the same thing I told Hugo when Elizabeth died. You were there for him. That's all that mattered."

"I could have done more," Alice replied as she buried her head into his shoulder.

"You did enough. Trust me." Oliver patted her on the back. "You did enough."

"What do I do now?" Alice asked.

"I don't know, but if you need anything, *anything*, let us know."

"Thank you," Alice said as she pulled back from Oliver. "Is Carol okay?"

"I'll talk to her. Don't worry. She's probably still in shock. Go home. Get some rest. It's the best thing for you right now."

Alice nodded.

Oliver continued, "We'll figure this out later. Together."

"Thank you."

"Do you want us to keep watching Max?"

"Thanks for the offer, but I think I could use her company right now," Alice said. She took Max's leash and clipped it to her collar.

"We're just a phone call away," Oliver said.

"Thank you," Alice said. She opened the door and headed for her SUV with Max leading the way.

~

MAX BOUNCED INTO THE HOUSE, excited to be home. She ran around downstairs, searching for Hugo. She went down the hall and into the kitchen. Unable to find him, she ran upstairs. Her toenails clicked against the hardwood steps. The clickity clack of her nails were like ghostly footprints from above. Unable to find Hugo, she ran back down to the entryway.

Alice stood in the doorway. She tried as much as possible to hold back her tears, but couldn't. They continued to flow. Guinevere entered the home and floated into the living room. She took her usual spot next to the red velvet couch.

Max followed in her pursuit of Hugo. Something caught her attention. She sniffed the hardwood flooring—the very spot where

Hugo had perished. She circled, dragging her nose across the floor to smell everything.

She stopped. Max scratched the hardwood floor with her paw. She sniffed again before continuing her scratching. She laid down on the spot where Hugo disappeared from this earth. She whined and whimpered.

Alice couldn't hold back. She buried her head into her hands and released another gush of tears. "I'm sorry, Max." Her voice was muffled by her hands. "I'm so sorry."

Max let out a low, drawn-out whimper.

After a long cry, Alice removed her witch's hat and black tailcoat. She placed them on the coat rack at the base of the steps. With a snap of her fingers, her boots untied themselves. She kicked them off, one at a time, stretching out her toes in her stockings. She climbed up the stairs toward her bedroom—their bedroom.

She grabbed her purple pajamas, neatly folded on their bed. She removed her shirt and black pants. The cold morning air brushed against her bare skin, sending a slight shiver down her spine. She put on her pajamas and turned down the bed covers. Hugo's pillow caught her eye. She picked up the pillow and held it close.

Alice went over to the laundry basket on the floor, waiting to be washed. She pulled out one of Hugo's black T-shirts. She slipped it over the pillow. Alice then climbed into bed and clutched the pillow tightly. She laid her head on the pillow.

It smelled of his cologne—the familiar vanilla and cedar scent. The scent convinced her soul Hugo was in the bed with her. One more time. One more time she was in a loving embrace with her best friend, her lover, her fiancé. Yet, when she attempted to wrap her arms around him one last time, the emptiness delivered the disappointing news he was really gone.

She breathed in the last remaining elements of his aura. The intoxicating scent of vanilla and cedar. Her eyes closed as she drifted asleep, holding the T-shirt covered pillow and dreaming of her Hugo.

One last time.

"Hey!" Alice's reflection yelled. "Get your morose ass out of bed and get in here."

Alice opened her eyes. "Leave me alone."

"Get your ass in here right now," her reflection demanded.

"Why?"

There was a thump, as if her reflection slammed into the side of the mirror. "Get in here, or so help me I'll scream and you'll never sleep."

Alice exhaled her annoyance. She got out of bed, carefully placing the pillow in her spot. She trudged into the bedroom and flipped on the switch. "What?" Alice shouted. "What could you possibly want right now?"

Her reflection glared at her, arms crossed with a look of determination. "Get him back," Alice's reflection said. "Bring him back. Right now."

Alice ran her hand through her purple hair and then smacked the side of her thighs. "How am I going to do that?"

"You're a witch; figure it out."

Alice placed her hands on her hips. She furled her eyebrows and turned her head to the side, unable to face her reflection. "With what? There is no body."

"I don't care. I don't care how you do it. Bring. Him. Back!"

"I don't know how!" Alice shouted.

"Figure it out!"

Alice clutched her head with her hands, trying to calm the pounding sensation. She desperately searched for a thought, any thought, but the overwhelming anger muted her thinking. Her hands fell to her sides. "Shouting won't bring him back."

"But you can," Alice's reflection said. "You're a witch. You know witchy things. Ez knows witchy things. Bring him back. Not for me, not for you, but for everyone."

Alice sighed. "I don't even know where to begin."

Alice's reflection paused. She placed her hand to her chin, deep in thought. "What if you don't bring him back? What if you went to get him?"

"What?"

"What if you went to go get him?"

"Don't be ridiculous."

"Ez has to know. There has to be some way."

"Even if I could, do you know what you're asking me to do?"

"Yes. That's why I'm asking you to do it."

"Out of the question."

"What else are you going to do? Lay around crying all day? Get moving on this. Go. Go. Go."

"He's gone," Alice shouted. "He's gone. Let him go!"

Alice's reflection's laid eyes on her, and a solemn silence filled the room. Her face was blank and expressionless. Alice recognized her stoic, unmoving expression—the face of feminine rage. Seething rage bubbled under the surface, held back from exploding on the spot.

With a low whisper, Alice's reflection said, "Then why can't you let him go? Why are you the one sleeping with a T-shirt covered pillow?"

Alice's teeth chattered. The coolness of the early autumn morning sent a shiver down her back. She was frozen at the words spoken by her reflection.

Alice's reflection leaned forward, placing both hands on the side of the mirror. "Since you can't let him go either, and you know I'm right, then figure out how to bring him back," she said, her voice raising to a near shout.

Alice covered her chin with her hands. She exhaled into them before dropping them back down. "Are you prepared for me to bring him back?"

"Whatever it takes. Wherever you go. Whatever you have to do. Bring Hugo and his reflection back," Alice's reflection commanded. "Bring. Them. Back!"

CODA

A STRANGER IN A NOT SO WONDROUS LAND

The long oar splashed into the water as the ferryman maneuvered the flat bottom gondola down the river. A wooden casket laid out on the bottom of the boat. The ferryman was covered in a dark cloak with its face hidden in a black icky void. It said no words and made no sound. It only rowed the boat toward the casket's final destination with its skeletal hands.

A lantern attached to the end of the gondola lit the way. Its light shone on the rocky, cave like surface surrounding the river. A light appeared in the distance. It grew brighter with every paddle of the oar.

The boat emerged from a cave into a small lagoon at the bottom of a sheer, rocky cliffside. The jagged mountain disappeared into the swirling black clouds which rolled in the sky. The boat crossed the lagoon to a waiting dock. Six ghoulish creatures, their faces shriveled and darkened, stood ready to receive the boat. Using wooden poles, they latched onto the gondola and pulled it next to the dock.

The boat rocked as four entered. They took positions at the corners of the wooden casket. They grasped underneath and lifted it above their shoulders. The two remaining on the dock stretched out and pulled the casket over the side of the boat. Together, they helped carry it up onto dry land to the back of a waiting carriage. They slid the wood box into the back and closed the carriage door.

The horse-drawn black carriage carried its occupant toward a final resting place. The horse was black as night, with seeping wounds on its side. Glass windows allowed viewing to the wooden casket held within. The wooden spoked wheels tumbled over the cobblestone pathway. A rider in dark robes jostled with every groove in the road. He tugged the reins, forcing the horse in the direction of his choosing.

The dark, swirling clouds rolled like a vengeful sea overhead. The occasional lightning bolt shattered the sky, illuminating the ground below. The sky was like dusk—dark, yet not completely descending the realm into darkness. Lanterns attached to the side of the carriage provided some light for the journey of the dead.

The funeral hearse made its procession down the winding street of mismatched houses of various colors and from various time periods. Great fissures in the siding revealed the soft wood underneath. Pieces of roofs, gutters, and shutters ripped from them, as if the whole house was rotting and decaying. Twisted trees and dead plants decorated the yards of the homes.

They passed one house, and three knocks rang forth through the air. It was constant. Non-stop. Three knocks. The sound of wood against glass, like something was trying to escape.

Wails filled the air. Wails of ghoulish voices. Tormented souls meandered throughout the landscape. Their faces discolored as if they wore painted skeletal masks. White with black around their eyes, nose, and part of their cheeks. Their bodies gaunt. They shuffled about without purpose or intention.

The three knocks filled the air again. Unending. Desperate.

The hearse continued its journey. The houses it passed appeared as if they were plucked out of many different time periods to create a surreal environment. Some new. Some extremely old. All containing the wails of torment within. The hearse approached a Folk Victorian house. Purple and black in appearance. It too had the appearance of a decaying corpse. Pieces missing. Fissures in its siding. A twisted, familiar sight no doubt to the occupant inside.

A rider on a black horse, next to another horse-drawn carriage, observed the proceedings. He was shrouded in a black hooded robe. His face was unseen like the ferryman. A sword and sheath were held at his side. Fire spewed forth from the horse's nostrils with every breath. It shuffled at the approaching hearse. The rider pulled on the reins to control the great beast.

Three more knocks rang out against the glass.

The hearse stopped in front of the purple and black house. A group of four ghouls stood ready to greet the new arrival. They approached the back of the hearse and opened the door. The ghouls pulled the wooden casket, passing it down until it was free from its glass prison. They struggled with the weight of the box, but held firm. Without speaking, they turned and began carrying it up the walkway toward the gray porch.

Three more knocks echoed throughout the land.

They moved the box inside the awaiting house. They turned a tight corner and placed the box on the floor of the living room. It was filled with a Victorian style red couch, a black high-back chair, and an assortment of macabre items filled every available space. It was dressed to resemble the home of the occupant of the casket.

A woman followed the procession. The ghouls stood at attention, their backs straight and arms at their sides. She was dressed in a black Edwardian gown. She wore matching lace gloves and held a collapsed, black parasol. Her face was painted white and black to look like a skull. She tapped the end of the parasol on the floor.

"Where is the warden of this house?" she demanded.

The leather soles of boots tapped against the wooden floorboards and sent an echo throughout the house. They grew closer as he left the kitchen and entered the living room. He was a burly man wearing a green coat. Gold buttons running down the center held it closed. He wore an oversized, leather tricorn hat. The leather was tanned and brown with age. Unlike the others, he had no painted skull mask. He held a cup of tea and took a sip.

"I'm here, your highness," his booming voice said.

She pointed the parasol at the casket. "I expect you to complete your job as soon as possible with this one. He's special. He's from *my* town."

Thaddeus Price bowed his head. "Of course, your highness. I'll do my best."

"Your best won't be good enough. This is the one we've been waiting for. He drank from the spell. This is the one who will set us free from this prison," she said. She pointed the parasol at Thaddeus. "No mistakes. Or else the Rider will see to it this is your last one. Is that understood?"

Thaddeus peered from under the leather brim of his hat. "I won't fail you, Ms. Sinclair."

Madeline Sinclair smacked the floor with the end of her parasol. She turned and exited the house.

Thaddeus took a sip of tea from his cup. "Open it up," he said. "Let's greet our new visitor."

The ghouls grabbed the lid of the wooden casket and flung it open. Inside, with his arms crossed, laid the body of Hugo Dodds, resting peacefully in eternal slumber.

Thaddeus kicked the head of the casket. "Time to wake up," he bellowed.

Hugo's eyes sprung open. He gasped for air, filling his lungs as if he hadn't taken a breath in ages. Hugo sat up and touched the wooden sides of the box. His eyebrows furled and eyes narrowed while taking in his new surroundings. He touched his chest, finding a hole where the stake had stabbed through his heart.

Hugo gasped at the sight of the ghoulish figures towering above him. He scooted back as far as he could in the wooden casket, holding steadfast to the sides. He examined the room once more before his eyes focused on Thaddeus.

"I'm sure you have a lot of questions," Thaddeus said. "They'll all be answered in due time."

Hugo breathed heavily. His eyes darted back-and-forth from Thaddeus and then to the ghouls.

"Now don't work yourself up. Please remain calm," Thaddeus said.

Hugo furled his eyebrows and locked onto him. "Where's Alice? How did you get in our home?"

Thaddeus set the cup down on a shelf. "I'm going to need you to remain calm and still."

Hugo stood and jumped out of the casket. He backed into a corner of the living room. The ghouls turned to face him, moving close. His breathing labored. He picked up a statue to arm himself. He snarled, elongating his vampire fangs. The ghouls stopped moving.

"Where am I?" he asked.

"A place most curious and unusual," Thaddeus replied.

"What happened to me?" Hugo shouted.

"Well, Mr. Dodds," Thaddeus said. "You're dead."

To Be Continued

Alice and Hugo Will Return In

THE NEIGHBORHOOD GHOST

ALSO BY CHRISTOPHER M. MASON

THE NEIGHBORHOOD SERIES

The Neighborhood Witch

The Neighborhood Vampire

The Neighborhood Ghost

ABOUT THE AUTHOR

Christopher M. Mason is an author fueled by a lifelong passion for gothic and paranormal stories. In 2023, he introduced readers to a magical and intriguing world in his award-winning debut novel, "The Neighborhood Witch."

Christopher is a graduate of Wright State University, where he learned the art of storytelling. By flickering candlelight, he creates new characters and imaginative adventures for readers. He holds the belief that stories are a source of light amidst the darkness, allowing the ordinary to escape into extraordinary adventures.

www.christophermmason.com

www.ingramcontent.com/pod-product-compliance
Lightning Source LLC
LaVergne TN
LVHW050303141224
799066LV00001B/26